ORIGI

NEW WRITING FROM
BRITAIN'S OLDEST PUBLISHER

Risk-taking writing for risk-taking readers.

JM Originals was launched in 2015 to champion distinctive, experimental, genre-defying fiction and non-fiction. From memoirs and short stories to literary and speculative fiction, it is a place where readers can find something, well, *original*.

JM Originals is unlike any other list out there with its editors having sole say in the books that get published on the list. The buck stops with them and that is what makes things so exciting. They can publish from the heart, on a hunch, or because they just really, really like the words they've read.

Many Originals authors have gone on to win or be shortlisted for a whole host of prizes including the Booker Prize, the Desmond Elliott Award and the Women's Prize for Fiction. Others have been selected for promotions such as Indie Book of the Month. Our hope for our wonderful authors is that JM Originals will be the first step in their publishing journey and that they will continue writing books for John Murray well into the future.

Every JM Original is published with a limited-edition print run. This means every time you buy one of our covetable books, you're not only investing in an author's career but also building a library of (potentially!) valuable first editions. Writers need readers and we'd love for you to become part of our JM Originals community. Get in contact and tell us what you love about our books. We're waiting to hear from you.

We Could Not See the Stars

Elizabeth Wong

JM ORIGINALS

First published in Great Britain in 2021 by JM Originals
An Imprint of John Murray (Publishers)
An Hachette UK company

1

Copyright © Elizabeth Wong 2021

The right of Elizabeth Wong to be identified as the Author of the Work has been
asserted by her in accordance with the Copyright, Designs and Patents Act 1988.

A CIP catalogue record for this title is available from the British Library

Trade Paperback ISBN 9781529338898
eBook ISBN 9781529338904

Typeset in Minion Pro by Manipal Technologies Limited

Printed and bound in Great Britain by Clays Ltd, Elcograf S.p.A.

John Murray policy is to use papers that are natural, renewable and recyclable
products and made from wood grown in sustainable forests. The logging and
manufacturing processes are expected to conform to the environmental regulations
of the country of origin.

John Murray (Publishers)
Carmelite House
50 Victoria Embankment
London EC4Y 0DZ

www.johnmurraypress.co.uk

For Mum and Dad

'Imagine that you are a Kalahari Bushman and that you stumble upon a transistor radio in the sand.'

Incognito: The Secret Lives of the Brain by David Eagleman

Part One
Kampung Seng

The Storm and the Dream

I n silence, they waited for fish to appear in their nets, but none did. The salty sea heat stuck to the pores of their skin. Through the makeshift roof of old fishing nets came the piercing light of the afternoon and, along with it, shadows that stippled their limbs. *So hot today, hot until can die*, as their ah-ma would say.

'Very hot.' Lim Chong Meng, son and heir to the Lim Fishing Company, nodded.

No fish in the river mouth – what you expect lah? his cousin Tan Yong Han thought. *Water stagnant here, never move wan, and the river silt blooms in clouds. Only the small kecik-kecik fish come here to hide. Waste of time.* But he kept silent. Chong Meng would never listen to him, anyway. Instead Han said, 'Yah lor, so hot, no fish in the nets somemore. Let's go back.'

'You boss or I boss? Just now I heard a big shoal of mackerel swimming here. Clear like anything only. Heard their beating fins, their hearts. You wait and then you see.'

Han fed one end of the net into the water. The buoy made a gentle plop, then the weights, before the current pulled the sleepy net into a wall, its whiteness blooming in the darkness of the water. The rope chafed against his hands, tugging, wanting to drag him into the spills of the net, but he held strong, and looped the other end of the rope onto the boat.

Each of them had a smoke and a pee, as if both activities were in a combination set menu: Combo A – one smoke, one pee. Combo B – one yawn, one swear word, one smoke. At the back of the boat, the worker at the steering wheel snored, his head in his hands. Some time passed. They pulled the closest buoy and its nets back up onto the deck. Mostly chau hu: smelly fish that were not for eating and destined for fertiliser. Some prawns, but not many. The prawns twitched frantically as Han held them up in the sunlight, peering through their translucence. There were other inedible fish: a jellyfish, small eels, a puffer fish, two starfish and what looked like a tiny shark, but was likely a marine catfish. Han dropped them into a bucket for discards, where squid ink swished. There was even a cluster of fish eggs. He scooped up the little translucent blobs with dark centres like eyes and felt them watching him. Not fish, not yet. He let them slip back into the sea. Nothing in the nets that would have brought them money. The workers' 30 per cent cut of zero was still a big fat zero.

'Next time sure got mackerel wan,' Chong Meng said. 'Throw the nets in again.'

Han stared in the direction of land and wondered what Ah-ma would have cooked for dinner. Rice, a splash of soy sauce, fried anchovies and steamed bayam.

'Not going too far out,' his uncle, the tauke Mr Lim, had told him that morning. 'Easy, easy day. In fact, only you and

4

one other worker need to go out to join Chong Meng. Take the coastal boat.'

Chong Meng leading the boat? His cousin was never good at spotting fish. Bad luck Chong Meng, the other workers whispered. Suay, very suay – fish-cursed, they said quietly, so that the boss's son would not hear. But the coastal boat had advantages. They would return to shore mid-afternoon before it got too hot. There was time to take on an evening shift of washing dishes at Song Kee restaurant. And Han knew that the last deep-sea boat came back half-empty because of the winds sweeping in from the Boatbreaker Seas. Half the profits, half the pay.

As they waited, Chong Meng said, 'You know yesterday right, I was at Boon Chee restaurant, eat dinner like normal only lor. But then, I met this Mr Ng from the capital. Very confident man. He even shouted at the captain taking orders at the restaurant last night: this food is terrible, your vegetables are too soggy like anything only! Why am I paying for this? My mother also can cook better.' Chong Meng laughed, and the rocking of the boat rose with his laughter. 'So rude, can you imagine? Somemore hor if you see his right hand, there are two big gold rings! Big-big wan! Bigger than my father's ring! Then on his left hand leh? Big gold Rolex somemore! I asked this Mr Ng, "Why someone like you come here? What is there in this small village?"'

What was there in this small village?

In their evenings, they lingered in the parking lot of the former Golden Star cinema. The last rays of sunlight flared across their motorcycles as they smoked their cigarettes, and the dust clouds from the main road billowed around them. Sometimes they would race from Golden Star to Liu's prawn farms on the other side of the village, and back again. Han's Honda C70 was almost as old as he was, so he watched as others sped away.

As the dust ebbed into the muggy night, and the warm sea breeze rushed through their clothes, inevitably they found themselves in either Coconut Flower or Boon Chee, both solidly run restaurants, chosen each night on the performance of their air-conditioning units. They would have beers, Marmite chicken, razor clams in garlic and stir-fry sweet potato leaves. Their armpits would always be sticky. If they were at Boon Chee, they would watch football matches that were showing on the twenty-year-old Sony TV that hung over the entrance, next to Laughing Buddha looking down at them. 'Eh, boss, boss, more beer, peanuts also, why like that so slow?' Chong Meng would holler, and the workers would scurry.

By the time Han got home, Father and Ah-ma would be watching a serial drama, maybe a love story, or a love scandal, or both, with Father giving the TV a sharp hit to the side to make it work. On the altar, Mazu and Mama's spade watched over Father, Ah-ma and Han. Father would head to bed first, but spend most of the night awake because of his back. Ah-ma would be next to her room, and Han last, unrolling his mattress in the corner of the living room.

Han was not sure how to explain this to Chong Meng, who in any case, was not looking for any answers but his own.

That afternoon, with their fishless nets, they half listened to the chattering radio: now an upbeat hit from one of the capital's many pop stars, now the news of the Peninsula, now an advert – a woman enthusing over the pleasures of a soap that could wash off even tough stains without the use of hot water.

Only 11.99 at your nearest supermarket, she added. If you buy two before the first of the— but she never got the chance to finish, for she was interrupted by the local frequency: *Storm, from west, coming in quickly.*

There was the heat of the languid afternoon, and then, on the far side of the horizon, from the Boatbreaker Seas where the sea touched the sky, there was a deep, funeral-white blankness, and a roar arose from somewhere that was yet to be named, a crushing beginning of things. Nothing existed in the white static as it erased everything in its path, taking with it islands and calm heat and radio chatter. *Storm, storm from west, watch out, storm.*

'Maybe fifteen minutes before it gets here,' Chong Meng said. 'Pull the nets, get ready to go!'

They hauled the nets into the boat as fast as they could. Their hands were sore as the ropes tumbled in wet and buoys whipped through the air. Now the mangrove swamp that lay across the estuary like a protective hand was gone, swallowed into the storm as if it had never existed. The winds grew in speed: first a timid breeze poking at the edges of their boat, then increasingly rough, rocking them from side to side.

A few minutes later, the large gaping mouth of the estuary was gone too, swallowed into the storm. Stronger winds followed, pummelling the fragile frame of the boat, and their bodies juddered as the patchwork of balau planks strained at the joints. 'Only the best quality I give you wan,' the boatyard builder had said, but everyone knew that was a lie, that the balau planks were scavenged wood, junk from some shipwreck found washed up in the roots of mangrove trees, or tangled in fishing nets like drowned women.

'Go back now, to the docks! Go!' Chong Meng shouted to the worker at the steering wheel. The first drops of rain began to land.

Did the worker hear? What was that man's name again? For one long stretched moment – a chant exhaled in a single breath, a cat mewling into the night – their limbs were petrified stillness, captured in flashes of lightning as nothing moved, and the roar of the storm enveloped the small boat. Their feet felt the planks underneath them but nothing moved in that moment.

'Yes, boss,' came the desultory reply.

Now the rain fell in large stoney drops, striking their flesh, and the once-flat sea burst open. Waves exploded on the side of the boat like firecrackers on the New Year. *Bang! Bang! Bang-bang-bang-bang-bang!* The sky sparked.

'Eh you, what you doing back there? Fai di lah! Faster!' Chong Meng shouted to the engines. He jumped to the back of the boat. 'Oi, bodoh ah? Stupid! Cannot listen ah?'

A meagre roar escaped from the engines. *Vroom-vroom*, the engine said, unhurriedly, even as more water poured onto the boat, from the sea, from the sky, everywhere; their ankles drowning.

The boat rocked its way back up the estuary. The waves came at them fast, forcing the boat to turn sideways, and then pushing the sides of the boat. The bow was tipped high into the sky, and in the next moment, dived down low so far that they grabbed whatever they could to stop from falling into the sea. The deck disappeared beneath their feet, and their bodies lurched like jiang shis.

If the boat capsized here, who would say prayers for their bodies? Trapped between the river and the open sea, a dirty, lazy place. And, more importantly, if Han was gone, who would feed Ah-ma and Father?

'Turn, turn! Kai yau!' Chong Meng shouted.

The engine gave another roar. There was a burst of energy from the boat. *Vroom-vroom-VROOM.* The unnamed worker at the back swung his entire weight at the wheel to turn the bow so it faced the waves straight on. Another burst of energy, and suddenly they were striding through the water, cutting each fresh wave with confidence.

The shoreline approached, lined by hundreds of docks. Here, even more large fishing trawlers and small two-man sampans were tethered. They banged loudly at the shock-absorbing tyres and drums that lined the docks, usually an auspicious sign of welcome, but now an early warning as the waves rushed in from the storm and rolled all the way up the estuary.

The docks of the Lim Fishing Company appeared in front of them, where a land man was already waiting. Han threw the guiding ropes to the man, who pulled the boat in, jostling them into position against the old tyre bumpers, before both ends of the boat were tethered to the posts. Their meagre catch was forgotten.

'Faster cover!' Chong Meng instructed, even as they knew what to do, stretching a thick grey tarp around the boat. After the last corner was tied down, the storm reached the docks of the Lim Fishing Company. Dark rain beat down their eyes and ears. They ran into the warehouse, their faces slick with wetness. A semi-stray dog opened an eye at them as they sloshed in, but immediately went back to sleep among the thunder and lightning.

The sorting workers were long gone, the concrete floor had been hosed down earlier and was now dry, Mr Lim the tauke himself was back in his home, and the warehouse and docks of Lim Fishing Company were silent. The concrete floor was cold. Winds whipped into the exposed warehouse, and its temporary inhabitants grew colder, wetter.

Outside, chewed lollipop sticks, empty packets of Twisties and Magnum wrappers bopped around in the rushing water of the road. A lone motorcycle leaned awkwardly in a pothole, riderless, abandoned. *Engine's underwater*, Han thought. *Who would be so stupid to be riding in this rain?*

He changed out of his wet clothes into a spare T-shirt and pair of trousers that his ah-ma made him take so that he would not always smell of fish. His feet were wrinkled from the water. He collapsed into a heap of fishing nets, the rain falling in heavy drops across the corrugated iron roof. The great, incessant roar filled his ears, washing out remnant noises of everything else: breathing, barking, sleeping, sighing, squeaking. He felt the noise as if it was pressing his chest, drowning his ears, until he was a small, cold fleck, alone in the barren warehouse. He brought up his weary knees closer to his face, trying to find the gentle echoes of his own heartbeat; the calm of a baby in his mother's womb.

Chong Meng was already sprawled out on the pile of fishing nets next to Han's. As if on instinct, he opened his eyes sleepily. 'I want to go to the capital,' he mumbled. 'Once I went to the capital's port. People everywhere, people mountain, people sea, crowding the streets. So difficult to walk around, and hard to breathe. Imagine, seeing a person once in your life and never seeing them again. I want to go to Bawahsiang, to the Eastern Port, all these places we heard of only. Only hear, never go.'

He closed his eyes fractionally, then lifted his lids again. 'Eh, that Mr Ng told me this story. Don't know whether true wan or not. But you must promise not to tell anyone. Somewhere far away, there was a tower, he said.'

*

Imagine that you are walking through a forest in the dark. You step over the tree roots, with mud and leeches riding up the sides of your legs, and outstretched branches brushing your arms. Suddenly, the ground falls away and there, in front of you, a perfectly circular hole emerges in the ground, like the deep nostril of a ghost. The hole so large that you can't see what is on the other side, and you wonder if the hole ever ends. Perhaps all the land in this world drops off a cliff edge, down-down into the ghost's deep nostril, where there is no light at the start nor at the end.

Then you see something in the distance. At first, you think that your eyes have tricked you. There is no light here, you think, it's all dark, it's all same-same only, same-same for a man who cannot see, same-same in the deep nostril of the ghost, no start, no end. Yet your eyes insist that this is something new. This is different. Dark on dark, a mountain of black rock rises from the large hole.

You never knew that different types of darkness existed before, yet here these shadows exhibit themselves to you, like a light show, except in inverse: *A dark show*, you think to yourself. Against the canvas of emptiness, the outline of this mountain can just be seen, conical in shape, with smooth sides that gently roll off its peak.

Here, too, in this same-same darkness, on this same-same mountain, right at its peak, yet another object reveals itself. Is that a lighter shade of darkness, a different type of darkness? You cannot be sure; all colours are relative and, right now, you can only explain what you are seeing in the context of the overwhelming darkness. For this object that you are seeing, in the hole where there is no light, is a golden tower.

You cannot understand how you are seeing a golden tower in this dark-on-dark world, where every object is as dark as the stretched-out emptiness of the empty sky without stars. This must just be another shade of black, you think, and for some reason, your mind interprets the colour as golden. Bright, brilliant, dazzling, shining like a star against the long night!

When you turn your head away, the brightness of the golden tower dissolves back into the ancient darkness, and reappears when you look at it directly. What is this – a trick of light? You have never seen a tower like this before. How could you even begin to describe what you are seeing? This symmetrical structure that bends away from you in perfect circularity, the smoothness of its walls that contain no visible markings, no windows, no joints, and most importantly, no top. For the top of the tower cannot be seen; the tower continues to climb high into the night, where it disappears. There is no end, you think. Only a sense of everything beginning: here, start, go. The golden tower sings a promise to you, that the darkness is limited, temporary.

You can see a long, thin line in front of you. There is a bridge that connects you to the tower. You place one foot on the line, then another, then another. The darkness of the hole rises up around you, like noxious fumes from floating rubbish. You start choking. Your mind wants to shut down, to reduce itself to a state of nothingness, to join this darkness. You can no longer see your feet or your fingers, or even the bridge itself. You lift up your left leg to test if you can do so, and your muscles twitch and your leg feels like it has moved, although you are not sure.

You say a few words out loud to remind yourself that you exist in this place. 'Hello, I am here, I exist,' you say, in the most insistent voice you have, feeling small as you do so. You expected your voice to echo in the massive cavern that is the hole, but it does not.

Instead, there is silence. I don't mean that the place is silent; rather, it is as if the noise has been sucked from the surroundings, leaving a vacuum. All around you there is a weight, a burden of silence that has been pressed onto you. There has been a death, you think, for no place is ever this silent, except at a funeral.

And because nothing has prepared you for this, because you live in a world of sound, you constantly expect to hear something, as if all this is a big joke and, sooner or later, the person-in-charge will let you in on it. But you don't hear anything. You continue not hearing anything. For there is nothing to be heard. This is a place of same-same darkness; this is the dark nostril of a ghost. There is no light here, even as the golden tower shines before you.

A door stands at the end of the bridge. It is the door to the golden tower. You push it open.

When you enter the tower, it is as if you have always been in the tower, as if you never left. As if you lived there your entire life, and everything that happened outside the tower was just a dream.

Did Chong Meng tell Han the story of the tower that day? He was not sure – the memory felt second-hand, as if Han was remembering a memory of a memory. Perhaps he had originally read the story in a book and dreamt it into the sequence of events on that day. Perhaps someone else had told him the story; but the memory was trapped there, an unyielding knot in that day's weave.

Mama's Spade

The next morning, Han woke up shivering, even as the warmth of the sun flooded his nest of fishing nets. Chong Meng had already left for home. A warm mist clung low to the ground, like the persistent exhale of an engine. Somewhere in the estuary, early morning trawlers sputtered out fumes as they headed to sea. Han rode home on the Honda C70. Father was awake, watching a morning talk show on the TV, sitting in his favourite red-blue-white rubber string chair, on which he was slumped low, resting his feet on the extended footrest. The ceiling fan lurched in slow loops, as if unclear on what to do next.

If not for Han's company, Father would sit in front of his TV or his radio all day, listening to never-ending bad news that he had no connection to and had no power to change. On and on the newsreader intoned: Corrupt politicians in the capital. Declining trade from the Eastern Port. Problems brought by immigrants from the Desert of Birds. The latest storm coming in from the Boatbreaker Seas. Volcanic eruptions in the Hei-san archipelago.

'Rain last night, got stuck in the warehouse,' Han told Father. 'How are you feeling now?'

Father nodded. 'Better. I think it's the new medicine. My back is no longer so painful. Maybe I can go back out to sea next week. See what the doctor say.'

'Where's Ah-ma?'

'Still sleeping. Last afternoon she worked too hard on the garden, planting kangkung and chilli. Seventy-five-year-old woman gets tired easily wan you know. When I was small, she used to work eighteen hours a day. Sell kuih door to door with her baskets, grow vegetables, raise chickens. Now, just two hours in the garden and like that also she tired already,' Father said.

Han nodded. These were stories he had heard many times before.

They went for their usual Sunday breakfast in Kopitiam Liong, where, on plastic stools, conversations of the people of Kampung Seng unfolded.

'Eh, you going to the temple tonight ah? I heard they are putting up new lanterns woh.'

'My daughter-in-law is so dirty and so lazy wan. Only one month she moved into my house, already I cannot stand her. If not for my son I surely would have kicked her out already loh! Put plates everywhere, never wash up, somemore expect me to cook dinner. What you think I am, maid ah? She should be cooking dinner for me.'

'Doctor said I need new medicine for my stomach. She said this one not strong enough, no wonder I keep vomiting after I eat food. Ai-yah, old like that, all parts break down. Haha!'

16

Han ordered a kopi-O and Father a kopi-C. They slowly pulled off corners of three pandan buns. Father had bought the newspaper but ignored it as they chatted about Mr Lim opening his third prawn farm at the far end of the estuary.

A man approached their table. He did not say who he was but Han recognised him from the gold Rolex on his left wrist.

Han had imagined Mr Ng as a tall, fair man with polished shoes. Upper-class, like all the people from the capital. Instead, he was dark from working in the sun too long. Another surprise: he was as tall as Han was. Grey streaks ran through his thinning hair. His cheeks looked as if they had once been puffy but were now sunken in. An old polo T-shirt and grey, nondescript trousers hung on him, along with the pungent stink of several-days-old unwashed clothes.

There was a raised mole the size of a coin on the left of his chin, out of which grew three strands of hair. Sign of prosperity, Ah-ma would have said. But Mr Ng's eyes and mouth were small and thin, which Ah-ma would have said was a sign of stinginess.

'Hello sirs, can I join your table on this fine morning?' Mr Ng smiled as he tilted his head. 'No place liao, kopitiam this morning so full. Ah-hmm, okay, can anot?'

A brief moment passed before Father gave the barest hint of a nod, unsure of what this stranger wanted. Mr Ng slid into the spare chair at their table in the swiftest of motions, so swift that it remained unclear whether he had waited for the nod from Father, or not. In any case, Mr Ng seemed like the type of person who never waited for permission from others to do exactly what he wanted. Permission for a man like Mr Ng was something nice to have, but not a must-have.

Mr Ng snapped his fingers in the direction of the workers in the restaurant. 'Hello? Hello? I want roti bakar, and this white coffee too, like this man here.' Mr Ng nodded in the direction of Father's kopi-C.

A worker slid over a cup of kopi-C. Some coffee escaped into the saucer.

Mr Ng smiled again at Father and, as an afterthought, looked in Han's direction. 'The storm yesterday – wah, so bad hor! Radio in the capital also talk about storm. Say longkang in the capital clogged up, rubbish floating on the streets. And then the New Villages on the outskirts flooded now. Even the Desert of Birds got rain they say, first time this year.' He drank most of the kopi-C in three quick gulps.

Father asked Mr Ng why he was here. If Father wasn't mistaken, Mr Ng had arrived in their small village four days ago. 'The barber told me about you. Said you were some kind of reporter or something.'

'Ah-hmm, reporter hor, super good at investigating things,' Mr Ng replied. 'I'm something like that, what you might say, someone who finds things for other people, something like a reporter but not really.'

'What is there to find in this small village?' Father asked. 'There's nothing in Kampung Seng. Only fish and prawns! This season, storms so bad that fish also cannot find!' He shook his head. 'The Boatbreaker Seas too rough to go out most days. Storms keep getting worse and worse, how fisherman like me can survive? Hard life.'

'You think here got hard life? I been to the Desert of Birds. There really got hard life. Nothing there, not even water. At least here got water, got fish, got trees. You lucky man, blessed by gods, you just don't know it,' Mr Ng said. 'Eh, if you don't mind me asking, Mr . . . Mr Tan, issit?'

Father nodded.

18

'Mr Tan, I ask around, just ask-ask only, and everyone seems to think you would know about something I want to know about. Now, I see on your face you might be worried. Eh, don't worry, nothing to worry about, I chat-chat only, okay? People say you might know about someone. People say, ask Mr Tan, but they don't say why. Now, ah-hmm, Mr Tan, I'm looking for a woman who came to Kampung Seng a long time ago. Beautiful woman, long hair and fair skin. This is a drawing of her.' Mr Ng pulled out a piece of paper and pushed it over to Father. 'Don't worry, I'm not looking to marry her,' he added, with a lopsided smile.

Han peered at the drawing; she looked like his mother, who died when he was four.

Mr Ng continued, 'Maybe she has something that I am looking for. Do you know where she is now? I just want to speak to her. Just talk only wan.'

Father stood up. 'Why are you asking me this?' His face was like the roots of a mangrove swamp, tightening in the edges of the sea.

Mr Ng continued, smiling. 'Everyone in this village said, ask Mr Tan. So Mr Tan, I ask you, you know this woman? I just want to speak to her. Don't worry, I'm not police, hah.'

'Why you ask me these things?' Father turned his head away from Mr Ng. 'Go away.'

Mr Ng looked at Father and Han but said nothing else. Then he picked up the drawing and left. Kopitiam Liong was silent as people carefully avoided looking at Father and Han. They would later gossip in private, nestled in the hum of prayers at the temple, or within the cacophony of the morning market. It would be too rude – and maybe even bad luck, suay, they would say – to say anything in front of Father and Han, especially if the topic was about Han's mama.

At that moment, the worker brought Mr Ng's roti bakar to the table and was confused when he found Mr Ng's empty chair, lingering as if wanting to ask Father a question.

Father waved the worker away, and went back to picking at the pandan buns without saying a word. He never spoke about Mama's death, or even what it was like when she was alive. Father could speak at length on whether Ah Huat gambled too much, or whether the price of cigarettes had gone up, but never about Mama. Even after all these years, his feelings were so raw that a stranger asking about Mama made him angry.

Ah-ma had woken up by the time they arrived home and was mending nets in the kitchen.

Father said, 'Bad back,' and disappeared through the door of his bedroom.

'What was Father like when he was a boy?' Han asked Ah-ma.

'Your father – your father was a very obedient and filial child. Nothing like you –always so stubborn!' Ah-ma pinched Han's ear. 'He was always so serious. Your kong-kong never had to scold him. He would do his homework on time, pack his bag and get ready for school the next day. Then, he would ask us whether we needed help with chores. Sometimes, we both wondered whether he was too serious for a child. Not good for a child to be so serious, you know!' Ah-ma whispered, 'Did something happen to him? Sometimes I worry that your father is thinking of the old days.'

Han told her about Mr Ng looking for Mama.

Ah-ma was upset. 'Who does Mr Ng think he is? Talking about the dead? So rude. Si liao better left buried in the ground. People from the capital all the same wan, no manners.'

*

They sat for the rest of the afternoon in the kitchen, mending nets together. Even as Ah-ma's eyes declined with age, her hands remained sensitive, feeling the patterns with her fingers. She had done this to earn extra money ever since Han was little: intertwining fingers, threads, net.

Han had joined her since he was eight, when he had wondered why Ah-ma was sitting on her knees near the kitchen window. So that the light from outside would fall on the cords, Ah-ma had replied, and when he looked at the tangle on Ah-ma's lap, he saw a mass of shifting silver lines, moving as if they had a purpose. Let me teach you. They worked in mirror images of each other, him learning the basic mends, Ah-ma teaching, as moonlight fell upon their hands. He learned to connect two halves of a broken cord, and then connect more, and more. A new pattern appeared where six fingers were, a thread connected where his hands worked, a bundle of knots transformed into a full mesh. Patterns appeared where there were once ugly knots.

Han did not remember much of his mama. His few memories of her were like broken pieces of driftwood: once from boats, or docks, or warehouses, now turning in the broken waves of the swash, origin unknown, with no end or beginning.

His first memory was of opening his eyes. The world was a dark thing and unfamiliar, and he found comfort in her breathing, in her warm centre. His next memory of Mama happened just before she passed away. Han had put on his special blue shirt as it was his birthday. They were having cake! But he was sad; his special blue shirt was getting too tight. Look here, look here, Mama! I couldn't button this button. Mama said that he was growing into a big boy, and he should wear his shirt more before he got too big.

He remembered Mama's funeral. He and Chong Meng ran underneath the coffin between the stands, playing kejar-kejar, before they were told off by Chong Meng's mother, Mrs Lim. 'Stop laughing, this is a funeral!' She smacked them on their arms. They stopped laughing, and Chong Meng stared at his mother and rubbed his arm. Han walked around the stands, wanting to see Mama inside the coffin, but he was not tall enough to look at her from above. Finally, Ah-ma lifted him up in her arms where he could look at Mama sleeping.

'Why is she holding a picture of me?' Han asked.

Because you were her favourite person, and she wants to remember you when she goes to heaven, Ah-ma replied.

'Why is she going to heaven?' Han asked.

Because that is what people do when they leave this world, Ah-ma replied.

Cold rain fell on the day of the funeral, and droplets of water condensed on the inside of the windows.

Mama married Father when Han was a baby. There was no mention of who Han's real father was. Here in this small village, where sometimes life was an unrelenting storm and Mazu forgot to send her grace, and the only land in sight was a slippery rock, people adopted other people's children freely; neither curiosity nor protocol mattered, only that Father called Han his son and that was that.

Of course Mrs Lim disapproved of their marriage: 'My brother, always making mistakes. Marrying that foreign woman with baby from don't-know-where. I told him no, but he never listen. I intro him to nice women but they don't want him, say he poor. See lah!' For the benefit of her mahjong kakis, Mrs Lim would shake her head. 'Somemore now, worship spade! On the altar! I told them to put a picture of her instead but they don't listen. No common sense!'

Mrs Lim's altars were made of real wood, the expensive kind, not like the imitation rosewood that her brother had. They were the best type of wood: Only the best for you, madam, her supplier said. Got real mother-of-pearl inlays, import from the Hei-san islands. Somemore these carvings of dragons by a master carver; dragons bring you ong, protect your household. And here, got additional features, like this pull-out drawer at the top of the altar.

'Pull-out drawer for what?' she asked.

'To put the swords lah,' he said.

Why need swords for the altar? she wanted to ask, but didn't dare for fear of looking stupid.

'Make sure you put your main altar facing the main door for maximum feng shui,' he said.

Her main altar was as busy as the morning market. Statues of gods and deities peered over each other's shoulders, as if they were related. Choy Sun Yeh, the god of wealth, was placed on an elevated stand in the middle, while Mazu, Tua Pek Gong, Guan Gong, Ji Gong, Gong Choo Gong, Tiger God, and other minor deities gathered on the platform below. She didn't even know most of their names. There was the usual incense bowl, plate of fruits, and three small tea cups, but no burning candles for her altars. Her friends told her that electric candles were the modern thing. 'So your walls don't get black lah! All that soot from the candles not good for you, you know.'

The ancestral altar had eight pictures of their deceased relatives. On the kitchen altar, she placed Chau Ang Gong overlooking their one-of-a-kind, antique marble dining table from the Bercahaya Empire era. And outside by the cempedak tree, Datuk Gong had his own altar with offerings of betel nuts and fresh flowers.

In contrast, her brother had two fake-wood altars. They worshipped Mazu on the main altar; on the smaller altar, they placed that woman's spade! Somemore put joss sticks! Offerings of tea and fruits also got! Really beh tahan!

Once, she'd even seen her brother ask advice from that woman's spade. This fact Mrs Lim didn't dare tell her friends, pai seh, later they think Mrs Lim siao like her brother. Somemore the spade look so ugly, not like her noble sword. Odd, knobbly object, about the length of her arm, dull silver, not polished. The blade of the spade was large and shaped like a triangle that had a knock on its head. Some inscriptions on the handle that no one understood.

Her mother asked her, 'Why you so busybody wan? Your brother's spade none of your business also. Pray let him pray lah. The spade is the one thing that Swee brought with her when she arrived here.'

'The spade not the only thing she brought. She also brought Han what,' Mrs Lim replied, which was met with silence from her mother.

Mrs Lim could not understand these kinds of people; no wonder her brother never got anywhere in life.

No other spade looked like Mama's. The handle was engraved with lines and dots; a language no one understood. Their words for the spade were lost; they were primitive cave dwellers before history or language, and they had looked up into the Milky Way and its stars, gathering into layers tens of thousands of light-years deep, bending the space around them with their immense gravity – this they could not understand, except to say, Lights in the sky at night.

'Cha pah toh,' as Ah-ma would say, waving her hands, like when she was describing her lack of measurements for cooking. Their language was born in working sweat, in the vats of boiling bones for stock, or in hoisting nets of fish. There were approximate measurements ('about half a thumb of water above the rice'); imprecise dates ('wedding start around eight evening'); and locations defined by social relations ('near Goh's house, around the corner but facing Ah Meng's motorcycle shop, won't get lost wan'). So, in all, perhaps 'spade' was as good as any other word to name the object.

The Before

In the afternoon, Chong Meng visited their house, which was a surprise to everyone as the last time Chong Meng had come over it had been the second day of the New Year, several months before.

'Chong Meng!' Ah-ma exclaimed. 'What brings my first grandson here?'

She brought out the tray containing jars of pineapple tarts, yam biscuits and kuih kapit. 'Nah, have some treats. These kuih kapit very nice wan. I just bought them last week from Mrs Cheah. Very light and thin.'

'No thanks, Ah-ma. I have already eaten.' Chong Meng was embarrassed, his large body hunched over in an attempt to make himself a more similar size to his grandmother. Chong Meng had never spent much time with Ah-ma, other than the occasional Saturday evening when the two families had dinner together at either Boon Chee or Coconut Flower restaurant.

Even on the eve of the New Year, they had had the family's reunion dinner at the Lims' house. 'I know not tradition for the married daughter to host, but we got maid to cook, better for everyone, no? Somemore our house got air conditioning,' Mrs Lim had said.

Mrs Lim kept their family apart – with drops of contact permitted between the two families – lest the Tan family thought themselves of a similar social status. 'Don't spend so much time with that side of the family. Their house is so ancient, they don't even have air conditioning. So hot! And they only have those ugly rattan chairs and old string chairs to sit on, must be at least fifteen years old hor. And don't be too friendly with them at work,' she said to Chong Meng. 'You are the boss, can't let this get to their heads.'

So it was a surprise to Ah-ma and Han when Chong Meng, perched at the edge of the rattan two-seater, said, 'Ah-ma, you are going to the hairdressers tomorrow morning, right? For your new hair perm?'

'Wah, Chong Meng, you came here to ask me that ah?' Ah-ma laughed.

Chong Meng always wore an air of nervousness and deference in his attitude towards Ah-ma; too scared of showing disrespect, or of being above his place as a dutiful grandson. He only spoke in polite generalities to Ah-ma, and even those usually ended after fifteen minutes, when Chong Meng would say that he had to go. (Mrs Lim often reminded Chong Meng many times to respect his elders. 'Must have values, Chong Meng. Don't simply chit-chat with her. She is not your friend, she is your grandmother! Your cousin, that Han, is a bad influence. What kind of people do you think we are?' she had said.)

28

Chong Meng replied, his head bobbing: 'Ah-ma, I just wanted to tell Han to be at the docks tomorrow early morning, another day trip out to sea. And I wanted to ask Uncle Tan help with fish sorting in the morning, because there is a deep-sea boat coming in.' He peered furtively at the jar of pineapple tarts. 'I know that his back is still painful but we need the extra help.'

Han nodded, surprised, as his rota didn't call for him for the next two days, but he had no time to think about it as he had to start on his second shift in the Song Kee shortly. He hoped that he wouldn't be falling asleep on the boat tomorrow.

Years later, when Han was to think about everything that had happened, he would pinpoint the next day as marking a before and an after: there was a Before, where everything happened in his life happened before; and there was an After, as if he had sailed out to sea on a brilliantly hazy day, as the heat skipped restlessly through the waves, and found out that he could not turn the boat around to return.

The next day started at dawn. Han shuffled out of bed. Ah-ma had put the kettle over the gas stove several minutes before. Han would remember his grandmother this way for years after: Ah-ma half watching the kettle come to the boil as it shook in its seat. The flame from the stove cast a warm glow over her, intermittently broken by the overhead fluorescent light that flickered across her person. Sweat formed small beads on her brow and intermingled with steam rising from the kettle spout. When Ah-ma pushed away the excess sweat on her forehead with the back of her hand, he noticed how her skin rippled into itself with every exhalation and inhalation, that every dark sunspot trembled within its folds, and how she placed her right hand on her lower back for balance. Han could feel Ah-ma getting smaller as he grew taller. *One day our roles will be reversed*, he thought.

Outside, a rooster began its morning routine, with long, loud crows to the neighbourhood, as it shook itself ready for the first rays of sun to appear. '*Goukokoko*,' it warned. '*Goukokoko*.'

'The sunset was red yesterday evening, means today is going to be a hot day. See lah my perm, it's so hot, now my hair going straight! Lucky I'm going to hairdresser today,' Ah-ma said, before giving Han a once-over. 'Ai-yah, how can you wear those clothes? Wear some fresh ones, after people think we are poor.'

Han examined himself. He wore the same brown pants and T-shirt from yesterday. He must have fallen asleep right after he got back from his shift at Song Kee. Ah-ma gave him hot Milo in an enamel mug. He drank it all, even the dregs, tilting his head back to slurp any remains, leaving behind trails of chocolate sediment.

Only the streetlamps were awake that morning, watching as his motorcycle bumped over the potholes.

When he arrived at the warehouse, Mr Lim was at the docks, giving instructions over a small radio, while squinting at the horizon, where a black dot appeared. 'No, bring her in slowly! It was just repaired! What you lot doing out there I also don't know.' He was speaking to the crew that had been out for a week on the deep-sea boat. These boats were three storeys high and several times wider than the coastal boats, with an accommodation deck that could hold thirty mattresses laid side by side.

As Han walked onto the docks, Mr Lim gestured to him. 'Han, you go take the coastal boat, with Chong Meng. Bring two workers with you.'

Chong Meng was already waiting on the boat, eating a yau char kwai that he had bought from the stalls in the dead-end alley at the back of the wet market, near where the Tang family lived. He wiped the grease on his hands onto his trousers. A few stray sesame seeds clung to the corner of his mouth. 'Ready to go? Ready?' he said, when he saw Han arriving. Another stray sesame seed waited in the gap between Chong Meng's two front teeth.

There was nothing to do while the boat rumbled out of the estuary, so Han got out his pouch of old tobacco leaves, rolled them around in paper and lit up one of the ends. He drew a long breath on the other end, then exhaled. The acridity and bitterness sat on his tongue in layers. He unfolded his legs and rested them on the fishing nets, his feet brushing the ribs of the boat, tired after his night shift. Near his feet, in the deep inner corners above the overflow holes where excess water could return to the sea, a dozen silverfish also slept, unbothered.

They were in a large trawler and everyone was motionless but him. Han reached over and shook the person next to him. It was Chong Meng. 'Wake up,' Han said. No one stirred. Their eyes were carefully shut, as if possessed by a ghost. The trawler itself was floating in the sea, with no land in sight, nor any stars either. His eyes hurt from the perpetual blueness of the bright sky. Everything was impossibly calm, and only the gentle rocking of the boat reminded him that the world was still alive. 'Wake up,' Han demanded. 'WAKE UP.' No one heard him. His voice was hollow, absorbed in the waves. Time seemed to pass, measured by the uneven rhythm of waves chopping at the boat. One beat, one second; another beat, another second; and Han waited for everyone to wake up.

An eternity later, he stood in a dark place, facing a tap. The tap had been left running, and water poured from it, falling as rain onto the world. Han knew that if he could turn the tap off, the rain would stop. He took the handle in both hands and turned it clockwise to close it, but as he kept turning, more and more rain poured out onto the world. He tried turning it the other way, but the rain wouldn't stop. He knew then that there was no way he could turn it off, but he had to keep trying all the same. His palms burned with effort, his fingers were raw.

The stars, a voice said from somewhere in the darkness. Han knew, without any doubt, that it was the voice of his mama, except his mama had been dead for many years. Look up at the stars, Mama told him.

Instead, Han looked down and found that it wasn't rain pouring from the tap, but nets. Lengths and lengths of nets spurted from the tap, spilling out over the whole world, weaving themselves into intricate patterns. He knew that he knew what the patterns meant, even before he saw them, but the meanings burned into trails of smoke whenever he looked at them. The knowledge didn't, couldn't, translate into his conscious mind – something was blocking it, like a locked door, a secret word. Then he was swimming in those nets, and the whole world transformed into a sea. And for the longest time, he was drowning in nets of incomprehensible meanings, spinning out into infinity.

The After

Han and Chong Meng spent the rest of their morning dropping nets off the coast. It was uneventful fishing. They returned to the docks; his watch told him that it was 14.11. The deep-sea boat that Han had seen arriving earlier that morning was now the centre of attention. Old T-shirts were left to dry from every available space, fluttering around the boat as if excited to be returning to shore. Dock workers swarmed the boat, unearthing crates of fish from the boat's innards and dragging them to the side, where they tipped out fish and ice into plastic drums to be carted to the warehouse.

A dolly stacked high with polystyrene boxes of differing sizes squeaked to a stop. Mr Lim yelled at the handler of the dolly: 'Eh, you! What you doing? I told you how many times, that one is not to go to the capital, that one is to sell to the wholesaler here wan. You deaf ah? You stupid ah? I tell you, tell you again also never listen.'

In the warehouse, Father was squatting next to the prawns. 'My back is very tired now,' he said to Han. 'I have been sorting these prawns for five hours.' Next to him were foam boxes full of prawns that had been sorted by size, as if the school bell had rung and each year had been herded into assembly: year 1, the youngest and smallest ones; year 2, only slightly larger; and all the years up through to year 6, the oldest and biggest prawns.

Father unfolded himself from his squatting position. Mr Lim waved them both home, saying, 'We got enough workers here by now. Most of the sorting is already done.'

They rode home sharing the Honda in the heat of the afternoon. When they arrived, they were drenched in sweat.

Father got off the motorbike first to open the gates. Han drove through and parked the Honda underneath the awning. They approached the front-door grille, Han automatically reaching for the padlock. It was not there, as he would have expected. He took several seconds to register the absence. He found the two ends of the steel chain unsecured, and the padlock was missing.

Strange, he thought. *Ah-ma must have removed the padlock.*

He opened the door in a slow yawn. The house was dark, for Ah-ma liked to close the shutters to keep the air cool in the afternoon heat. When his eyes adjusted to the dimness, he saw a figure lying on the floor in the middle of the living room.

'Ah-ma! Ah-ma!' Her eyes were closed and she was not moving. Han placed a hand on her neck and felt for a pulse – there it was, a slow affirmation of life. 'Wake up,' he said. Her head moved towards Han and her eyes fluttered.

The ambulance came. Two men wheeled in a stretcher. When they lifted Ah-ma onto it, her left arm jutted at an angle; her fragility lay like freshly burned ash.

34

'We're going to hospital now. One of you can join us,' one of the men said. Father jumped into the back of the ambulance without saying anything. Han followed behind on his motorcycle.

Han waited in the waiting area for a long time. The floor grew dusty at his feet. Sometimes, he sensed the seat next to him being occupied; sometimes the seat was empty. After a while, he noticed Chong Meng next to him.

'What happened? Is she all right? Why was she at home? I thought she was supposed to be at the hairdresser?' Chong Meng asked.

Han had no answer to give. They both sat there until a doctor came.

'Her arm is broken, but her condition is stable. She is able to wake up from time to time, but we'll let her sleep for now. Tomorrow, we will set the bone in a cast.'

They were let into the ward where Ah-ma was sleeping. The air conditioning was set at a temperature too cold, making loud hissing noises. Father sat wearily in a chair next to her, a blanket drawn across his lap. Han stood close to Ah-ma and carefully placed her hand in his. He felt her breathing, gentle and quiet. Her skin felt thin in his hands. A movement behind her eyelids. She opened her eyes.

'Hello,' she said, and smiled. 'I'm okay, just tired,' and closed her eyes again.

'Where are your parents?' Father asked Chong Meng, who was standing beside the bed.

Chong Meng looked up abruptly. 'They're back home; my father said that he needed to organise the lorries going into the city. And my mother has a headache.'

'That sister of mine. Her own mother is lying here in hospital and still she can't be bothered to come.'

Chong Meng shifted his weight from his left foot to his right foot. 'My mother and father said that they will pay all the hospital bills.'

'You think money will solve this? You think money will cure her?' Father gave a loud humph. Then his face softened a little as he said, 'I shouldn't get angry at you; you are not to blame. After all, you are not your parents.'

Chong Meng looked even more uncomfortable. His eyes flickered from Father to Ah-ma, his lips tightly pressed and his forehead creased. He looked up at the ceiling where the pallid fluorescent lighting pulsed at a low frequency, and then he looked down at the floor tiles.

'It's late now. You boys should go home and get some sleep. I'm going to stay here for the night,' Father said.

After some persuading, it was decided that Chong Meng would drive Father back home and Han would spend the night by Ah-ma's bedside instead.

The chair was stiff and unyielding, but Han managed to shape himself into a cocoon to sleep. He felt the chill on his arms. Sleep came and went. In one of these periods of sleep, Han woke up and found Ah-ma looking at him.

'Ah-ma, you're awake?'

'There is little time,' Ah-ma said. Her words rang like temple bells. 'In case your father never tells you the story – you know what he's like! – I want to tell you. We can't change anything about the past, but I should tell you now, even though it's bad luck to talk about, you know, death – very suay. But suay or not suay, you should know, as you are not a boy anymore.'

Once upon a time, Ah-ma began, a beautiful young woman arrived in this village where there was nothing but fishing. She had long, black hair and fair skin, almost as if her skin had never seen the sun before. When she arrived, people started talking about this young woman: how she came here with a baby, how a woman as beautiful as she could have no husband yet have a baby, how she ended up in this village, even though no one knew her.

Ah-ma heard from the hairdresser that the young woman was working as a cleaner at the new Rasa Sayang resort by the beach.

'They are hiring all these out-of-town workers, most of them staying in the dorms, in the old plantations there. They are flooding this small village!' the hairdresser complained. 'You know what these young ones are like, looking for husband to gorek money.'

A taxi driver proudly informed Ah-ma that the young woman's name was Swee, as if he had been privileged to hold the secret of her name in his hands. He added, 'In your language, Swee means "beautiful", right?'

Ah-ma's qi gong friends told her they saw Swee frequently making offerings at the Thean Hou temple. 'Don't know why she's so pious,' they said, huffing. 'Maybe she's trying to atone for something.'

Ah-ma first saw Swee at the Billion supermarket, where Swee was at the payment counter buying baby shoes, baby shoes for you, Han! You were a calm baby sleeping among the chattering shop assistants.

She closed her eyes and sighed, before opening them again. 'You know what, I only saw her for a second, but I thought she would make a good wife for your father. Your father was already old by then. I so scared for him, every time I go to the temple and pray. What if he is single for ever? Where got any mother want to see her son lonely? I die then how? So I pray and pray and pray at the temple – Guan Yin, please send my son a wife. And then I saw your mother,' Ah-ma said.

Father first met Swee at the banks of the Ghueh Niu river on the day of Chap Goh Mei ('But not from an orange,' Ah-ma said). Soon after that, they got married. They were a good match. Father was very protective of Swee, who was like porcelain that could shatter at the merest touch. Ah-ma was very happy to have another grandchild.

'Some people would look down on a woman who already had a child with another man. They say the woman is tainted, and the child will bring bad luck. But you were a beautiful, chubby child and who wouldn't love you?'

Swee settled happily in their family, or so they all thought. She kept the home clean and always had food on the table. She was kind to Ah-ma and to Father. But she never spoke about her past, where she came from and why she ended up there. Or other important details, like what jobs her kong-kong and papa did, what gods she prayed to, how she celebrated the New Year, if she came from another fishing village further down the coast, and so on. When asked about her life before arriving at Kampung Seng, she stopped talking, and walked away mid-conversation.

('So rude, that woman! Ask about her family also so sensitive. Drama this, drama that. Maybe she from some ulu tribe in the desert, that's why don't want to say wan lah. Too pai seh,' Mrs Lim whispered to her husband.)

We are all part of this world, Ah-ma explained, connected in this great shining net of humanity, and to belong in it fully, one needs a past, a history. Because Swee never spoke about her past, it was as if she was not fully present in the net. As if her thread was a stray one, woven loosely with the other lines, threatening to unravel as life tugged on it.

'Sometimes I think she didn't know her own history. As if she didn't remember who her family were. She was a lost spirit, floating to whatever place that would accept her,' Ah-ma said.

A few years after they got married, Swee was late for dinner. Ah-ma remembered that she had prepared steamed eggs with minced pork, and watercress soup. (What useless details one remembers, she said to Han.) They started eating anyway, thinking Swee had gone to buy new towels. Then there was a sharp, frantic banging at their front gates. Mr Liew stood at their gates, yelling, 'Your wife! At the beach! Your wife! Come, come now!'

At the beach they found Swee surrounded by fishermen, looking at her with solemn attention. Her clothes were sodden. Father ran to her side. He placed his lips to her mouth, giving her his breath. She was cold and blue and still in the falling light of the evening.

Someone from the crowd whispered to Ah-ma that Swee had run deliberately into the sea, exactly at the spot where dangerous rip currents formed. She was dragged rapidly into deeper water. Swee could not swim. The fishermen who were nearby had rushed to the nearest motorboat to try to save her but by the time they arrived, she had already drowned.

Deliberately? She ran into the sea deliberately? Ah-ma asked a fisherman. Father held Swee in his arms, not wanting to let her go.

Yes . . . it looked like it. The man nodded slowly.

The next morning, two policemen in their dark uniforms arrived at the hospital, just after Father came in with the newspapers.

'We don't want to disturb the rest of the patients,' they whispered, looking worriedly around the ward as if the other patients were going to infect them, before drawing the curtains around Ah-ma's bed. 'So, Auntie, do you remember what happened yesterday?'

Ah-ma had walked to the hairdresser that morning, but the hairdresser had a fever and was not there. ('Walk all the way there but then the others said ah-Kim was sick, so I just went back home lor,' Ah-ma said.) She had been weeding the vegetable patch out the back, digging out the roots with an old fork, when she heard the doorbell ring. She unlocked the padlock from the steel chain, opened the front-door grille, and tiptoed in her bare feet across the tiles of the front yard, hot in the morning sun. She peered through the gate. A man was outside. She had never seen him before, which was unusual, as she knew almost everyone who lived in the village. She had lived in this village all her life. (I even know both your mothers, she told the policemen. Your mother went to school with me – she pointed at one police officer – and your mother sells vegetables at the market, pointing at the second police officer.) Of the stranger at the gate, Ah-ma thought, this man was not one of those foreign workers from the resort. Too well-dressed. That was the last thing she remembered.

'We think he gave you a smelling drug, the ones that make you faint,' the taller police officer said. 'Then he climbed over the gate and straight into the house. We think that he carried you inside after.'

'Why? I'm an old woman; who would want to disturb me?'

'Your son said that he took an item from your house. A spade?'

Father said to the shorter police officer: 'I told you it was that good-for-nothing Mr Ng. I knew it from the day I met him. Asking about Swee.'

'This Mr Ng left Lucky Inn last night. We have his car plate number. To be honest, Auntie, since he didn't steal much, I think very hard for us to go after him. Got more important problems in Kampung Seng, like illegal workers without work permit. It's just a spade after all.' The policemen left. There was nothing else they could do or wanted to do.

Chong Meng arrived at noon. He said to Han and Father: 'I'm here to accompany Ah-ma for the day. You can both go back now, get some rest. I also heard about the spade. But it's been lying in the house for a while now, very old item, rusty, even. He didn't steal any of your other things, you see. Wouldn't expect it either, from a man like Mr Ng.'

'I stay here a bit longer,' Han said.

'Go, go have some rest. Don't worry,' Chong Meng said. 'Uncle, cousin, don't worry.' He looked at Ah-ma as if he was trying to solve a puzzle.

Father made his daily offerings when they got home. 'Stand in front of the altar, close your eyes, and ask Mama to send you good luck,' Father said to Han. They both closed their eyes. 'Nah, light these three joss sticks and put them in the censer. Tell Mama that yesterday was a bad day.'

Han stood in front of the altar, bowing his head. *Who are you, Mama? Why did you end with the sea?*

'I knew that Mr Ng was a no-good fellow when I saw him. What can we do? Nothing. The police have bigger fish in the sea to chase. We small people are not important,' Father said

41

with some sadness. 'It's life. We say thank you to the gods that nothing worse happened to Ah-ma.'

Han was determined. 'Father, I am going to find Mr Ng. I know he is headed for the capital.'

'No point, son, just let it go. Mama's spade was not going to be with us for ever,' Father said. 'The capital is so big, you're not going to find Mr Ng. You are young. You haven't even been to the capital before. What else can you do?'

You are young were the words that Han heard. He thought about staying in this village and with his family that he loved. But Ah-ma's words last night had awoken something in him, an uncommunicable desire to find the spade. There was a hole in the net and he had to mend it. A great wrong had been done, not just because a spade had been stolen, but because a man stole from their family, who had so few things, and so few memories, especially for a man who had lost his wife and a boy who had lost his mother.

Han said, 'Mama is dead. Dead.' His stomach was heavy. He had never said the word out loud before, and he half wanted to take it back. The provocation hung in the air.

Father stepped back, nearly falling over his feet before catching himself. 'You think I don't know? You think every morning I don't wish your mama was here? I put joss sticks every day for fifteen years! You don't even remember her.'

Something in Han broke, and for the first time in his life, he shouted at Father: 'Why you think I want to get the spade back? She's dead and I have nothing left of her!'

You – you are what is left of her, Father thought. Instead he said, 'Nothing you do will bring her back.' His words were quiet but dispensed like heavy, heirloom plates, tucked away in the cupboard, brought out only on special occasions.

42

Han could feel the weight of Father's feelings, and the long years that Father had spent guarding them. Nevertheless, he could feel his next sentence tumbling out of his mouth, knowing that they would hurt. 'Easy for you to say do nothing. You . . . you just sit at home every day and do nothing.' Maybe he wanted to hurt Father purposely, to get him to react, to say something, anything. 'Put joss sticks, pray to your gods, for what?' Why did Father not say anything about Mama in all these years? Why can't he just talk about it? 'Mama's still dead! Her spade is gone! Pray also pray no use wan!'

Father said, nearly growling, biting, 'Fine, go to the capital. You think you are so smart? What do you know?'

They stood in an angry silence, before Han turned away. 'I have to find Mama's spade. Take care of Ah-ma until I get the spade back.' *I love you, Father*, Han did not say.

Father said nothing. He looked at the empty spot on the altar where the spade used to stand, as the afternoon light shone through the dusty louvre windows.

Chap Goh Mei

It had been the night of Chap Goh Mei, the final hours of the New Year celebrations, when he had met Swee for the first time, seventeen years ago. He had picked up two oranges that had drifted towards the banks of the Ghueh Niu river. The oranges were dark and pimply, and any phone numbers that had been written onto these misshapen spheres had rubbed off. He sighed and thought, *No luck, Ma. See, I came to the river like you told me to, okay? Got oranges but no phone number also. Enough, enough?*

Obviously he knew what his ma would reply: 'You got try hard, anot? Don't just stand-stand there and pick one or two oranges, alang-alang only. Pick more orange. How else can find wife? Go go go.'

All along the banks of the Ghueh Niu river were young women and men, bright in their hope, the women throwing in oranges with their names and phone numbers written in dark ink, and the men eagerly retrieving the oranges with the contact details. These women and men stood in small, single-sex groups for protection, chattering, standing in open crescents, their bodies facing inwards, while their eyes searched, watching the other groups, thinking, *Where is my future wife? Where is my future husband?*

He had been about to ride his Honda home when he first saw Swee and her fine hair that drifted to her shoulders. She stood high up on the bank, away from the groups, white cloth wrapped around her body and, nestled within, a sleeping child. She looked like the goddess Guan Yin. Her eyes scanned the banks, before she noticed him, another solitary person, staring back at her.

They were both instantly embarrassed, having been caught looking at each other. He was about to move away, eyes turned down, when she smiled at him.

'Have you found any oranges?' she said.

'Uh, yes, uh, no, not really. I found oranges, but they had no names on them. What about you? You throwing oranges?'

She shook her head. 'Not throwing oranges. Only for single, unmarried women. Just came here to look.'

'You have a husband?' he asked, even though he already knew the answer.

'I don't have one. I have my beautiful child,' she said. There the words tolled, so definitive, so final. *I have my beautiful child* were her words, and no shame tarnished their pure expression. 'His name is Han,' she added.

The bells rang in the temple. New Year celebrations were about to close. It felt like an ending and a beginning.

'Are you going to walk home, miss? I can give you a ride,' he said, and then stopped, as he realised how his words could have been construed.

Swee looked in the direction of the river, where it flowed darkly into the open sea. The clouds shifted and there was the moon, the first full moon of the year, and of the rest of their lives. Then she stared at him, and said, 'Yes, please. Han needs to get home to sleep. Just go slowly, okay?'

He visited these memories often, when he was tired, or lonely, or when he simply missed her. These memories lay like flowers waiting to be picked over and over again. He would remember the nights when they slept huddled next to each other, and she would squeeze his hand several times, waking both of them up. He would remember them arguing about whether the fan was too loud for Han to sleep. Or when she brought him yellow chrysanthemums from the market ('Every Friday they sell cheap-cheap').

And then there were the times he told her that he was going on the deep-sea fishing trips.

Deep-sea boat, he said. Good money.

No, don't leave me. Don't leave us, Swee told him.

Ma can keep you company. Don't worry. She cook you food. She cook Han food.

Why do you always do this? Why must you keep going on the deep-sea boat?

We need the money to buy meat. It is just one week.

Don't eat meat is okay. We won't die wan. We can eat eggs.

After Han grow up to be short, how? Eat vegetables only, then short like me. Already he is shorter than his cousin. Short-short, get teased in school, not successful, you know. He needs to eat meat, Swee.

Just borrow money from your sister, she will lend you wan. She got so much money. Only for short time. Just tell her you need it for this month! Just ask her!

47

My sister? Already she is so sombong. Stuck up like anything only. Only because she marry Mr Lim. Now got money, now suddenly better than us. You know she talk behind our back, say how poor we are, say you are bad luck, suay. She say why I marry foreign woman from don't-know-where. You crazy? You forgot?

Swee turned away. He was instantly sorry. He wished he could comfort her, to tell her that everything would be okay, and he did all this for her, for the three of them. What was she so afraid of?

He looked at his feet and mumbled in way of an apology, a concession: 'I only go one week. Don't worry, okay? Deep-sea boat. Twice the pay. Share of profits. Ma will cook you watercress soup. Your favourite.' His words were repeated over and over again, like a charm to ward off evil. *Watercress soup. Your favourite.*

Okay, she said. And then, almost as an afterthought, she said, The nights are long.

She looked at him, as if she wanted to say something else. He could not read her expression. The moment was past.

Could he have helped her and could he have stopped her? he thought later, but he was just a kampung boy from Kampung Seng and there was nothing more he could have done, only to accept what had happened. That was what he told himself, anyway.

In any case these were his memories and there was no changing them. For there was no more her to create new stories, new memories. No more new Swee; just the Swee of the past, repeating in an endless loop. Like the sea in the dead afternoon heat, when no wind blew, and chau hu swam in permanently slow circles; that was how he remembered her for the rest of his long years. Maybe that was to be his punishment.

He wished she was alive, partly because he missed her and also because he wanted to share with her what Han had become. What would she have thought of her son now?

'What a strong and filial young man,' she would have said.

Swee would have been a proud mother.

Part Two
Suriyang,
Eighteen Years Earlier

Swee

To the east of Kampung Seng, east beyond Liu's prawn farms, further east past the paddy fields, as far as you can go, beyond the Western Range, further, further, into the desert highlands, past the sand-choked villages of the East Coast, leaving the great Peninsula behind, and the unnamed sea where all the maps end, to the east of *that* sea, the Hei-san islands lie in their thousands.

There was an unnamed woman on one of these islands, on her first day for the rest of her life. She had small cuts on her face and on her exposed arms. She was in a forest, carrying a crying baby. What do I do with this thing? A wetness developed on her breast. The baby was turning to her – her – as the provider of his needs. She felt wanted. Another feeling surfaced, strong like the trunk of trees, to give the baby everything she possessed.

Oh, you beautiful thing, she thought for the first time.

She held the baby, and his warmness touched her skin. He felt small and alive. His head moved wildly against her chest, his nose turning left and right as he searched for her breast, ferocious until he found her nipple and latched on. Some time passed, maybe no time passed.

She found herself carrying a large bag. In it were small, brown cubes, and she placed one in her mouth. The cube dissolved instantly, and tasted of muddy rain puddles, of far-off woody rustles, and a further thousand sensations that she could not name, for she had no memories to compare them with. The growing pain in her middle disappeared and her head cleared.

There were other objects in the bag, too – a Bag of Objects. Later, she tried to guess the function of some of the items. Food, matches, bandages, a spade – but not one for digging holes in the ground. There were many objects whose functions she could not even begin to guess. A silver blanket with a long rope attached to two corners? An eight-sided object that was warm to touch, even on the coldest nights? A cylinder the size of her palm but as heavy as a sack of rice?

This unnamed woman arrived at the mountain village of Suriyang. The bottom of her trousers was torn, where the forest undergrowth had tugged at the hems repeatedly. Her skin was pale, as if she had not seen the sun very much, and glowed with such translucence that one could almost see the blood flowing through her veins. Although she did not know it yet, she was considered – in the villagers' eyes – a spirit.

The first villager who saw the spirit was a young boy picking rambutans in the orchard, who ran away to his mother, crying, 'I saw spirits, Mama! They have come back!'

Here was a new one, the villagers chatted nervously when they heard the news. A spirit has come again. They had not seen a spirit in such a long time; the last one had visited more than twenty years ago. Parents told their children: Here, here, come and see her, but keep your distance, because the spirits bring bad luck. The durian trees are less fruitful, and the black dust blows from the Burnt Islands and covers our homes with darkness. Remember this day so that you can tell your own children. The spirits visit our village less and less, and each spirit may be the last spirit. One day, we might never see the spirits again.

The village sinseh approached the spirit, as was customary. Unlike the other sinsehs on the island, this sinseh was a woman, and young. At last count, the sinseh estimated her age to be somewhere in the early forties, having given birth to a child over a year ago. She was good at curing ailments and the villagers respected her.

'Do you have a name?' the sinseh asked, even though she knew the answer already. These spirits came out of the forest with no memories. They could not remember anything. Like blank sheets of paper. They had no names. They could not remember what they had for dinner yesterday. They could not remember the cold seasons, or the hot seasons. They could not tell you whether they lived in a hut or under the trees. It was as if the Urang Api-Api had burned any writing of their past. They were human, but not one of them.

'No,' the spirit replied. Her words came out in soft, rhythmic patterns, with a lilt that was not at all like the local accent of Suriyang. She struggled to form her next words, as if the muscles in her mouth were not used to moving. But her meaning was clear enough. 'No, I don't. I don't remember my name,' the spirit said.

The spirit's tools for communication had remained intact, even though her words had no personal meaning. Her tongue and her mouth made the sounds automatically, without interference from her active thoughts. She did not know what these sounds were but had started to realise the relationship between her thoughts and the sounds. These were skills she did not know she had.

If she could have looked into her own eyes, she would have found the same expressions that she saw in the villagers': curious, wary, but desperate to connect.

She opened her mouth and focused her attention on a thought that she wanted to communicate to the sinseh. 'I . . . I am thirsty. I would like some water if you are able to offer me some.'

More words came to the spirit: *Sinseh. Looks after the villagers' health. Prescribes herbs.*

Villagers gathered around them, but the spirit was concentrating on drinking the glass of water given to her. Her baby looked around contentedly, unaware of the level of interest surrounding them.

'I will give you a name,' the sinseh said. She paused to think. 'Swee, that will be your name from now on.'

Swee. The sound was strange to her, but she accepted it.

'And for your baby, do you have a name for him?'

Swee shook her head.

'Then your baby's name can be Han,' the sinseh said. Han gurgled as if in acceptance.

What black magic had led to this? The sinseh knew that her herbs and medicines would not cure this disease of the mind.

The clouds that had occupied the afternoon sky gave way to a small opening of blue and, for a moment, as sunlight poured onto the land, the pale skin of Swee and Han shimmered.

Swee and Han were given permission to stay in the village's temple hall.

'But you can't leave the temple grounds ah? Need to ask me or the temple caretaker first, okay?' the sinseh said.

A partially uncurled bamboo mat was left out for Swee to sleep on. A frayed blanket lay to one side. Han cried, his sharp shrieks clouded the air. She rocked him, feeling the weight of his little body in her arms. She scanned her surroundings – different shapes of grey and black, unfamiliar to her. They were nameless shadows; she who did not know the names of anything in this world. If Swee had dreams that night, they were jumbled thoughts that made up the first night of the rest of her life.

'This is a small temple,' the temple caretaker explained to Swee. Several strands of white hair limped across his forehead. 'A small temple for our small village. We have three altars here. The centre altar is for Tian Gong, the Jade Emperor. The other altar is for Mazu and her two guardian generals. And the one on the outside, the small altar out there, is to appease the local spirits. You know, *your* kind.'

Dawn was the hour of Breaking the Quiet. Swee woke up before anyone arrived at the temple. She rolled up her sleeping mat into a tight circle. Then, she raised burning joss sticks to Tian Gong at the front door of the temple, as the caretaker taught her. *Thank you for bringing me to this village*, she prayed, as she knelt in front of the altar. The giant statue of Tian Gong looked down on the young mother and her baby with benevolence, perhaps reminded of his own heaven-bound daughter, separated from her lover by the depths of the Milky Way.

The temple followers would arrive later to say their prayers, their heads bowed at similar angles as they chanted. At night, when the heat had left the temple walls, Swee would sweep the compound, then give the place a quick mop as the floors usually got sticky with the sweat of others, before rolling out mats for Han and herself to sleep on.

Days passed with the aimlessness of a ticking clock, with the exception of festival days, where everyone visited the temple. Children ran around in bare feet, and there was an excess of incense and food offerings: sweet ang ku kuih, tong sui, kee chang, thi kuih and ong lai; fruit of mysterious shapes and colours; and even, depending on what festival the temple celebrated, a whole roasted pig. They would say prayers for a prosperous future and make their joss-stick offerings to the god being celebrated. And then the community feasted together in the same way that their parents, and their grandparents, and their great-grandparents before them had done.

On one of the festival days, she asked the caretaker, 'Why are we making these mi koo?' She pointed at the little pink buns shaped like tortoises, freshly steamed in their baskets.

'It's what we have always done, ah-girl. The recipe was passed down seven generations. Look, look, new flavours for this year! Banana, pandan and pineapple.' He turned away excitedly, having already forgotten her question.

Sometimes they asked her, 'What ancestors do you pray to? Who brought your family into this world?' Some looked at her with pity, some looked at her with disapproval. No culture, no traditions, no ancestors, no family, no husband, but a baby!

58

The Spirits

At Suriyang, the memories that Swee created were the foundations on which she stood for the rest of her life, and sometimes clung to, like a desperate prayer. Her mind absorbed every waking moment, even simple things like using a spoon and fork, sitting on the toilet, kneeling to say prayers. Each memory was a precious stone that she delicately placed in her box of memories. Each memory was taken out again and again, examined in the smallest detail, until any impurities had been polished away to a dull shine.

But a gigantic hole of memories defined her existence. Sometimes she stood at the edge of the dark hole, and the soles of her feet felt the accelerating change as the ground dropped into a sharp cliff, beyond which there was nothing and nothing else. It was against this hole and her lack of memories that she felt a deep anger; she wanted to rage, shout, throw things into this loss. But she could not. All her anger could not collect into a core because there was nothing she could be angry at. Anger that she had lost something, but she did not know what, even as she felt its loss.

She told the temple caretaker of this. He was her only friend in the village.

'You need to accept it,' he said. 'Like the others before you.'

The caretaker was several decades old and had a wife (who had died last year), six children (three dead from dengue as children) and ten grandchildren. He told her that the spirits had appeared in their village for as long as anyone could remember. 'Your kind has always been near our people. We have you in our histories; you are part of this land as much as we are.

'Our land is fertile. We grow jackfruit, vegetables and paddy on stepped terraces in valleys that rivers have carved out. Frequent storms bring fresh water from the mountains. The black soil is rich and brings us prosperous harvests. The gods have brought good health and fortune to our ancestors.

'On the Day of Ashes, we make our offerings to the God of Black Cranes. One roast pig, which will bring us crops and animals for the rest of the year. And white chrysanthemums, kiok hoe, so that the forest will not take our children,' the caretaker said.

There was power in the forest – black magic in the same black soil that the village grew on. It gave things, like water from the mountains, but it also took things. 'It took your memory, and it took everything that you had been,' the caretaker said. 'The forest gave birth to a new you and to the others like you.'

It also took the children of the village. Their mothers told them to play only where the river was wide and the forest was

60

thin. 'Don't play-play in the forest. Got hantu will gigit you.' Their fathers would beat them with a rotan if they disobeyed. But children went into the forest anyway, and some never came back. Fathers and mothers entered the forest to look for their child, but sometimes they too did not return to the village; and those who did, had lost their memories.

'Perhaps it is better that they do not remember what they lost,' the caretaker said.

The caretaker's grandaunt had told everyone who would listen, of the time when she found two spirits in the orchard shed. She was only fourteen then. They were sleeping with their arms around each other, with bags of brown cubes standing guard beside them. They looked like a middle-aged man and woman, but she knew better. 'Go away,' she told these cursed creatures, bravely. They quickly packed up their moultish belongings and skittered into the night.

Going further back in their family's history, the caretaker heard that his great-grandfather had found a group of them on the street one night – three men and two women – huddling together like lost deer. They had the same strange clothing, with the same translucent skin. They carried large bags. 'You can sleep on my porch,' his great-grandfather said.

But his great-grandmother was superstitious and did not want any of these dirty spirits near her. 'Bring bad luck, you know,' she had said, so the story went. 'But don't make them angry, in case they curse us. Maybe just say nicely that they can't sleep on the porch; they have to find somewhere else.'

These spirits are suffering from retrograde amnesia, a foreign visitor called Professor Toh later noted.

Think of it as such: When asked, *Who are you?* the spirits had no answer to this question, not even the recollection of a long-lost dream. When asked, they delved into the expansive seas of their souls and surfaced with . . . nothing. No life swam in their seas, no fish swam with the great currents, pushing through the meadows of bright corals, no boats passed over the surface and no people flailed in their depths. Their souls were featureless oceans that reached into the great deep of the abyssal plain, where no light and no life had ever warmed the cold ocean floor.

The professor asked: When did the spirits first come to your village? How long before the Great Eruptions? Were there more of them, once upon a time?

The villagers had no answers. For the villagers, these questions were in the same category as what caused the Great Eruptions, what killed off the Bercahaya Empire, what do you know of your ancestors? We are simple people, we pray to gods, and we have honourable lives, the villagers said, and together they folded their questions away into their daily chants and into the stern protection of the gods. Why was it necessary to know when the spirits started arriving in their village? Why was it important to know which direction the spirits had come from? The villagers of Suriyang did not care. They lived like pebbles stranded in a mountain valley, their village so remote that it took thirteen days to walk to the sea. Once a week, a lorry brought in goods from the coast: children's toys, sweets, cigarettes, and stories of other islands and the distant Peninsula beyond.

The spirits never left Suriyang, either. They worked in manual-labour jobs that no one else wanted to do. They lost their translucence after several months under the sun, and their skin turned into the villagers' brown. Many of them died young, as if the weight of their absent histories was too much to bear for one person.

These spirits are not meant for this world. They are just passing through, like ash clouds, as the caretaker's grandaunt used to say.

Hungry Ghost Festival

On the fifteenth day of the seventh month, Swee cleaned the altars in preparation for the Hungry Ghost Festival. She was wiping the crumbs from the food offerings, clearing old ashes from the censers and giving fresh water to the flowers, when she found, in one of the drawers of the altar, a framed picture that lay nestled within dust and old prayer paper. She held the picture up to the light.

A spade, sketched in rough, black ink, now faded with age.

'What is this picture?' she asked the caretaker, who was in his room. The room that he lived in was adjoining the temple, built simply with four walls, two windows, a roof and a door that opened directly into the temple hall, but was frequently kept locked so that temple devotees did not accidentally wander into it. Not that there was much to steal: his only possessions were a few photographs and a large piece of cloth stretched to form a hammock to sleep in.

'I don't know,' the caretaker said. 'I kept it in the drawer because the hook that held it up had fallen from the wall. Never got the chance to fix it.'

'Where does it come from?' she said.

'I don't know,' he said again. 'These things are not important you know, ah-girl. Who knows how old that picture is? Maybe a hundred!' he said. 'Are you concentrating on your cleaning? This is the Hungry Ghost month, first day somemore. The gates of hell are open, ghosts are let out to wander on earth. People arriving at the temple soon to make their offerings!'

Swee slipped away to the storeroom, with Han sleeping in a wrap high up on her back. Here, her Bag of Objects was hidden among the many dusty bottles of prayer oil. Her hands shook as she undid the straps. She sifted through the items until she found what she had been looking for: her spade. Just like the one in the picture. It was as if the artist had drawn Swee's own spade, with its misshapen blade and too-short shaft. She traced out the carvings on the handle with the tips of her fingers, feeling its energy; as if the spade had been much more than a spade, once upon a time.

Someone else has seen the spade before, she thought. Her hands trembled as she held the object, feeling the unbalanced weight of the handle. She wondered about the people who had held it before. Her past was like a starless night sky but, as she studied the drawing of the spade and the spade both, she felt the sun's warmth creeping along the curved edges of a distant horizon.

Han stirred from his nap. Somewhere, they belonged somewhere once, in some place, some time ago. There were tears in her eyes, from happiness or sadness or both, as she sat on the storeroom floor, and she wondered what it all meant.

Perhaps there could be a future for us, too, she thought.

That night, the villagers visited the temple to burn items for their ancestors. Among the items – made out of joss paper – burned were hell money, in honourably large denominations; gold bars; bicycles; servants; and clothes. These were tossed into the furnace outside the temple's main gates.

'We have to provide things for our ancestors. We do this by burning hell money, and anything they might need in the afterlife. Now my grandfather will get the bicycle he always wanted when he was alive,' the caretaker explained to Swee. 'Also, if we don't please their ghosts, they might come back to haunt us and bring bad luck to our family down the line.'

Into ashes, the items burned. The paper dissolved and their smoke trails curled in the air, where they rose to the sky. A loose bundle of billion-dollar hell money, signed by the Bank of Hell, burned rapturously and then there was nothing but dust. Smoke gave a hazy veil to the night.

A family gave Swee some of their joss-paper items, so that she could offer her ancestors some wealth.

'But I don't know who they are,' she said.

'Just in case, you never know.'

She tossed a few gold bars into the furnace.

What ancestors do I pray to? She watched the fire as it consumed item after item, roaring as more gold bars were thrown into it. More, more, it craved, seeking appeasement from the crowds. More, it cried, licking at the walls of the furnace, wanting to escape. More, it cried to ancestral spirits roaming the earth that month, looking for entertainment and food. We are the dead, and we will accept your riches!

Next to the temple, in the corner of the village school's playing fields, getai performances were being held on a stage, which had been specially built for the Hungry Ghost Festival. The stage was made up of several planks of wood slapped together and held fast by rusty nails.

Swee had visited the stage earlier in the evening, before the temple's prayers had started. She had sat on an empty seat in the front row.

'This seat is reserved for ghosts, you know. Can't you read?' A woman with white hair waved her umbrella at Swee.

Yes-yes, Auntie. Swee nodded meekly and shuffled off to stand by the side.

A troupe of acrobats was on the stage making a human pyramid. They twisted themselves so that their legs were pointing up in the air, while they held themselves aloft with their forearms. They contorted their bodies into shapes – a chair, a seesaw – even as they maintained the pyramid. Swee was fascinated: everyday gossip in Suriyang was her usual entertainment. As the night went on, the performances became more tawdry. Disco lights flashed furiously, blue, green, yellow, red; lights pulsing, flooding the village in a garish performance.

She had rushed back to the temple for the scripture readings but did not remember much of them. The night ended with a woman singing about drinking rice wine in the morning, afternoon and in the evening, at home, in a restaurant and in a bar, because her lover had left her and she had nothing else to live for.

When the music was over the crowds left, and the temple was empty once again, only now sticky with sweat from the soles of its visitors. Swee swept and mopped the floors.

68

The fire was still burning in the furnace. Wads of hell money and paper cars waited their turn to be burned. Swee and the caretaker looked at the flames.

'Leave the fire to die down overnight and you can rake it in the morning,' the caretaker told her. 'It will burn itself out in the furnace. There are no houses nearby, anyway.' The temple was located on the far eastern side of Suriyang, beyond the last house and only reachable by a small dirt road.

That night, Swee placed the spade next to the mats before lying down, as she did every night since she found the picture. Her sleep was intruded on by a warm presence that bathed her with light. She basked in its glow, before it melted into greyness. The air swirled, pushing and pulling her in the faceless grey. *Fight it.* She punched into the thin air, but that only made her sweat. The greyness collapsed on her and there was nothing left but fire.

She woke up.

Around her, flames ate the wooden pillars of the temple. Heat and smoke warped the air. Burn, burn, and so it all burned. The only light came from above, where flames had reached the ceilings. Swee crouched down low, where the air was still clear and the concrete floor cool to touch. Han! He was still asleep. Her spade lay by his side. She grabbed a sling and quickly tied Han to her front, and then started crawling towards the entrance. As an afterthought, she turned around and grabbed the spade with her left hand – the smallest of hunches, a thought from somewhere, a life before, a life after. *Maybe this spade will protect us, bring us good luck.*

The entrance to the temple was partially blocked: carvings of vines and fruit had burned off the beams and collapsed onto the floor, and were now scorching, faceless wood. The once-strong wooden pillars that marked the temple's entrance were now blazing with bright-red heat. It hissed at her, full of fury. She recoiled. Everywhere the fire was erasing the temple, burning the wooden fibres and the stories that it held into flames, and then blackness.

Her eyes teared and she could not see. The heat: she felt as if she was burning too, burning with the flames, her skin crinkling like prayer paper and her hair on fire. She wanted to cry – it was too hard, the fire was too strong. Maybe she should just give up, the memory-hole within her whispered. Disappear into the fire; the fire would release her from the anger of nothing-knowing.

Then she felt Han's little fingers scrabbling at her neck. His feet pushed at her ribs. He was awake and screaming, kicking, his head thrashing from side to side, crying for her. She had to get out, or Han would die. She needed to save him. She could not let him burn, not him, not his gentle skin or fine brown hair or perfectly shaped ears. He cried and cried and she knew what she must do. She hissed at the fire: *You do not get to take my son!*

She lifted her left hand up and found that she was still holding the spade. A shield. It felt cool to her touch. She got down on her elbows and slithered through a tunnel of flames. A burning log fell on the upturned sole of her left foot. She bit on her tongue to stop herself from jerking away. Her palms were a mess of blood and blisters.

Suddenly, she felt a cool breeze hit her face and, all at once, the envelope of heat dropped away. They were outside.

It was a dark, new-moon night in the courtyard. The air was saturated with smoke. The fire was raging by the north gate, where the flames had overrun the furnace. The south

70

gate remained clear. She found a simple chain looped around the gate, secured by a padlock half-eaten by rust. She used the force of her hands to slam the lock into the metal bars of the gate. The harsh sound startled Han. But the lock did not fall open.

The gate was made of simple standing bars with spear-tops. The bars were spaced widely apart, enough that Han could fit through the gaps. Swee unwrapped him from his sling and knelt, carefully sliding him between the bars and resting him on the ground on the outside of the gates. She placed the spade next to him.

With her body free from carrying Han, she grabbed the lock with both hands again, and hit it against the bars of the gate. It juddered violently, and then fell open. She threw the lock to the side, the chain joining it. Using her entire body weight, she leaned against the bars. The gate sighed heavily and opened onto the dirt road that led to the village.

Han was still crying. Was he okay? Was he burned? She placed a hand on his face. He was fine, just distressed. She kissed him and placed his cheek against hers, hoping that it would calm him. He smelled of gentleness.

'There, there. What a beautiful, brave boy you are,' she told him.

She watched as the temple collapsed on itself, its walls falling into rubble. Some time passed. The flames died down. A dull, leaden feeling grew within her stomach. She had forgotten about the caretaker. He would have been sleeping in the room next door.

Where the temple and caretaker's room had once stood were fragments of familiar objects that she knew and loved. Blackened statues of Thousand-Mile Eye and With-the-Wind

Ear. A large bell that had hung in the temple hall had fallen to the ground, one half of its face now melted into a deformed mask. The charred beams pulsed with latent heat. Swee tried to step closer, to see, just maybe, and the ghost of smoke and heat threatened to swallow her. And there, in the south corner, next to the half-burned door, curled as if he was asleep, the caretaker lay broken, surrounded by ash. Patches of his T-shirt had melted on his body, colouring into yellow and black stains. His mouth was open.

A sob escaped from her throat, her eyes stinging from loss, tears or smoke, or all three. She willed time to stop; she watched the sky for signs of the sun arriving. Stop, so that it would only be a short time from when the caretaker was alive and the temple floors sticky with people's sweat. Stop, so that the memory of the caretaker would always be close to her.

With every passing moment Swee felt the caretaker moving further away, his ghost joining the other ghosts in the underworld. She felt she was living two split lives: in one life, the caretaker died and the temple burned down; in the other life, she had raked the fire tame in the furnace last night, and they slept in blankets that wrapped them in residual warmth, waking up in the morning as they always did. She could see the caretaker preparing offerings to each god, while she placed burning joss sticks in the censers. The temple followers would arrive one by one, rosy-cheeked in the morning wet. They would chant and bow their heads. The sun would move through their kneeling shadows, that morning and every morning after that. This was the life she was supposed to have lived.

Instead, flames were fading in the darkened abscess where the temple once stood. *If only I could have saved him*, she thought. *If only I was lying in the ashes instead of him.*

But another feeling arose in her, a feeling that was as fierce and old as the land. *I have to protect Han.* She pulled him closer to her chest, finding comfort in his baby-smell, and was surprised to find herself holding the spade. At least she had saved one thing from the fire, she thought, and her heart ached.

Light rain fell upon the valley. The last of the flames fought the drops and spat sparks, and eventually the flames fell quiet too, pulling back into protected nooks where the wood still pulsed with heat, and even that subsided into a glow, and then there was nothing left but the damp ashes of the temple. Now there was really nothing, not even light.

Swee and Han slept under the protection of a small bush for the rest of the night. Swee did not get much sleep, waking at every sound. Tigers prowled on the margins of Suriyang, sniffing out a goat or two. Or a baby.

When the first sun rays rose, a weighty groan reverberated through the air. *The weekly lorry*, Swee thought sleepily, *goods from the coast.* She felt a tickling at her elbow. Grass. She jumped up, startling Han, before she remembered what had happened last night. Her panic giving way to a dull pain. The villagers would blame her for the fire. The only person she could turn to was now dead.

She had to see the temple grounds again. She didn't expect to find anything, except she knew she had to see it.

Ash slept in thick layers. Statues, altars, carvings, prayers, photographs – gone. Sent to the heavens, the caretaker would say, though Swee was not sure whether there was a heaven for any of them. This was a graveyard of prayers. She looked for her Bag of Objects, but she could not find it.

The temple followers would be there very soon, and she could imagine what they would say. 'You are so suay, only bring bad luck to this village.' Even the nice Mr Khaw who offered chicken herbal soup to Han would not be so nice to them now. He would believe that she was bad luck too. There would be no sympathy or forgiveness for someone like her. She and Han would be sent into the forests from where they came, this time to die.

They needed to leave the village. When the temple followers arrived that morning, they would see the ashes, and they would believe that she and Han were dead, burned in their sleep. The village would be sad, but no one would look for them.

Perhaps the villagers are right; perhaps I am bad luck, she thought.

One day she would cry for the caretaker, for the loss of her first home, and for the loss of her first memories. But, this day, she had to find her way to the coast.

Part Three
The Capital

For All the Distant Cousins

Han stood in the front entrance of the Lim Fishing Company warehouse, a small bundle of belongings at his feet.

His uncle, Mr Lim, had told him, 'Now, boy, I'm doing your family a big favour, okay? Pulling in strings so the lorry will let you sit as a passenger. Somemore you can get a job through my connections in the capital. Happy you have a successful fishing tycoon as an uncle?'

His cousin, Chong Meng, rubbed his hands together and said, 'The capital will have a lot to offer young people. One can really become somebody there!'

Even his ah-ma said to Father, 'Never mind, he is only young once hor. Must let these young people go and see the world a bit, after they go crazy. See only Kampung Seng, hear only Kampung Seng. Must enjoy sikit lah. Where got all young boys like you, never go anywhere wan!'

*

After a six-hour drive south along the coast, the lorry driver dropped Han at the wholesale market, the largest in the capital. Look out for the name 'Chua and Sons', Han was told. Somewhere in the northwest corner.

The wholesale market was an imposing structure, several times larger than the Lim Fishing Company warehouse, and even larger than his school hall and all its attendant buildings. There were no walls, only concrete pillars holding up the panels of corrugated iron that was the roof. Air blew in through the various halls, keeping the market cool, even in the afternoon heat. It swept through the market like the early morning traders and the buyers, swerving around chicken stalls, flower stalls, vegetable stalls, and blowing old cabbage leaves into the path of a broom. The halls were nearly empty by this time, as waves of buyers had bought what they needed and gone home; the only people left in the afternoon were vendors packing up, and lost tourists.

The west hall smelled of the sea. This was where the fish sellers gathered, with their mountains of dirty ice, metal trays and rubber boots. The sign *Chua and Sons* hung above one of the stalls, its lettering nearly rubbed off. An old woman moved around fishscale-stained water with a large push broom.

'Excuse me, do you know where I can find Mr Chua?' Han asked. 'I'm supposed to be working here as temporary help.'

The woman straightened her back. 'I'm Madam Chua. Mr Chua died long time ago lah. Yes-yes, my usual temp boy went back to his hometown. His ma sick.' She squinted at Han. 'You the replacement? Come early tomorrow. Two in the morning. You need to stay until noon, otherwise no pay. Okay?'

That night and the rest of his nights in the capital, Han slept in a dorm of twenty beds that the lorry driver told him about.

When he arrived, most of the beds were filled with sleeping bodies, a few stray arms and legs poking out from sheets, or draped over the sides of the beds. The lights were left on at their full brightness. It was a hot, stuffy room, and there was no fan; the only air came from a small, squat, louvre window perched high on the wall, barely ajar.

Han placed the bag that contained his clothes and the herbs that Father had made him bring along to the capital (In case you get sick, Father said) in the locker next to his bed, and lay on the mattress until the lights were turned off. Occasionally, a cough rose from one of the bodies, but for the most part there was only snoring and rustling noises that drifted together in the night air, and the room was calm.

The early morning of the wholesale market was different from the slow scenes of the afternoon. Ice buckets of squid jostled for space in the passageways, barrows of lotus roots were pushed over unsuspecting toes, and rambutan-laden boxes towered dangerously on their dollies. The unmistakable deep-fried fragrance of yau char kwai spread through the air. Han bumped his way through to the fish section, and just in time too, for there was already a buyer – a cook from a nearby restaurant, who needed twenty kilos of ang zhor, twenty kilos of koay gau and ten kilos of squid.

'Fish tank broken,' the cook said, resentfully. He had complained about the tank's pump too many times to count but had been ignored. 'Have to get fish directly from market.'

Han could not speak to Madam Chua about his search for Mr Ng until later in the day, once the buyers had disappeared.

'His name is Mr Ng. Do you know where he is?' Han asked.

'Mr Ng? Mr Ng what? No more details ah?'

'Middle-aged man. If you tell me where any of the Ng family stays, then I can go and ask them. Or if got two Ng families, then I can also ask both.'

'You crazy? Got hundreds of Ng families in the capital! Not like I can know all of them also,' she said, her permed curls swinging from left to right as she shook her head.

'Hundreds? You mean, hundreds of families with the surname of Ng? Cannot just ask people about the Ng family – a Mr Ng, cousin, or uncle, or brother to someone? Someone must know him.'

'You think what? You think the capital is like your small kampung, issit? Here got so many Ngs, so many Tans, so many Lims, so many Chuas, so many of everything. Ai-yah, whatever surname you name of, sure got many of the same-same in the capital wan. My family name Chua, you say special, but in this market alone, got six Chuas. Two Chua flower sellers, three Chua vegetable sellers, and then there is me. So you tell me, you tell me lah, Mr Ng like that name so common, find also how to find? Who can point you to the right Mr Ng?'

Asking Madam Chua had been the extent of Han's plan, and now he felt lost, an overwhelmed kampung boy standing in the breeze of the capital. How many Ngs? How many people? Why wouldn't she know all the Ng families? He had not expected this.

'Surely, you can point me to one Ng person? Maybe I just ask only. Nothing to lose. Since I am here, might as well,' he said, dazed.

Madam Chua sighed. She picked up a dense book from the counter and handed it to Han. He flipped the book open to a random page. Inside, the text laid itself out in orderly rows and columns, repeating over and over again in a pattern.

'See this phone book, got the names of all the Ngs in this capital. You so smart, you try to find one lah.'

Ngs. His eyes followed down the rows and rows of Ngs. Ng Ming Ming. Ng Wai Ling. Many Ngs, hundreds upon hundreds of rows of people, all with the family name Ng, derived from a common ancestor once upon a time. They swam in their Ng-ness, largely unaware that each of them was somehow bound together, that they shared blood and perhaps much more: common languages, common traditions and dreams of their ancestors. Each family of Ngs was a disparate branch that reached away from each other, the tips of their branches scraped at the sky and the sun, up, as high as they could go, hundreds and hundreds of them, all different and all the same, and forgetting that in the past, and still in the present, they were attached to the great sturdy trunk of their ancestors that bore their weight and held them secure. They would not know this. They would choose to forget; they would believe themselves to be alone, their words and thoughts lost in the streets and among the houses, where no one knew them, not even their third nephew or great-aunt. In their hearts they carried a sadness for all the distant cousins they did not know, and the family histories they had forgotten. They had no name for this sadness; indeed, they did not even realise they were sad, and yet the sadness clung to them for their whole lives, like a deepening shadow.

It was with optimism and some naivety that Han had decided to go through the list of Ngs in the phone book, visiting each of the listed addresses in order after he had finished work at the wholesale market. He had visited forty-six homes of Ngs with no luck, when, one afternoon during the monsoon season, around the corner from the wholesale market, he saw Mr Ng, the same Mr Ng whom they had met in Kopitiam Liong, dark from the sun, with his raised mole, thinning hair and the gold Rolex.

Mr Ng was walking east, where the sun was beginning its descent. His strides were long and purposeful; he was a man who wanted to be somewhere. Han followed from a distance. Not for the first time Han asked himself, *What would a man like Mr Ng want with Mama's spade?*

They walked to a part of the city lined with well-kept town houses, where the windows were not dusty or broken, but framed by linear curtains. Here, children jumped over kerbs, and found themselves next to storm drains that were too wide for them to cross. Look, so many tadpoles! they told each other, and their excitement bounced over the general hum of the metal-caged air-con units, whirring in abundance on the outside wall of every home. Gutter water dripped onto awnings. The pavements were swollen with afternoon heat, and somewhere in the hills, thunder boomed. Women – perhaps mothers, maids or grandmothers like his ah-ma – peered onto the streets from time to time, and upon seeing that everything was okay, withdrew back into their inside worlds, while men sipped at their kopi-Os, and had conversations about only Important Things, No Women No Children Allowed.

Mr Ng had arrived at a corner house at the intersection of two streets. The front door was made of solid jati wood, distinct from the other metal-grille doors of the houses next to it. The door opened, and closed, and Mr Ng was gone.

Han observed that the house was narrow, with white walls and several shuttered windows. The now-familiar metal bars crossed these windows.

Robberies in the city were increasing at an alarming rate, complained Madam Chua. Her wedding jewellery of twenty-three years had been taken from the top of her dresser, and her prepared ang paus, ready to be given out in the New Year, had disappeared when she was at work. 'Somemore I even hide the ang paus inside the toolbox, and still these blardy robbers managed to find it. All that money gone. No ang pau for the neighbours' kids, how? Cannot show my face!' Madam Chua had told him. 'So unsafe this capital. Where I grew up, you know, on the East Coast, even though the city was almost as big as this, a lot less robberies and break-ins. Sometimes the ground-floor windows don't have metal bars even!'

Han followed the house around to its side. There was a second entrance there – a smaller, less impressive door. The door opened.

He jumped. He was ready to run away. He had not thought much about what he would say or do if he saw Mr Ng – would he confront him? Would he demand the spade back? He was relieved when a young woman appeared. She looked about Han's age.

'Why you are looking at this house? I haven't seen you around before. And you are too young to be the police.'

'Miss-ah, I am looking for a man, Mr Ng. Is this his house? He went inside just now.'

The woman's face softened. 'This is Professor Toh's house. The man who just entered, he is a detective of one kind or another. He tried to make an appointment for a while now, but the professor is a busy man, you know.'

Han tried to peer into the house. The woman stood in front of the doorway, blocking his line of sight. Afternoon sunlight shone from behind Han and cast long shadows of their bodies into the house, where they merged with the darkness.

He said, 'Oh, okay. Are you the professor's . . . wife?'

'I'm the housekeeper. Well, if it is not Professor Toh you are looking for, then I can't help you. You should not be loitering around. Just so you know, the professor is not responsible for anyone else. All detectives must sign a contract saying that they are liable for their actions and the consequences.'

Han stared at her. 'What are you talking about?'

'The reward.' She stared back. 'Information on the forests of Naga Tua. You know, the professor's research. Professor Toh is the most famous expert on the Naga Tua island. No one else knows more than him. He is published in many journals and has appeared on the TV many times.' She peered at Han closely and said, 'What are you looking for again?'

'Miss-ah, I'm looking for this Mr Ng who came to this house. He stole an item from my family. It belonged to my mama.'

The young woman looked as if there was more she wanted to say, but struggled with the immensity of the words, and had given up a long time ago.

Instead, she said, 'I can hear them talking in the room. Sounds like they are unhappy. Come back tomorrow; the professor said Mr Ng has another appointment then.' There was a disconnect between what her face expressed and what her words said.

Han wanted to stay longer, to feel for what had not been said, like a blind man mending nets. But the woman looked anxious, so he stepped away from the house.

She called after him, 'What is your name?'

'I am Han,' he said.

'Min. My name.'

Mr Ng

When Mr Ng first held the spade in his hands, he was let down by its insignificance. *What is this?* he thought. A misshapen ugly object, only just fit underneath the front seat of his Volvo 240 hor. That Chong Meng, don't know what he talking about. He think this spade is what? Say-say very valuable, Swee's only possession wah, until Mr Ng think, this spade is like a sword, can chop a person until they die. Like the swords in the kung-fu shows.

Instead, this spade . . . really is a spade wan. Not gold, not silver. That dead woman Swee probably stole it from someone. The professor won't pay him any money for this stupid piece of junk. Still, at least the spade was something. When Mr Ng first arrived at Kampung Seng, he had long been fed up. Why his luck so suay wan? His mother would have told him to make more temple offerings. Maybe one of the gods was angry at him, she would have said. But he always prayed at the temple on Thursday evenings, made his offerings to Datuk Gong with betel leaves, lime paste and tobacco, and asked for good wealth and riches. Maybe he had not given enough paper money to his ancestors at the Hungry Ghost Festival last year. Maybe Grandpa Ling was still angry at his offering of the bicycle.

Three years, and look, only a spade. Some old spade! Three years since his initial meeting with Professor Toh, when he was first hired. If he had known that woman Swee would have been so hard to trace, he wouldn't even have started. The professor had told him, 'You will earn big bonus if you track her down. Somemore, I will credit your name in my research, in my papers. People at conferences will know of you. You will be famous! You will be important in science! And everyone will remember your name, even after you die. This is a kind of immortality, you know?'

Ai-yah, bullshit, all of it, except for the money. Mr Ng would not be here if it wasn't for the money.

Once upon a time, so it had been whispered, there was a detective named Mr Ooi, with a wife and small kid. This Mr Ooi managed to find something in the forests of Naga Tua island, but no one knew what. He came back cuckoo. 'What did you find?' the other detectives had asked Mr Ooi. The replies Mr Ooi gave were, 'I don't know. I can't remember. I can't remember anything before the village. I can't even remember my wife and child.' And then he cried; he always cried when asked this question. A grown man crying – weak man, really have no shame, the others said.

Others said that a demon possessed him. An old and cruel demon, perhaps a vengeful soldier from before the war. A tang ki was needed to exorcise this demon, and he did so by entering into a trance, chanting scriptures, brandishing a sword and offering pomelos. But no matter what scriptures were chanted, what sticky, sweet offerings were made, the old Mr Ooi was now gone, and in his place stood a new man who shared the same name and face as Mr Ooi, thirty years of age, but with only a few months of memories.

Professor Toh had refused to say anything about Mr Ooi, but had honoured his agreement by providing Mr Ooi's family with a regular income. ('Ai-yah, of course he had to pay Mr Ooi's family big reward, otherwise which other fool in the future would accept work from the professor again?')

Mr Ng knew about the risks. But his mother was old, and he had no family and no wife. Even if he forgot everything, not like he would know it also! At least he would have enough money to live on comfortably for the rest of his life. New or old Mr Ng, doesn't matter. What mattered was the money. Life with air con, beer, and even a maid to serve him. If he lost his memory, was that really so bad?

'There's a good salary and bonus,' the professor said, in their first meeting.

'Where do I start?' Mr Ng said.

'What do you know about the Hei-san archipelago?'

Professor Toh said, What do you mean, you have not heard of the Hei-san archipelago? Further east than the East Coast, across the sea. The archipelago comprises nine hundred islands at last count. And the Bercahaya Empire – never mind. Here, I'll put it in terms you can understand. From the capital, you have to sail south along the Peninsula. There is one cargo ship that sails from the capital to the Hei-san islands. Take this ship, even though it is slow and leaves only once every two months. The ship lurches forward with the inefficiency of a government employee on their second afternoon break – too much air bandung and cucur pisang. Your comfort and time are of no concern to them.

The ship loads and unloads goods at ports along the coastline of the Peninsula, with both captain and crew wearing a tidak-apa attitude, until it reaches the southernmost tip: Bawahsiang, the last port before the ship leaves the Peninsula. When the ship finishes loading itself with supplies, it leaves Bawahsiang and sails east through the open sea, with no comfort of any land in sight. Two weeks of sailing, and the only thing you see is the curve of the horizon. You feel dizzy, not knowing exactly where you are, only that you are sailing east, and that the sun moves from the front of the ship to the back of the ship, every day.

Until one day, perhaps in the middle of the night, or in the first light of day, if you are lucky, a black speck is seen, like a forgotten smudge of ink or a small buzzing fly. You see it, you stare at it, because it is something different.

The ship sails closer, the edges of the speck fuzz even as your eye is drawn to its centre, and then the speck splits in two. Where there were once two specks, now there are four, now eight, now sixteen, and now your eyes count black specks that number in the hundreds, maybe even thousands. You are gripped by a primordial fear, you see predators expanding exponentially, multiplying through the sea and bursting into the air, a sense of something never-ending, all-consuming, devouring you and your land and the resources of the world. These specks are now a swarm of thousands of black fly specks; still their number keeps on growing. Run away, your brain tells you, turn the ship around and sail back to the Peninsula. These specks will swarm at you, lay millions of eggs in the crevices of your body, until they hatch into blobs of hungry larvae, squirming as they eat you from within. When you open your lips to speak, black flies come out, their tiny wings beating on the roof of your mouth.

You run to the large block at the rear of the ship, known as the castle, climb up several floors, through the accommodations and common areas, and arrive at the bridge, desperate. But the captain ignores you, as he has done for the past month; he waves you off with a flick of his hand, and a roll of his eyes, mouthing the words 'Land people' to his second-in-command. The ship sails on. The blackness approaches. There is nothing you can do except hide in your cabin.

Land, land, you hear some of the crew cry out, uncertain whether their cry is in relief or despair. You rush to the deck; the ship has pulled closer to the face of the blackness. This is the moment when you realise that the specks – they are not flies. They are clusters of hills and mountains rising from the sea, black mountains as dark as night. Some are small, more like common hills, their rounded mounds shrouded in green as they peep modestly above the waves. Others could be the highest mountains in the world, for all you know.

At their base, a swathe of leafy, green trees and grass masks the deep darkness of the rocks. Even the aprons of black pebbles that have travelled down the mountains are blanketed by green. Green mangrove trees grip the loose banks of black sand. Grass is tucked in the gaps between the dark pebbles. Slivers of black rock wedge themselves in, like a stubborn infestation. There is an invisible war going on here, between the black rock with a lifespan of several millennia, and the green trees whose lives can be measured by the turns of the earth.

When your eyes leave the skirts of green, you will find the black walls climb high into the sky, their darkness eating away at your vision, their long lines piercing the still-sleeping air. Their cliffs are so steep that their angles are not found in nature; they appear to have no consideration for the laws of energy and matter. Some of the lines end in jagged peaks, and some are obscured by sweeping clouds. You will not be able to see where they end.

Dizzy, you take a step back. The islands appear to propagate faster than your vision allows. For a moment, you are awed; the word *infinity* occurs to you. Your gaze softens to take in these multiplying islands: from the northernmost ones, the Burnt Islands, appearing just like their name; to the southernmost islands, which are greener and teeming with life. Here is the Bulan-Bulan cluster, here are the Pinnacles, here is the Jadi-Jadi cluster, here is the Naga cluster. Here is the Solitary Island. On the starboard side, you see the hills of the Dahun-Dahun cluster, a group of fifteen islands with black mounds that look like swollen boils. On the port side, you see the islands whose hills get higher the further away they are. Most of these islands are unnamed, identified by the academics of the capital only by their location: 21/4-B, 21/5-A, 32/8-A, 10/2-C. Who would be so imaginative as to give each of these same-same islands a unique name?

This is the Hei-san archipelago of a thousand islands, past the unnamed sea, beyond the edge of the map. The weather on the islands is as hot and humid as our capital. There are littoral villages scattered throughout, transient structures, as each generation of people shifts to where the best fishing grounds are, and where fresh water can be found. Only the Burnt Islands are completely uninhabited, due to the constant eruptions.

You arrive. The island that you want is located on the Naga cluster. Naga Tua, it is called. There is a small but working port on the island, necessary for the lives of the villagers in the south-central islands. There is a lorry that leaves from the port for the villages in the mountain valleys. Ask when it leaves. Take it to the valleys. You will arrive on a pebbly floodplain where three streams meet.

Suriyang, the locals call this village. See what you can find out about the spirits. I am not sure whether you will be able to learn much, but you are the one tool I have now. The locals do not want to speak to me anymore. They treat me like some type of disease, those ungrateful things.

Mr Ng could never be sure whether the professor was just talking cock about the Hei-san islands. He had sailed there as soon as he was given the job. Upon his first sight of the islands, he had thought, *Nothing so great about these islands also.* And the villagers of Suriyang were just ulu kampung people living in the backside of nowhere.

'Our ancestors settled here a long time ago. The soil is fertile and the water is fresh, and we farm in peace,' said the village sinseh, her short white hair undisturbed by the wind. 'Sometimes the local spirits come to our village. The last one was many years ago; she died in a temple fire.'

'None alive anymore?'

Most of them died very young, Mr Ng was told. Some sort of disease.

Mr Ng stayed in Suriyang for several weeks, just to see what gossip he could dig up. Old men, nothing better to do than sit in kopitiam and complain here, complain there; old women, nothing better to do than to go to the marketplace and sembang-sembang: how the world is changing, how the foreigners caused the price of bayam to go up, how Ah Heng's daughter ran away with a sailor. To the Peninsula, they said.

Uncle, how are you doing this early morning? Auntie, come, let me help you with your basket of vegetables. How is your son, by the way? No problem lah – of course I help to rebuild the temple.

'The temple was burned down fifteen years ago, but only now we have the materials to fix it,' the butcher said. 'Our temple was very old. It has been around since my grandfather's days, grandfather's grandfather's days even. Then she arrived at our peaceful village and a few months after, *boom*, the temple burned down in one night.' The butcher shook his head. 'We don't need her kind here, is what I told the sinseh.'

The shutters of the medicinal hall were drawn low on hot afternoons, keeping the place cool and dark. Like other medicinal halls, the air was a special kind of musty, flavoured by the smell of dried roots and herbs. Mr Ng secretly believed that he too would become preserved if he stayed in the hall for too long, his skin flaking in the dry air and his nails falling off.

Today, Mr Ng was not alone, for a Suriyang villager – a Mr Tay – wanted something from the sinseh.

'My son, so short, somemore fifteen years old already. For a man, terrible to be so short. How will find wife like that? Ai-yoh, I'm growing old already, one day I die, and my son will still be short. Sinseh, you can help ah? You have some herbs for my son to grow taller?' Mr Tay said.

The sinseh nodded. 'Ah, yes, Mr Tay, I have some roots for your son. Just boil for several hours and give him the soup.' She perused the hundreds of jars in the medicinal hall, round and made of clear glass, standing neatly in multiple rows, floor to ceiling. Each jar was the size of a human head. What is in them? Mr Ng once asked. The accumulated wisdom of generations she said: dried angelica roots, ginseng, dates, goji berries, mushrooms, herbs, seeds, berries, saffron, birds' nests, and the powder of the ground horn of a rhino.

It was during this conversation with Mr Tay that Mr Ng first noticed the yellowed newspaper clipping of the temple fire, tucked between old ledger books on the shelves. When the sinseh was not looking, he pulled it out and saw a picture of the burned-down temple, and another picture of a young woman. This was that spirit, Swee, he thought. Pity she died in the fire.

He visited the sinseh often during his time at Suriyang; partly because she knew of the gossip-gossip of Suriyang, partly because she could not shoo him away if he came to her medicinal hall, and partly because she too welcomed someone else to talk to. The village sinseh was a difficult job, mediating arguments among the living, consoling the sick, listening to the dying. She was happy to hear about Mr Ng's stories of his travels, which were mostly stories of how terrible the outside world was. Crew on the ships were so cho loh and spat everywhere. Men in the capital sought working women to pass the time, Mr Ng whispered. He finished his stories with, 'If only the world could be more like this peaceful village, aih, we would all be happier!' Mr Ng's greatest talent was to obtain the trust of kampung aunties.

'Aih,' she said in response to his stories, her expression crestfallen. 'Sometimes I think about travelling outside this village. But so many bad people out there. Maybe I am not missing anything.'

One afternoon, as Mr Ng recounted another version of the world-is-scary story, and as the sinseh nodded in fear and sadness, she said something new that he had not heard before.

'Sometimes I wonder where she could have gone, young, with the baby somemore. Is she safe?' she said.

Mr Ng stood a little straighter. 'Madam, who is this?'

'Swee, the spirit. She is alive, you know . . .' Her words were addressed to no one but only the darkness of the medicinal hall. The air changed; time flattened for the sinseh, spirits were brought back to life, or perhaps they never died in the first place, in this world where everything – past, present, future – happened simultaneously.

The sinseh stood on the wet earth. The weekly lorry was parked in the village square; the driver having breakfast at his usual kopitiam.

No one else was around but Swee and her baby, their faces stained with black ash, their figures moving furtively like snakes darting in the shadows.

'Swee?'

Swee's head jerked in the sinseh's direction, her eyes wide. 'Help me,' she said. 'There was a fire last night. I didn't rake the furnace. The temple burned down. Please don't blame me; I tried.'

'Fire? The caretaker?' the sinseh said.

'He died in the fire.' Swee cried and the baby joined her, in the close of the morning.

Mr Ng stood in the medicinal hall and listened with interest as the sinseh spoke. The sinseh was a medium, communicating another reality that had occurred, was occurring – like

94

ripples pulsing outwards and meeting its reflection, destroying the other.

'Yes-yes, ah-hmm, where did she want go?' he said, wanting to encourage the story further.

He broke the moment. The sinseh blinked. 'Mr Ng, you are a traveller. Maybe you might have seen Swee. She left this village in the lorry, which brought her to the port. The driver later reported to me that she left on a ship for the Peninsula. He never saw her again.' The sinseh bowed her head. 'It has been many years since the temple burned down. For so long I wondered what happened to her. *Is* she safe? Her baby must be a teenager now. I wish I could know.'

He said, 'Sure sure, I'll try to help you find. But you know, it's not easy. Like trying to find an ant in a forest.' How much would the professor pay him in bonuses if he found Swee? 'You have a picture of her?' Easy money. Now just need to find out where she ended up.

At the port of Naga Tua, Mr Ng learned that Swee was thought to have found a job on a cargo ship before leaving the island. But no one could tell him which ship or where she went. So long ago how can remember? Mr Ng went through the old shipping manifests of each of the shipping companies that might have docked there.

After several months, he traced her journey to one of the quieter ports on the northwest coastline of the Peninsula, one that most of the bigger container ships bypassed. It had one half-asleep shipyard. Dock workers slept in shady nooks wherever they could find them: underneath a building overhang, inside half-finished boats, in little corners of a stairwell.

The shipyard was empty when Mr Ng arrived to investigate. In the kopitiam next door, a group of old men were finishing their daily gossip and breakfast. They used to be lorry drivers; now, they were retired.

'Morning, sirs! I was just wondering ah, you can be so kind to help me? Looking for kind soul.' Mr Ng unfolded the picture of Swee, the cut-out from the newspaper. 'Tell me, sirs, you seen this person ah? She might have come to this port a long time ago, eighteen years ago. Carrying a baby.'

These former lorry drivers squinted at the worn picture. It waved like a flag above the table of Milo kosongs and kopi-Os, and roti bakar crumbs.

'Ai-yah, so long ago, how to remember exactly! You siao,' the former lorry driver with the least grey in his hair said.

But one of the lorry drivers said, 'You know what? I remember her. She arrived at the port, during the monsoon season. Didn't say much. I gave her some advice, you know. Young woman like you shouldn't be travelling like this. Where is your husband? Find yourself a husband because it's not safe for women out there.

'She said that she just wanted a job. I took her to the Rasa Sayang resort to find work; there, the five-star luxury wan, where the rich people stay. The resort always need a lot of workers.'

When Mr Ng heard this story, he sped off to Kampung Seng, a 45-minute drive away, all the time thinking: *This is it! Bonus day akan datang!* Wait until he told the professor, with his posh words and his atas face.

But when he asked around Kampung Seng for Swee, the villagers whispered to him that Swee died many years ago. Village folk were so pantang to talk about death, not wanting to tell him, as if her ghost would come back and haunt them. She died very young, just like the others. Bad luck spirit. Too much time, too much money spent. Find what? Find nothing.

He drank away his disappointment in bottle-sized coconut toddies at the Boon Chee restaurant, and rambled about the professor, or the island of Naga Tua, or a nonsense story about some tower in the forest. One evening, after he ate a plate of fried bihun meant for three people, the boy Chong Meng told him about Swee's spade, inadvertently: 'My auntie married into our family. So lucky, otherwise she would just be a worker somewhere. My mother always said that Swee stole that ugly spade from her last employer.'

Mr Ng never knew where any of his assignments would end up. Like a dog, he just had to follow the trail wherever it took him, just follow only. Don't ask why-why, don't question why strange; the strangeness was why he got paid. His job was not to find the answer to the story. His job was just to take. Take things! Take people! Take information! Most taken things were useless, but Mr Ng's job was not to be fussy. So when that Chong Meng, that kampung boy, mentioned the ugly spade, Mr Ng's nose twitched. Take!

'Eh, Chong Meng, you got a lot of talents. Someone like you will do well in the capital, be a successful rich businessman. You see my Rolex? Work hard, and one day you can own one, too. A man like you shouldn't be stuck in this fishing village, you know. If you come to the capital, I can give you a leg up,' Mr Ng said.

Of course, that Chong Meng, bodoh like anything, give wrong information to Mr Ng. Easy task like that also cannot do. Ask if anyone was at home the next morning, and Chong

Meng said, 'No one at home, my uncle and cousin out fishing and Ah-ma going to do her hair at the hairdresser's.'

Mr Ng was not a bad man. He went to the temple and prayed regularly to Datuk Gong. So he was not a bad man when he hit the grandmother on the head. Sometimes in order to be successful, one must do certain things.

Look at where he was now. He drove his Volvo 240 back to the capital, and parked outside his mother's house, in the grubby area where there was free parking. He wrapped the spade in wads of old newspaper and placed it in the boot of his car. No one would bother looking in there for the spade; besides, the newspapers stank like the capital's river after a bad storm.

He took a stroll through the lanes of the neat town houses, to the professor's house. What would he say? How much would his bonus be this time? More than the time he sourced the orphans? Mr Ng was already thinking of what he would buy with the money.

Empty Houses

When Han went to the police headquarters in the capital to report Mr Ng, a police officer told him, 'You want to report the theft of a spade? Your mama's spade? Look, you're young so let me tell you, okay? This is small fry. If got murderer, rapist, or even if your money stolen, then is important. Someone stole your spade, so what?' The police officer rolled a pencil across the table. 'Just buy a new spade lah! Hai-yah!'

The next afternoon, Han packed the remaining crabs into ice boxes, and hosed down fish entrails from the counters and floors.

'I finish for the day?' Han asked.

Madam Chua waved him off. 'Okay, you can go. Go. Tomorrow same time, okay.'

'All this extra sotong, can I have some? Tomorrow surely spoiled wan.'

Madam Chua nodded, so Han wrapped the translucent bodies of three large squid into sheets of yesterday's newspaper, and then he went off to see Min.

At the side door of the town house, Han knocked, and the door opened. Cool air-conditioned air leaked onto the street.

'The Mr Ng you are looking for, he came this morning instead,' Min said.

'I was just coming to give you some sotong,' Han said. 'To say thank you for telling me about Mr Ng. Too many sotong caught this week, fishermen giving them out for free. I even removed all the innards.'

Min blinked, perhaps startled by sunlight that flashed off the tar road, or by the smell of fish bones and old vegetables that Han emitted, or by the gift of squid tubes. She was not a person to receive many gifts. 'Thank you, thank you.' Her brow furrowed, and she half turned away, before she stopped and said, 'You, you – you hungry ah? There's some perut ikan cooking in the pot. You can have some.'

A ladle had sunk into the depths of the pot and reappeared full of a stew filled with chunks of pineapple, perut ikan, aubergine and green beans. Warm smells rose into the air: the tangy sourness of pineapple, stewed for several hours until it lost its sharpness to the gravy; the lightness of coconut milk that cut through the dense clouds of fermented shrimp paste.

The kitchen grew happy with the anticipation of its purpose being fulfilled: to feed; to give joy to stomachs; to encourage the transformation from part to whole, of lemongrass, shallots, chillies, belacan, fish stomachs, aubergines, long beans, tamarind, hay bi, daun kadok, mint leaves and coconut milk, transformed into a stew that bubbled for hours. Chau Ang

Gong watched from above the kitchen altar, approving of the abundance.

'Perut ikan! The restaurants or the street stalls don't cook it. Last time I ate it, my ah-ma cooked for me,' Han said.

Min scooped out a flat paddle's worth of rice and slid it into a bowl for him. 'You look very hungry.'

Han drew out a stool from under the kitchen table. He sank his spoon into the bowl of perut ikan and emptied its contents into the rice bowl. This transference of perut ikan onto the rice was repeated several times, until the rice itself was swimming in gravy. Joss sticks on the altar burned to their ends.

As Han ate, he explained that Mr Ng had stolen their family's spade and pushed his ah-ma to the ground, breaking her arm. 'But the police won't do anything,' he added.

Mr Ng had an appointment with Professor Toh for next Thursday afternoon, Min said. That was in ten days. He would be meeting the professor in his office upstairs. 'This kind of people are so thick-skinned; you must confront them in front of an audience. Otherwise, he won't listen to you. I see people like this all the time. They just take and take.'

'You can help me confront Mr Ng?'

Min paused. She did not like people relying on her too much. She felt a deep aversion if they showed signs of needing her help, wanting her to fulfil something missing in their lives. Their needs were always so arbitrary, unpaid, with unspoken expectations.

Her job as the professor's housekeeper was a comfortable one. The professor needed her services, but these were well-defined duties, and paid for. She cooked, she cleaned, she managed the house, and in return, she was given a room and a salary. She had a fixed value. She knew that she would not be kicked out of the professor's house for not fulfilling some unexpected role or task or not reaching some standard.

But now, here, was a new feeling, a pulsing warmth. She first examined the feeling in her mind, turning it over, checking for hidden edges. It looked for water, and to her for nourishment. It cried to her in mewls: Let's help. We'll help. We can make his life better. There was a softness within Han and it made her feel protective. Maybe she had been soft like him, once. Maybe if her ah-ma or her kong-kong or Ma or Pa had loved her and protected her and saved her from the Cliff of the First Wei Leep and the Bone Fields, or maybe if Kuang was still alive, she would have kept some of her softness, too. She asked of this new feeling, this wanting to protect, What if I had to crawl, in the heat, in the sun, across ground so hard that each step tore away the skin at my knees? What if I left the shade and walked through the thick heat only to find a cave, empty, with my footsteps echoing off the stone walls because everything soft had died a long time ago? What then?

She packed the feeling up in a box and closed the lid. She said to Han, 'No lah, after I let you into the study, I'll stay in the kitchen. If the professor find out, how? I might lose my job.'

It was deep into the night, and the feet of moths were warm on the glass of streetlamps. Their wings fluttered minutely as the wind passed by them, and Min's head and body had long fallen still, her chest rising, falling. The stiffness of the mat beneath her no longer bothered her, nor the coldness of the floor, nor the darkness or the humidity, until a voice came up through the clammy walls and the rickety staircase, 'Min-ah-Min, come here, girl! Make me some tea. Hurry up, ah-girl, you got so much time, issit?'

Min ran down to the front hall, where the professor had just shuffled in. 'I'm so *exhausted*. Those Health Ministry officials – how many times must they ask me? I already told them I don't know!'

'Professor? Is there anything I can do?'

'No, no.' He waved her off irritably. 'Nothing! Just boil some tea, can anot? Po lei, open the new tin. It doesn't matter; just open the new one, don't be so cheap. The tea in the old tin so stale, no more scent already. I'm going up to my office. Bring the tea upstairs. Hurry up, don't dilly-dally.' He held his stomach and creaked his way upstairs.

She carried up a steeping pot of po lei and two of the professor's favourite teacups. The room was poorly lit, with the side and table lamp casting oblique shadows. The professor was peering at the paper on his desk. Min noticed that there were new sheets of paper, fresh white ones. Underneath lay a bed of variously yellowed paper; every new layer burying the older layers like sand dunes marching over the desert.

The tray was set down next to the lamp, and tea was poured. Steam was released. Min wondered what new information he had received. Surely he could not be planning another field trip; there was no one left to do his dirty work. Even that despicable Miss Gan had grown increasingly guarded about her volunteers. People were nosy, starting to ask questions, she said. Priest, prayer group leader, even the doctor. There were only so many police officers Miss Gan could bribe.

Despite herself, Min was curious. She lifted her head discreetly as her eyes quickly scanned the sheets on the table. Not for the first time she saw the map of Naga Tua, gridded up, divided into areas, most crossed out, but two areas highlighted.

And, what was that? A drawing of a puller, or something that very much looked like it. How did he get that drawing? A whisper came to her, and she was reminded of skipping pebbles in a sandstorm.

The professor looked up. 'Min, we have busy day tomorrow. First, a morning appointment with one of them, the ones with the memory condition. The orphans. Make sure you get kuih talam. Don't buy any more fried bananas.'

Min shivered. These appointments were the worst. They arrived like empty houses, with their walls and windows present, but nothing on the inside. In the house, the walls were hard, and there were no beds or chairs or warmth from the kitchen stove. Professor Toh said, Disease in the forest, parasite, virus. Don't ask any more, girl. Focus on your work.

How could she? When they came with their empty eyes, dark and solemn, not understanding, and it seemed that the only person who did remember was her? She felt the weight of their memories that they left behind for her to keep.

'Then after lunch, I need to see the doctor again. They said they need to do a few more tests. Don't know why they bother. So many tests, it's not as if the results would change.'

The professor shuffled papers into neat stacks and placed a glassy, black stone on top of each stack. He collected the pencils on his desk, and placed them into a jar, one dropping on the floor as he did so.

'Next week, I'm going on a long research trip with Mr Ng. Don't make any more new appointments for me. Don't cancel the others yet. Wait until I leave first. After people come and ask why I cancel. These other researchers so pat kua.' The professor yawned. 'I am nearly there, Min.'

104

He must be going on another field trip. Had Miss Gan sent him new volunteers? Then she remembered Mr Ng's assistant, the young man that accompanied Mr Ng that morning – carefree like the orphans, she thought. She tried not to think about what would happen to him. This problem was contagious, a smudge that only blackened when rubbed. Not her business, she reminded herself.

That night, her sleeping mat was colder than usual. The concrete floor had absorbed the moisture from the afternoon thunderstorms and released its coolness at night. Her bones could not rest. She took her mat up into the spare bedroom – the professor wouldn't know, she told herself – and laid her mat squarely over the mattress, aligning corner to corner. She tried to sleep. There was one dream that came to her, over and over again – Mr Ng's assistant, sitting in the second visitor chair in the professor's study, his floppy hair covering half his head. The hair brushed out of the way, and there was no face behind it, no eyes or ears or nose as expected, only smooth, unbroken skin where his face once was. An empty shell of a person who cannot see or talk.

Why don't you have a face? she screamed, and her words were buried in a dust storm. Sand filled her open mouth. She was angry. Stupid, stupid man! So bodoh wan you, face also don't have. Why no face? Why?

When she woke up, her tears had wetted the soft sheets on the mattress beneath. Better get up now before the professor finds out. She straightened the sheets as much as she could and moved her mat back to her room. The patches of wet on the sheet would dry soon.

Min had been young once. She remembered the violent dust storms of the dry season, of long ago. They scraped through

105

the bare rock, raking through the thin soil for sand particles to scatter over the land. Sometimes these storms would carry her along as she held her ma's hand, floating above the mud-topped roofs of the homes in their valley. This is your people, her ma had said. This is the ancient spring of our valley that brings water to us, created by the First Wei Leep who descended from the skies. This is how we worship our god. You are young yet.

One day you must do this by yourself.

One day she was twelve years old and woke up in a flat basin. The Bone Fields, they called it. Her soft body felt every bump and stone on the ground as it lay, broken in all angles, like a doll carelessly flung. Sunlight pricked her eyelids. The Cliff of the First Wei Leep towered in straight steep columns that rose so high she could not see the top of them, but she knew that the cliff flattened out into a plateau at its highest point. Behind were serried rows of mountains, black and purple-burnt, as if they had been charred by a fire.

The ground was stained with scorched maroon. It was her blood. She could not will her legs to move, no matter how many times she shouted at them.

To the north, the first few houses of her village lapped at the edges of the basin. She shouted in that direction for help, hoping that the wind would pick up her words and carry them to her family. She hoped that they would not take long in finding her, as she did not want her family wandering in the hot desert. She wondered who would come to her first. Ma and Pa would search all the houses for her. Ee Po, who made her tau yew bak every third day, would worry why Min had not visited her yet. Tua Ku, who had promised that Min could join him on his trek to the Forgotten Lake next week, would search the springs in case she had fallen asleep near the bushes, like she always did when she was playing.

But no one came, even as she saw, far away, people standing like grey vultures. She could see their faces, observing. The sun turned to sting, pushing sharp needles into her head, the skin on her back; pinpricks at first, which grew into blisters that dissolved her skin. Her throat was dusty. She coughed up saliva into her mouth and swallowed it again so that her mouth was moist. On her face, tears dried into crusty salt lumps. *Why won't they help?*

Time passed in moments she could not remember. She found herself lying on a mud-cool floor, as Researcher Kwan gave her water to drink. Researcher Kwan said, 'No one would save you. They watched you from the village. I asked them, Why don't you save that girl? Can't you see that she is dying? I asked your family, your teacher, your friends. Your ma and pa were crying, but even they too looked at you as if they had accepted your death. I could not stand by my oath anymore – I had to interfere. So I walked out to the basin – so hot I almost fainted – and lifted you onto my back. You were nearly dead.'

Why did they leave me to die? she asked Researcher Kwan.

'Did you fail your people's coming-of-age test?'

'I don't know,' Min said, confused. She turned her head away and arched her back. She wanted to go home, back to her family, and she wept when she was told that there was no home for her to go back to. She must leave, go to a faraway place called the capital, a place where there was no ma or pa or ee po or tua ku, and there was no sand, only too much rain and a lot of people. She would never see her family again.

'They have forgotten you,' Researcher Kwan said, gently.

Her heart cleaved into two halves, with one half left in the sleeping sand. This half of her heart never aged; it would always be the heart of the twelve-year-old girl who never left her family or the Desert of Birds.

That morning, Min lit three joss sticks at the altar, then brought them to the front door to pray to Tian Gong: for the good health and prosperity of the household. And of other people too, she added. The incense of the joss sticks joined the dull haze of the capital.

In the greyness, cars and lorries and people moved in their own worlds, and in the gloom, one of them stopped. This one was a young female, several years younger than Min.

'You're early for your appointment. Where is your guardian? Where is Miss Gan?' Min asked. A disaffected matronly woman surfaced in Min's memory, wearing a grey samfu, smoking opium in the professor's office until the professor told her to stop. You try looking after these creatures, and then you can tell me when to stop. It's all your fault, anyway, Miss Gan had told the professor.

'Miss Gan didn't want to come. Said it was too boring. I'm here by myself.'

This was Sky Yang. 'But just call her Sky,' Miss Gan had said at the first meeting.

As Min explained to Han later, Sky Yang the girl was the opposite of Sky Yang the name. She was pale, with hunched shoulders that made her seem smaller than she was. Her figure disappeared under the drape of her clothes, a free Milo T-shirt that had been donated to the Mercy Orphanage, worn and washed so many times that the label had cracked into small hexagons, as if parched. The 'o' was no longer

108

visible, swallowed by the sea of ominous Milo green. Her hair reached her waist in greasy tentacles. There was no movement in her hair, or in her eyes. She appeared to be bored, uninterested, and one would assume that she was an average teenager, until one inspected her carefully to find nothing there at all.

'What do you mean, nothing there at all? You mean, like the kind never go to school wan? Stupid or what? In the fishing village, there are a few people like that, born wrong way. Nice but not very smart.'

No, no, not like that, Min tried to explain to Han. 'Sky Yang is not stupid. She is more like an empty house.' As empty as abandoned stone houses that perched on the slopes of a lake plain, where the mud, once softened by the rainy season, had now hardened into cracks. If one looked hard enough, one would find broken pottery charred from cooking fires. Once upon a time, families lived there but they have long moved out and taken everything with them. Now the dry wind blew at the sand, burying everything.

'Then the professor interview Sky Yang for what?' Han asked.

Sky Yang was an orphan, one of the many from the Mercy Orphanage who entered the forest and contracted a . . . disease, Min said, uncomfortably. Sky Yang's memory was empty, empty-houses empty, and the professor was keen to find out what her first memory was, just like the rest of them who went to the forest and got the disease. So far, his research had shown that there was no clear pattern in any of them: an old tree, stream with overhanging branches, a bridge, black soil, a boulder, darkness, the sky, two mousedeers. But they said the same thing: I didn't know what I was seeing. I had no

109

vocabulary, no capacity to name the tree or the branch or the bridge. Even now I can't describe these memories.

'You mean that there was more than one person who contracted the disease? Everything also forget can like that wan?' Han said.

Min nodded curtly.

Han was reminded of Ah-ma's words in the hospital. *Sometimes I think she didn't know her own history . . . She was a lost spirit, floating.*

At their meeting that morning, the professor asked his usual questions: Could you tell me what your first memory was? Any image that stands out? This picture showing the bamboo clearing, do you recognise it?

Sky Yang said, You want me to tell you? They ate it all: my speech, my eyes, they are chattering monkeys that attack at night, they cluster at streetlamps, then jump at you. Their fists are little but they send them into your eyes, and pull your ears from your head. They crack open your head like a watermelon, and scoop out your brain in big handfuls. All because I turned around.

The professor asked more questions, but Sky Yang would say no more.

'I only say what I know,' Sky said. That was the end of their meeting.

A series of sharp honks came from the street where Miss Gan had arrived in her car to collect Sky. Each honk was longer and louder than the last one, hinting at Miss Gan's growing irritation ('Why the stupid girl still don't want to come out wan? Like this also have to wait for her'). Sky Yang did not move. Min – who had been waiting in the professor's study

110

as her presence kept Sky Yang calm – eventually touched the bend of Sky Yang's arm. Only then did Sky Yang run downstairs without saying another word.

The professor frowned at his notebook. 'Useless, that Sky. At least we have her diary. I turn around now, she wrote. What does that even mean?' He shook his head and looked at Min, in the corner. 'Have you packed my clothes and equipment yet? Make sure you also pack my pills.' His instructions issued, he was about to wave her off, when he remembered something. 'One last thing. Come, I give you advice. Listen to me, Min.

'Someday, we must leave this world. Who will remember us? Our names forgotten, like sand in the wind. Most people are like common animals. They were born into this world, they live, and then they die. Just like that. No meaning at all. Their names are inscribed on granite tombstones so that other people will remember the names of their rotting bodies, buried in the ground. Pah! What kind of remembrance is that? Their children and grandchildren come to their grave on Cheng Meng and scrub their tombstones clean, and say some prayers, but they will die too. And then what? The tombstone stands on a mound, unvisited for years, their graves known by no one, their names forgotten. The green blades of lalang sprout through the cracks of their grave, and their bodies are erased by worms. This is the fate of the common person. They might as well not exist.

'But do you know what is permanent, Min? Accomplishment. Even five hundred years from now, we will still study the works of the great masters. You learned about the queens of the Bercahaya Empire, and their generals, the writers, the artists, the scientists, the adventurers? You know why?

Because their lives were worth remembering. These Bercahaya queens sailed across the sea to the Peninsula, conquered village after village, until their rule over the western lowlands was complete. This great capital, once a constellation of insignificant villages, was stitched together to make a city. Our civilisation was built on the foundations laid down by the Bercahaya queens. We inherited their ideas, and their languages. We dream their songs, we dream of ash and fire and the sea, we tell their stories to our children; now these stories are woven into our nursery rhymes and, in our hearts, their words beat. We remember them in our buildings, and in the temples along the coastline.

'So, Min, make sure people remember your name. If you don't, then what's the point in living?' the professor said. 'Might as well just die now.'

Jiang Shi

A mong the dirty ice piled high in yellow buckets, and the stacks of large metal trays full of sloshing fishy water, stray fishscales and broken-off fins, Madam Chua's phone rang. 'Han, pick up the phone. Busy with customer here. If it is the man from Keong Kee restaurant, tell them no more hung ngah, okay?' she shouted, before turning back to the person she had been speaking to and, continuing in the same breath, 'You only want three ang zho, where got discount? How I make money like this? This is not charity!'

Han approached the phone. It continued ringing.

Madam Chua yelled at him again: 'Han, what are you doing? Pick it up, pick it up!'

He lifted the receiver from its cradle, and said, 'Hello? Chua and Sons here.'

The response came back in jumpy, halting sentences, with a few words missing, as it percolated through the leaky telephone line. The person's voice was unmistakably Father's. 'Hello, this is . . . Sons? . . . speak to Han? Han . . .'

Father's voice arrived at the market in the same way fresh rain did, unsure of its place in the world. And then an image of Father appeared to Han, like a bowl of warm ginger soup.

'I'm here, listening to you.'

'Ah . . . son, are you . . .?'

Father's words disintegrated into static. *Father*, Han thought, and on instinct, reached his left hand into the air, as if it was an antenna, searching for the best signal. His hand remained aloft for a minute, two minutes, three: only static noise filtered through the receiver, empty, like grains of sand dropping to the floor.

Hearing his father's voice fade away, Han felt as if he had hidden something valuable; he hid it so well in the storeroom that the robbers could not find it, but neither could he. It was missing. Perhaps it was stuck behind the towers of damp newspapers that had built up because it had been several months since the paper lama man came around with his blue Nissan van to buy old newspapers for recycling, yelling through a loudspeaker: 'Old newspaper! Paper lama! Sau kau poh ji!' Han could not find it; it was misplaced: temporarily, he told himself. It would surface again, like the sun when it rounded off at the horizon each evening. The static noise deepened. His right hand started to ache from the effort of pressing the receiver tightly against his ear.

('Your worker, he's okay? Not crazy ah? Just put down the phone and call again lah,' said one of Madam Chua's customers, as he observed Han's behaviour from the front of her stall.

'Expensive you know. Kampung folk cannot afford to call, put down, and call again. Connection charges,' Madam Chua replied.)

114

Han hung up and was surprised to find the phone ringing again, instantly. Must be important wor, where got Ah-ma let him waste money on phone calls wan?

This time, Father's voice was clear. 'Han, I need to tell you something. Your ah-ma, your ah-ma, is . . .'

Is what?

'. . . very weak. She was discharged from hospital, getting better at first, but in the past few weeks, she has no energy to do anything. Even her garden also she doesn't take care of. The lalang grow all over her vegetables. She spends most of the day sleeping. Nowadays I do all the cooking you know, only simple meal wan, just one meat and one vegetable, no soup. You know my cooking hor.'

'Is she going to . . .?' Han could not bring himself to continue. Out of the corner of his eye, he saw Madam Chua throwing an empty tray into the corner for Han to wash up later. Other sounds of the market floated into his awareness: 'This fish not fresh, look at the eyes, cloudy already. You try to cheat me ah?' Big laughter from the two workers wheeling trolleys overflowing with brinjals and ladies' fingers. Overhead lighting hummed.

When Han finally spoke again, his voice was low. 'You think she's going to . . .'

'I don't know how long she will last,' Father said. Han imagined Father shaking his head. 'Come back, Han. Your kong-kong, before he got sick, he was like this, weak for several months, then, you know, he just left us.'

He just left us. Even after they died, still Father was too superstitious to say the word out loud: dead. As if saying the word would kill them; make them more dead than they already were. They died already, dead liao lor, superstitious also for what?

'The others . . . taking care of her anot? Auntie Lim? What about Chong Meng?'

'Ai-yah, that side of the family useless. My sister – she come visit, once a week, stay for twenty minutes then leave. When your kong-kong died also the same thing. And that Chong Meng; he's really one-kind. Go somewhere never tell anyone. Gone soon after you left. Said that he going with a friend on holiday. Where is he now? Everyone don't know.' Father said again: 'Useless, all of them.'

Several months before, Ah-ma had said that Han was of the age to start finding a wife. 'When I was your age,' Ah-ma said, 'I was already married and carrying your father in my tummy.' She was squatting by a large bucket. She had been wringing out soy beans in a large muslin, twisting them until white liquid seeped out into the bucket.

'There's a fresh cup of soy milk over on the kitchen table,' Ah-ma said. She got up to heave the contents of the first bucket onto the vegetable plot. Out fell the white mush of wrung-out soy beans.

'This is good fertiliser,' she told him, pleased. 'It will make the plants grow.' Her cheeks were red from the morning's activity.

Han found himself looking at the phone, his arms hanging loosely by his side. He needed to go back home. To his surprise, he found Madam Chua standing next to him; her presence announcing itself in a dense cloud of baby powder that she applied to her armpits in copious amounts every morning.

'You okay, ah-boy?' Madam Chua said.

'Yah, okay.'

116

'Got problem at home, issit?'

Han turned his head away to stare at the mountains of fish-stained ice.

'No need to wash these trays. I get the flower boy to come help. His fine hands need some roughening up.' Madam Chua added, 'The lorry leaves at six tonight if you want to go back home.'

Han nodded, not wanting to say anything but thankful for her kindness. Sunlight poured through the main windows as if a cloud had moved from in front of the sun, and a new thought appeared in his head: *Chua and Sons* – who did the sons refer to and why were they not helping out at the stall? In the sunlight, Madam Chua's hair appeared grey, and in that moment, she looked as old and as lonely as his ah-ma.

Han was late; he lost track of the time after that phone call. He had made a plan with Min to confront Mr Ng that afternoon. He ran through the streets in the heat, before the familiar side door appeared. He knocked.

Min opened. 'You are late you are late! Why are you late?'

'My ah-ma is . . . sick. You know, she's old,' Han tried to say. 'I need to go back home soon. Is Mr Ng there?'

But Min was too angry to listen. 'I waited all morning. I felt sorry for you. And I had also hoped – well, it doesn't matter anymore!'

Sounds came from within the darkened house: footsteps and the front door closing.

'The professor is leaving on his field trip. And Mr Ng and that young man, really just a boy, are joining him. I can't do anything!' She clenched her fists.

'Min, it's okay.' He tried to touch her arm, but she waved his hand away.

'No, it is not okay,' she told him. Her eyes looked at him, their red-rimmed whiteness sunken among folds of skin. 'No, it is not okay. You know what? They have not left yet. They are there, just at the front door, and I can hear them getting into the car. Go, say something, say whatever you had been meaning to say to Mr Ng. The spade and all that. Maybe you can stop them from going.'

'Going where?'

'Nowhere! Just go and do what you need to do! Go before it is too late!'

Han ran to the front door, where Mr Ng's Volvo 240 was parked. He recognised the dark brown paint peeling off in large flakes, the four wheels infested with rust, and a large dent on the side.

A tall, skinny man had opened the door to the passenger seat. He wore a shirt, brown blazer and brown trousers, like the ones Han had to wear for Monday school assemblies. This must be the professor. The probable-professor climbed into the car and closed the door with a click. The door locks were pressed down, the engine started.

Han ran to the car. Its occupants stared at him. First, the probable-professor, who checked that the door was locked with a tap of his hand. Next, Mr Ng, sitting in the driver's seat. He recognised Han and sneered. The third passenger sat in the back, in the furthest corner from where Han stood, obscured from view. Han stepped to one side to see better and, at the same time, inside the car, the third passenger leaned over, their eyes met, and they recognised each other.

Chong Meng? Han half said, half thought.

Han?! The half-uttered syllable left Chong Meng's lips, both a question and an exclamation, for he was as surprised and startled as Han was.

118

Caught in the same place and time, their fates touched fleetingly. Their destinies were no longer the tightly knotted nets of their youth but, instead, they were bright strands that extended to where they could see no further; whether the net would end or keep growing infinitely, neither of them knew.

Then the car drove off, and their destinies diverged. Han stared at the mud-streaked windows of the Volvo 240 as it roared away. Chong Meng going on holiday, pah. No, no, he wasn't; he was with that thief, Mr Ng. Did Chong Meng tell Mr Ng about the spade in the first place?

Han picked up an empty Pepsi can from the street and threw it at the roof of the professor's house with as much force as possible. It slammed onto the wall before dropping onto the road.

Min was watching from the doorway.

'The spade is gone,' Han told Min. 'Mr Ng took it. My cousin took it. I don't care anymore. This is enough. I need to go home and spend time with my ah-ma.'

'Your cousin? You mean that boy, that young man? The one in the car?' She gripped Han's forearm. 'He doesn't look like you. But, you speak alike. Oh, I hear it now.'

'My cousin, he can just go die lah. Always trying to be hero. Behind our back go and help stranger only. Maybe that Mr Ng offered him money.'

'Your cousin is going to die, you know,' Min said, tonelessly, looking far away, past Han's shoulder, in the direction where the car had sped off. Her previous agitation had disappeared, her head and shoulders drooped. She appeared to have aged ten years in the space of minutes. 'The professor and Mr Ng have sent him to die.'

*

Min explained, they are heading to the port now. We can't catch up with them without a car.

Once every two months, the cargo ship *Bintang Jelas* arrives in the port of the capital. It picks up goods and then sails for the thousand-island Hei-san archipelago. When *Bintang Jelas* arrives, the ship is emptied as its crew go through their changeover. The castle is cleaned out, and the holds are loaded with fertiliser, water, oil, dry food, grains and machinery. A fresh crew is put on. *Bintang Jelas*, now full from its banquet, sails south, hugging the coastline, dropping into the smaller west coast ports like it is catching up with old friends. Then the ship arrives at Bawahsiang, before sailing east, across the unnamed open sea that separates the Peninsula and the Hei-san islands. After these two weeks, *Bintang Jelas* finally arrives at Naga Tua island.

There, your cousin, and Mr Ng, and Professor Toh, will disembark. In two months' time, they will re-board the *Bintang Jelas*, but the cousin that you know will have disappeared for ever in the forests of Naga Tua, leaving behind an empty shell.

Every time the professor tells me that it will not happen again – No more, no more, he says – every time he leaves on one of his field trips to Naga Tua island, it happens again. Just one last time, he tells me, for his work is nearly complete. Just one more orphan to send into the forest to do his dirty work for him. He chooses the smartest, strongest ones. When they come back, their eyes are empty. He never cares.

Now you are angry; you are angry at your cousin for lying, for letting Mr Ng steal your spade, for cheating your family. Ah-ma was sent to hospital. You say he just sit there, two-faced, can smile and say nothing. But angry also angry no point.

You will be a stranger to him, even as you wish he could remember. He will not know his name. He will not know you.

Angry how? Angry also no point. He will be dead to you.

Remember that time when Ming Tat came last in the motorcycle race but didn't have any money to pay back the bet that he had lost? Remember, Chong Meng? His payment instead was to spend one night in the forest.

Which forest?

The one at the back of our school. The jiang shi one.

The story of jiang shi haunting the forest at the back of their school had been told to Han and Chong Meng so many times that they could not remember how the stories came about, or who told them. The jiang shi were foreign soldiers who were killed in the forest, and their bodies abandoned, buried in the earth that was not their homeland. Their spirits haunted the forest, looking for a living body to tumpang so that they could go home. No, no, that story was not true. The jiang shi were, in fact, villagers who were rounded up by soldiers, brought to the forest and shot without burial or ceremony. No prayer paper or gold bars were burned for them. No prayers crossed the lips of their families. Their bodies had been thrown in a small pit to rot. Just like animals, Mrs Lim had whispered. They were cursed to haunt living beings for the rest of their undead lives, robbing the living of their blessings just as theirs had been taken away.

Thus it could not have been said that Ming Tat was not warned. Even their teachers had told them about jiang shi: 'If you ponteng class and go lepak at the back of the school, thinking you're so smart, miss school somemore, then the jiang shi come and find you and eat your life qi and then you know lah hah!' their teachers said.

121

The one unexpected benefit of having jiang shi in the forest at the back of the school was that the school had the best attendance rate in the district, for no truant-to-be wanted to encounter a jiang shi, however boring their history class was. Even to ponteng class was difficult. The best place to hide was the block of toilets at the back of the school – and these toilets were also said to be lived in by jiang shi. While the living were naturally drawn to villages, cities and orchards of bountiful jackfruit trees, the dead were drawn to an absence of life – the toilet was the perfect place for jiang shi.

One time, Yee Liang was hiding in the toilets, having ponteng both his mathematics and geography classes. His normal hiding place was by the drains near the playing field, for there was a fresh breeze there and he could get a view of the fifth-form girls playing netball. But on that day, the discipline master was patrolling the hallways with his large rotan, ready to cane the palms of recalcitrant schoolboys. The toilets were Yee Liang's only option; if he was caught, he could always say he needed to use them.

Yee Liang had just lit a fresh cigarette when he heard breathing in the cubicle next to him. It sounded like a freshly exhaled breath. He looked about; there was no one there, the silence insisted, even as Yee Liang heard breathing all around. Then, in the air, at the base of his neck, his name was whispered, *Yee Liang* – his name and nothing else. He ran out of the block of toilets. From then on, he used the toilets near the teachers' canteen.

There were other stories, too: five primary-school children got lost on a school trip. The bomoh proclaimed that orang bunian had stolen the children but would return them many years from now. They never did.

122

Ming Tat knew these stories. He said that he was not afraid.

'Oh, did we forget? You can only bring one flashlight. And don't shine the light at the trees, you know, hehe – after orang bunian come and gigit you,' Chong Meng said, and the rest of the gang nodded, as they left Ming Tat in a small clearing in the forest at the back of the school.

'You think I stupid, I know lah,' Ming Tat had replied, waving them off, while shaking with the nervousness of a sixteen-year-old boy who had never spent a night away from his parents.

The next day, the rest of his motorcycle gang placed cigarette bets on whether Ming Tat would turn up to class. He missed the first lesson but arrived just in time for his science lesson. 'How was your night?' they asked him, before they realised the left half of Ming Tat's face – his left eye, left ear, left cheek – was not moving, as if it had seen a ghost and was frozen into silence.

The official diagnosis was that Ming Tat had been possessed by a demon. The tang ki who had been consulted explained that the demon had been lost in the forest, since before the long war, and was hungry and looking for food. It had managed to occupy Ming Tat's warm body and had lived there ever since.

'You can see its influence on your son, see – his face paralysed, controlled by the demon!' the tang ki told Ming Tat's father. The tang ki prescribed one home exorcism and weekly evening prayers to cleanse Ming Tat's house.

Ming Tat said, 'I tried to do everything properly wor. I said sorry three times before peeing in the bushes. I ate only vegetables, not meat.'

(When the hairdresser told Ah-ma the story, Ah-ma's comments were: 'Must have shine light on the trees, stupid.

123

Like that deserved to get possessed. None of my grandsons be so stupid yah?')

Two months after that fateful night, Ming Tat could move both sides of his face again.

There was nothing Han could do to stop Chong Meng from being sent into the forests of Naga Tua, Min told him.

'Just go home,' she said. 'Your ah-ma needs you. Your cousin, he chose his path. Even if you wanted to, you can't stop him. Maybe it's his punishment, karma of some sort. Remember, Han, the world does not give you anything for free. People take and take. None left for you. You can't do anything now, so you should just take care of yourself and the family who loves you; go back to your fishing village. Forget about your spade. Forget about your cousin; he will surely forget about you.'

Han could only see Chong Meng as he saw him last, the stunned expression, the guilt staining his face, as he stared at Han who stared at him.

Popiah

The late evening light cast the outlines of buildings in a deep burnt orange. Mothers and fathers pointed out the flame sky to their children: 'Nah, look ah, see how orange the sky is? Tomorrow will be very hot.' As the sun subsided in one corner, the rest of the sky unfurled with flutters of white clouds caught by the wind.

The evening prayer call sounded and then slipped away. Street football games were ended by mutual consensus, by groups of players in their separate games announcing end-game rules at the disappearing of the sun at the horizon.

'First side to reach seven goals wins.'

'First side to beat the other side by two points wins.'

In the school halls of the capital, floodlights were switched on, and badminton games were just starting. Players streamed onto courts and checked the feathers of their shuttlecocks for damage.

As the evening grew late, pasar malam vendors selling fruit and vegetables sensed their imminent closure and started giving discounts. They shouted, 'One for two, three for five!, lelong, lelong!'

'Auntie, if I sell you three for ten, then how do I make money? Ai-yah, okay lah, three-for-ten lah. But only this one time, okay, otherwise how I make money, Auntie?'

There was a long queue at the assam laksa stall, where one woman was furiously splashing assam laksa soup into bowls of fresh lai fun noodles. Her worker would take the bowl from her and scatter pineapple chunks, mint leaves and chopped chillies (for those who wanted it extra hot) on top. Next to them was a young man, yawning at his stall. No one stood in line for herbal eggs in a pot of simmering spiced tea. Across from them was the popiah man, rolling up popiah and drizzling kicap manis and chilli sauce as fast as he could.

'People mountain, people sea,' a grandmother grumbled. She was only trying to get home on her bicycle.

From the back of a converted lorry, the char kway teow man took orders that showed off his impressive memory skills: 'Two char kway teow. One small, with egg but without prawn. One large, without prawn and egg, and less spicy.' He tossed kway teow, cockles, chives and bean sprouts in a wok over the fire, until charred and caramelised by the dark soy sauce, before being plated, and another hand reached out to him to exchange worn leaves of paper money for the char kway teow, in one fluid motion.

In the fading sunlight, the stalls were lit by blue, green and orange fluorescent tubes. The vendors sighed, weary of a life that only knew work and long days; their sighs were buried under the pulse of music that blared from loudspeakers.

126

Someone was singing something, and a thrum filled the air, but it could have just been the power generators hissing.

Min had been weaving through the broken lines of pasar malam stalls for two hours, not thinking about food or much else. Her hands felt empty. She bought two popiah rolls on reflex: the future Min might be hungry. The pressure in her temples had not subsided.

Han had walked with her to the stalls but he had left early to catch the lorry back to his village. 'Might as well. Nothing else I can do here,' he said.

She promised to call him when the professor returned, even though she did not want to. 'Promise-promise, I'll call you as soon as the professor steps through the door.' She did not add, And Chong Meng, too. No more promises that she could not keep.

He only said, 'Thank you.'

Why thank you? She had done nothing, and nothings do not deserve thank yous. She was just a useless housekeeper. Blardy useless, go back to your desert, as the professor would have said.

Eventually, as the pasar malam wound down, Min went back to the professor's house and sat at the kitchen table. The two popiah sat curled in their tight rolls, now cold. She still did not feel like eating. Darkness closed in on the lone kitchen light. Chau Ang Gong observed her from the altar above the cold kitchen stove, not approving of the state of the household.

'I didn't feel like cooking today,' she told the kitchen god, as she lit three joss sticks and stuck them in the incense bowl.

She heard a knock at the door. She jumped; she didn't expect anyone else today – the roti man had already stopped by for her to buy a loaf of bread.

When she opened the door, she found Han.

127

'Eh, you supposed to go back tonight, right?' She looked at the clock in the kitchen. 'It's nine already wor. How come you here?'

There was another way to the Hei-san islands, Han said. 'Madam Chua told me, when I stopped to say goodbye. She comes from the east, you know. There is one train that goes to the East Coast, a government-run train, very slow but tickets cheap. Takes one week.'

'I never heard of train like that. How can, the train must take very long, going around the Peninsula,' Min said, sceptical.

'No, the train cuts through the Western Range, crosses the Desert of Birds, and arrives at the Eastern Port. And from the Eastern Port, we can take a ship to the Hei-san archipelago.'

It took some time before she realised what Han meant. All she heard were the words *the Desert of Birds*; words familiar and unfamiliar, estranged words. Did he even know what the Desert of Birds meant? she asked herself, knowing that Han and the pasar malam vendors and the char kway teow man and the assam laksa lady and the badminton players and Madam Chua and all the people of the capital, all the people of these lowlands, they could not know what *the Desert of Birds* meant: dust, sadness and endings.

Han misunderstood her reaction. 'Yah-yah, don't be scared, okay? The White Ghosts don't come into the Desert of Birds; the wall keeps them north. The train tracks are too far south for them.'

Scared? She was not scared of the White Ghosts. They never came into the Desert of Birds, especially not in the dry season. It was too hot for them – their skin would turn crisp in the sun and their pale hair would catch fire.

No, she was surprised. A train crossing the Desert of Birds? How improbable, how absurd, how fantastical, how astonishing.

Kuang had told her too many stories of foolish lowlanders attempting to cross the Desert of Birds on foot, with only one having survived – a woman in her forties, who arrived on the outskirts of the Eastern Port and collapsed at the side of a road, where a supply lorry found her. She had wanted to be the first to cross the desert unaided and had spent months preparing for the trek. She had studied old maps and she had fasted and she walked in the peak afternoon sun. But nothing could have hardened her for the dry heat. Her water supply had run out three days earlier. No water in the river beds, she said, or in the valleys, or found as mist in the morning air.

There had been no rain for many years.

Already Min found herself thinking about how the steel train tracks must swell in the burning heat, and whether the train had air conditioning, or if people fanned themselves in desperation to lift even just a bit of the sweat streaming from their pores, and how the sand grains must glommed to their clammy skin. A train! The desert people she once knew never spoke of a train, and so if it did exist, it must enter the Desert of Birds nearer the south, where the Western Range broke in narrow gashes, and there were established villages.

Only birds lived in that desert, the people of the capital said. The air is too thin for people; they'd have night-fevers.

Han continued, 'I called home just now. I spoke to Ah-ma. I heard the fan circling above her. Her voice sounded like motorcycle engines, you know, when the plug breaks and it's hard to start in the morning. I told her that I need to look after Chong Meng.

'She said that I needed to look after myself. "When I am gone, who will take care of you?" And Father didn't want to speak to me because he was angry.'

129

Han looked away from Min and stared out into the street. Rain started to fall with reluctance. Lights were turned on in houses across the road.

If your ah-ma dies in these two months, how? Min did not ask the question. Instead she said, 'When does the train leave?'

'Tomorrow. Only one train runs on the line. Go there one week, come back one week.'

She stared at Han. 'You going on this train, by yourself?' she said. 'Across the desert? Then find a boat to the Hei-san archipelago? And then look for the professor, Mr Ng and Chong Meng, somewhere in the forests of Naga Tua? Just to save your cousin?'

He stared back at her, with the naive fullness of a young man who has never travelled much outside fishing villages. 'Yes.'

The joss sticks had burned down to dull embers. The kitchen grew darker, and Min shivered as the cold gathered around them; the stove had not been used that day. In front of them, the table shrank as she watched, growing distant as if it belonged to a different reality. The two popiah, bought in some other life, had collapsed into the kicap manis and chilli sauce, their crisp exterior shells reduced to faceless, soggy sacks of vegetables.

'You okay?' Han said.

Min nodded to herself and said, 'We live two separate lives in the same house, the professor and I. I am like a cockroach that creeps by the wall, through the holes of the pipes and the cracks in the cupboards, while the professor *is* the house. Sometimes he wanders around the rooms naked, or with a sarong tied haphazardly around his waist – he doesn't care, he has a right to exist in all of its spaces.

130

She shook her head, her voice rising gradually as she continued. 'I'm so lowly a housekeeper, the stupid silly cockroach, there to keep the house clean or to be lectured at. So he speaks to me freely about his plans, his theories. But what he doesn't realise is that I am listening and I remember.

'You know what? I will follow you and I will help you. I will come with you.'

Part Four
Bintang Jelas

No People, Only Ghosts Here

C hong Meng was not happy.
　'What, need to work as deckhand? I'm tauke son you know,' he said. For indeed, he was the son of the tauke Mr Lim of the Lim Fishing Company. These kind of jobs for coolie only hor.

'No free passage on the ship,' Mr Ng said. 'You want to come along on this ex-pat-di-shun or not? So much pasal wan you. No gratefulness.'

What Mr Ng said stung. So much pasal wan, as if he was desperate to join them, as if he needed to be grateful. But he, Lim Chong Meng, had found the spade for Mr Ng! A sense of indignation rose in him and manifested itself as an itch below his chin. He scratched at it. There was a vague release of tension. 'The spade. I found for you the spade,' Chong Meng muttered, for muttering was the best he could do.

Mr Ng did not hear; he had turned away and was chatting to the professor animatedly.

It was just like being on a fishing boat again, only a much larger one with more shit to do. Many times he had grumbled to no one: what was he, some foreign worker? A coolie? *Bintang Jelas* sailed serenely on, and only the half-literate worker who identified himself as 'Third Officer' spoke to Chong Meng. He said that the ship was not a hotel, and that Chong Meng needed to do work, otherwise he would be sleeping out on the open deck.

Bloody hell. Ma hai. There was always work to do. Scraping and grinding off rust from surfaces. Walls that needed painting. Lashing gear on containers that needed tightening. In between the flurry of tasks, Chong Meng took to hiding behind the exhaust funnels just so he could have a smoke and to spite the third officer, Mr Ng, the professor – every single one of them – for making him work like some coolie.

On the second afternoon on *Bintang Jelas*, he was sent to the engine room. Opening the door, he was hit with the stench of burning oil. His nostrils felt like the air was eating away at their lining, so strong were the fumes. His lungs felt flooded with dark soot.

A mask hit Chong Meng in the face.

The wiper is sick today, someone said, from the darkness of the engine room. He got food poisoning wor. You need to wipe up the oil on the floor.

Chong Meng gingerly picked up the mask. It felt slimy. He slipped the elastic band of the mask over his head, covering his nose and mouth.

'What? Do what?' His words came out muffled.

Through the open door, he could see a single flickering light outlining the silhouette of a tall man. So great was the contrast between dark and light that his face was hidden in the back-flow of the pouring light. His boiler suit showed many creases, defined by their edges that formed a boundary between light and dark. Originally orange, the boiler suit was now stained all over with brown patches. The man's hair brushed the top of the door frame as he stepped through. The steel grating on which they stood shook. As the man unfolded into the pas-sageway, Chong Meng realised that this man looked different from any other man he knew: large, sunken eyes, protruding cheek bones, and hair the colour of Rasa Sayang beach sand.

Chong Meng had never seen a White Ghost, but the appear-ance of this man fit the stories.

'I am the oiler. But you call me Frank lah,' Frank the oiler said, although Chong Meng had asked no such question. He offered a grease-stained glove, and Chong Meng, stunned, unsure what to think, offered his hand in reflex. They shook hands. When Chong Meng pulled his hand back, he found grease had trans-ferred from Frank the oiler's glove onto his own.

'There, three piles of rags. Clean, dirty, very dirty. Mop up the oil first with a dirty rag. Dirty rag becomes very dirty rag. When most of the oil is gone, then use clean rag to wipe. Clean rag becomes dirty rag. Okay?'

Frank the oiler then disappeared into the ship's metal recesses, leaving Chong Meng in the company of the oil-stained rags, far removed from their original use as men's underwear and T-shirts. The constant churning hum of the engines added to Chong Meng's irritation, but he knelt on the floor and started wiping up the oil.

*

137

On the fourth day, Chong Meng's sleeping clothes were moved to the top bunk in his room.

'Wei, why my clothes moved there wan?' Chong Meng said.

The chief steward told him that there was a burst pipe on the third floor of the castle.

'Reshuffling,' he said, before adding: 'The room no more your own – you need to share now. Bottom bunk belongs to the Lady.' He caught Chong Meng's expression and said, 'Don't think anything funny ah. She belong to chief officer.'

There was just one female on *Bintang Jelas*, whose name remained unimportant – she had come to be known as the Lady. She walked around in shorts that rode up so high that Chong Meng made a special effort to scrape rust off the gangway, for a brief view of the smooth curve that started from the back of her legs and held her womanly hips. When she walked around in her boiler suit, the brown of her nearly bare legs winked through the side slits of the suit, which were meant for air circulation. The Lady did not wear any clothes underneath other than her black underwear, which was also visible in teasing, dark glimpses.

Chong Meng's experience of women was limited. He had a girlfriend back at school, Li Shen, whose father owned the hor fun stall in Restaurant S&O, but she broke up with him after three weeks when he tried to touch her breasts. Only light touch, he told her. Other people also let their girlfriend touch wan. She slapped him and did not speak to him for the rest of the school year. (Even more unfortunately, her father had also taken a dislike to him, and since then, whenever he ordered hor fun at their stall, Chong Meng was convinced that there were fewer prawns and less chicken in his bowl.)

138

The Lady was never once seen in his cabin. Her bags lay on the bottom bunk like abandoned dogs. Once, Chong Meng caught a whiff of fresh lemons that might have been her scent, or perhaps it was the cleaning detergent that the stewards used.

On the third night of her bags sitting on the bottom bunk bed, the chief officer took Chong Meng aside at dinner, and told him that he was not to go back to his room that night.

'Go to the game room, play cards or something. Make sure you stay away until midnight, okay, boy?' the chief officer said.

The burst pipe on the third floor of the castle was mended in three days. The flood in the toilets was mopped up. The bags disappeared.

In fact, Chong Meng rarely saw anyone during the day. The passageways were often empty, with crew members flitting in and out in sporadic bursts, so infrequent was their presence. Like visits to his kong-kong's grave in Bukit Temerlung. No people, only ghosts here, Han would have said.

The game room and sauna – who would have thought they would be deserted, every day and every night? One of the deckhands said, 'Fun? Here must work hard, work overtime. If I'm not working, then I'm sleeping. Why else I work on this ship? You think nice ah, be away from my family for so many weeks. I have a small girl you know, just three years old. In a few weeks she will be four. She is growing up so fast. If I work hard for a few years, then I can open up business in my village and be with my family again.'

Mr Ng, his one and only friend, could not be found on the lower levels of the castle. Chong Meng tried to climb up the steel staircases to the bridge to find Mr Ng, but was told by the third officer: 'You worker, not allowed at bridge.'

It was yet another evening when Chong Meng finally spotted Mr Ng, emerging from a corridor near the game room.

'Hello ah, sir,' Chong Meng said, stepping forward, holding out his right hand for a handshake.

Mr Ng frowned at Chong Meng's outstretched hand. 'Eh, you got see the professor around ah? He keeps to his room very often hor. Tell me if you see him, okay. But don't bother him too much yah.'

Chong Meng often found himself eating alone in the mess room. He memorised the entire variety of plastic forks: three-pronged, spork, heavy-duty, clear, and easily broken. Some nights, a flock of stewards took up residence at the long table at the back. They spoke in their local dialect, unfamiliar to Chong Meng with the exception of a few common words that dropped through the conversation like bird shit.

Just foreign workers only. Not as if I want to friend-friend with them also, Chong Meng told himself.

Chong Meng had visited the port side of the main deck, the 01 Level, every evening since he boarded *Bintang Jelas*. There no one told him what to do; there was only the setting sun and the sea and the jagged peaks of the Western Range, just visible in the falling light. He spotted small fishing boats that flitted about in the sea, nimbly darting in and out of the coast, their steel frames dancing in the waves. These boats were small compared to *Bintang Jelas*, but even the smallest boat out here was larger than any boat owned by the Lim Fishing Company. A few boats even had cranes. Those fishing boats would not need extra workers to move the nets of fish. And

140

their steel hulls would need a lot less maintenance than his wooden boats, which had to be repainted every few months.

They never lost sight of the land, as the ship visited the small ports that were scattered on the western coastline of the Peninsula, so unmemorable that their names were immediately forgotten. The Peninsula itself was constantly changing, from muddy banks near the capital, into pebble beaches, into gentle hills with their green, bare backs, into mountains where the sea ate into the cliffs. Fishing boats grew scarce and dropped back and, eleven days into their journey, Chong Meng realised that he had not seen a fishing boat for several days.

Here, the jade sea was much more agitated, and its waves threw themselves against the cliffs. People did not belong here, the cliffs were for birds only. Like spectators in a stadium, the birds watched *Bintang Jelas* from a safe distance, their webbed feet perched on the stepped tiers of the cliffs, high above the waves and boiling sea foam.

A solitary pile of rocks emerged from the monotony of the sea. It was capped by green trees, and it increased in size as *Bintang Jelas* approached. Prison Island. Mr Ng said that a boat of prisoners was dumped there, instead of in jail, as a punishment. It was unclear whether any were still alive. The coast looked deceptively close to the island, close enough to swim, but the sea was white-topped in its rage, surely drowning anyone who attempted to cross. A cold-tinged wind chilled Chong Meng's cheeks.

'Why they go to prison wan?' Chong Meng asked Mr Ng in one of their rare encounters. Only misplaced items, household arguments and unfilial children darkened the wooden white doors of Kampung Seng's police station. Chong Meng

141

himself had only been to the police station once, when his mother threw a saucepan at his father and a neighbour called the police.

'Usual reasons lor – maybe the prisoners did something the govmen didn't like. You know govmen lah.' Mr Ng gave a shrug. 'So quick to catch if you say something a bit bad about govmen. But then robbers, thieves, all – they just close one eye.'

More days passed. There were many temple ruins, appearing one after the other, uninhabited by people. Some appeared to be completely inaccessible: perched on pinnacles with cliffs on all sides, with no footpaths or bridges joining them to the mainland. Some were clustered, as if they sought out each other for comfort in this strange, new world. Worn-out stone lions guarded them. Trees grew within their sheltered walls, turning their faces away from the strong sea breeze.

Chong Meng saw a seagull that was perched on top of a stone lion. The seagull lifted its wings, and for a moment the lion appeared to move along with the flurry of flapping wings. Then, the seagull rose into the sky, and the lion was once again stone, immoveable, forgotten.

They were approaching Bawahsiang.

Last port on the Peninsula, a deckhand told him. We get two days here. Better get off if you can, otherwise you won't see land again for two weeks.

Got people in Bawahsiang? *Our* type of people? He wanted to ask Mr Ng but dared not.

Professor Toh

Professor Toh's favourite place on *Bintang Jelas* was at the bow, the only spot where he could hear himself think. Away from the tremendous roar of the ship, away from the grunting of men and engines, here was a silence at the very tip of the deck. One could never entirely escape the churn of the engines and the *thunk-thunk* of maintenance work, but a temporary truce had been called here, in this triangular area of grey deck that was separated from a fall into the ocean by a few flimsy pipes of railing.

He stood watching the limitless sea drift beneath the ship. The pain in his stomach was mild, almost forgettable, today. About a four on the pain scale. What would Dr Yip say? Have you taken your pills? Yes, doctor, I took the pills this morning. I washed them down with a lukewarm teh tarik.

Put some more condensed milk in my teh tarik, he had told the trainee cook this morning.

Can't wor, said the trainee cook, an uneducated eighteen-year-old boy. This teh tarik not make from fresh wan. It's three-in-one teh tarik, premixed powder. I just stir in hot water only.

The professor's teh tarik had been followed by several helpings of nasi lemak, with two deep-fried chicken legs, two fried eggs and a large scoop of sambal, which the cook had made extra spicy for him.

Dr Yip had told him, With your condition, you can eat whatever you want. Won't make any difference anymore.

The professor clutched at his stomach.

How long more? He had finally asked Dr Yip that day.

Zziowatt. A loud sound wafted from behind him, somewhere on the open deck, where the crew continued their maintenance. The sound manifested in a knot that hardened above his left eye. *Zziowatt*. No wonder these men were unthinking animals. The sound rose and subsided in jagged fits. *Zziowatt*. Any lulls were soon punctuated with sharp, shrieking wails. *Zziowatt*.

Two deckhands squatted by a hatch cover. As the professor arrived, they turned off their tools. The sound stopped.

'What are you doing?' he asked.

Scraping rust, they said.

No peace for a man this morning. Surely his cabin would be quieter. He decided to leave the bow. The steel door of the castle was decorated with coils of steel chains. Off to the side lay a pile of grease-stained, once-orange, once-luminescent boiler suits worn by the crew. The pile moved. The professor jumped. A head appeared, a bobbing ball that floated above the coils of chains, and the pile revealed itself to be a deckhand. In his hand were greased rags.

'Morning, Professor,' the deckhand said. 'You sleep okay ah last night? Got storm wor, wind and everything hor. Like that how can anyone sleep.'

The professor averted his gaze and muttered a reply. Who knew what this one wanted? They always wanted something; so desperate, all of them.

A few moments passed before the professor remembered. That was the kampung boy, wasn't it? Cheng . . . Cheng something. Cheng Meng? No, that was the festival. Chong Meng. That was it. Not the cleverest one, despite his name. A shame that Sky Yang came out of the forest the way she did. She was the smartest of them. Would this one even survive? Would he be washed up in some stream somewhere, like some of the earlier ones? Not for the first time, the professor wished he had more time to find better candidates.

The ache in his stomach subsided as soon as he entered the corridors of the castle. An emptiness replaced it. The grey walls and grey floors echoed; no one scuttled about. Good. They should be out on the ship, working. One never knows with these foreign workers, always loitering somewhere, hiding from honest hard work. Ship crew were the worst.

He climbed several levels until he reached his cabin, the largest one on the ship with the exception of the captain's. It had formerly belonged to the supercargo, before the professor had insisted very loudly, in words and in money, that he needed that room (the room had a large safe, the professor knew). In any case, the supercargo was willing to trade away his room. In the casinos and gambling dens of the capital, he had lost the company's voyage profits in several bad hands of chor dai di, and needed money to mask the company's losses.

Mr Ng appeared in the passageway, huffing, sweating, ingratiating, grinning; his humanness was like the putrid stink of durian.

For the first time in the course of their acquaintance, Professor Toh was temporarily comforted by Mr Ng's presence.

'Ah, Professor! Ah-hmm, I was looking for you. Where you go always in the morning wan? Your door always locked. I look high and low in the ship still can't find you. Bridge also takda. The two TV rooms also takda. I even go down to the engine room – also takda. Dinner also you come late leave early. Wah, you really miss out hor! Yesterday I found out that the captain has non-alcohol beer. Special treat he said. Damn shiok wei. Taste like normal beer only, if I close eyes don't see label lah! Haha!' Mr Ng laughed for several moments, before whispering, 'Eh, eh, Professor, I help you lot already. We good friends yah? We need to make plan wor.'

'Mr Ng, I'm very tired today. Need to take a nap now.'

'But we must talk, about the boy, you know. Remember ah, Mr Ng find for you wan!'

'Mr Ng – tomorrow, tomorrow we talk. All right?'

Mr Ng made a sound in his throat and skulked away.

The professor was alone in his cabin now. His bed sheets were smooth, featureless like a flat sea, calmed by the invisible stewards. The smell of their intrusion lingered, partly masked by the jasmine air-freshener that they had applied in copious clouds. He checked under the bed, and opened the curtains of the shower. Empty. He locked the cabin door, then pressed down the handle to make sure the door was, indeed, locked.

Then, with giddy steps, Professor Toh approached the cabin's safe, large enough that an adult man could sit inside comfortably. The steel monolith captured the professor's growing

146

reflection on its surface – the bright eyes, the shaking hands – holding his image sharply as if saving it for another day.

The code: two-eight-nine-nine-six-two. His fingers had memorised the sound of each click at the end of each turn, so much so that he could feel the *wrongness* in his fingers when he made a mistake. Paradoxically, he wished for someone to challenge this skill, to break the safe and change the code, so that for a few fleeting moments he would feel the unfamiliar clicks running through his fingers, the strangeness of the new language that had been imposed upon him. Not this time, however – the knob clicked into its grooves with ease, and the door opened.

The professor's left hand disappeared into the safe and reappeared with a metallic object that spanned all of two feet.

Mr Ng did not know the importance of what he had found in the backwaters of Kampung Seng. There were few people in this world who knew the purpose of this object.

Aleum. The tool sat unremarkably in the professor's hands, like a great container that had landed in the hold of the cargo ship, silent about its contents, going to a destination that was long decided but secret to the crew. His fingers caressed the deep ridges along the length of the tool; inscriptions written in a language whose manifest was missing.

Several weeks ago, Mr Ng showed up for his appointment at the professor's house. Mr Ng is the one with the gold Rolex, Min reminded the professor. He has been trying to meet you for one month now.

Afternoon rain fell in sharp strokes against the house. Mr Ng entered, followed closely by an unknown young man.

'Professor Toh,' Mr Ng said, solemnly. 'I found her. I found Swee. The spirit. She did not pass away in the temple fire in Suriyang. She married a fisherman this side of the Peninsula.'

'You found her?' Professor Toh gripped the edge of the table.

'No, she gone already. To the heavens. Bye-bye liao,' Mr Ng said.

These people and their primitive superstitions about death and dying. Could not even say the word *dead* out loud.

'My aunt passed away long time ago,' the unknown young man said from behind Mr Ng, his tone helpful, eager.

'Chong Meng!' Mr Ng barked at him. 'No need to talk. Just bring the spade here.'

A two-foot-long object had been placed on the professor's table.

It had taken all of the professor's willpower not to jump up and grab the spade with his hands, to run his fingers over the rough-serrated edges of the blade, to feel the grooves made by the inscriptions, to chant the word *aleum*, over and over again, as in a fever dream. The professor shuffled the papers on his desk instead.

'Professor? What you think ah?'

The professor said, 'Yes, yes, Mr Ng. I don't know whether it is of any use to me. This . . . spade, it is not useful to my research. Just another common household object. Look at it! It might lead to something more important, but maybe not. I'll keep it for now, but I can only give you a small bonus, since you didn't find the spirit, after all. I'm sure you understand.'

Bawahsiang

Chong Meng's eleven years at school were filled by mornings of tearing out the middle pages of his exercise books, folding them into dense wedges, and shooting them into girls' hair with the careful spring from an opportunistic rubber band; the afternoons found him sleeping at the back of the classroom, his hair tousled like overgrown lalang.

It was safe to say that he did not remember much about the teaching or the teachers in those eleven years – teachers who sailed in and out of his classrooms, impressing Chong Meng's palms with fervent, red, cane marks. Not doing homework, the teachers had said. Talking to friends while the teacher was teaching. Shirt not tucked into trousers, flapping everywhere. Make sure you tuck in properly!

Chong Meng endured school lessons like a bad tummy ache.

So it was to Chong Meng's surprise that Mrs Leong's words about the Peninsula rang like a bell in his head. There was only the unnamed sea beyond the Peninsula, and nothing more, Mrs Leong had said. Mrs Leong, the geography teacher who sometimes wore a red dress with buttons that gaped in the front and a bra that could be occasionally glimpsed. There was only the sea.

Until Mr Ng told him differently. 'Teachers, they know nothing these days,' Mr Ng said. 'Of course there is land beyond the Peninsula, what you think? Boy, you know how lucky you are, anot? How many people from your kampung get to see outside world? You will become Chong Meng, the big shot of Kampung Seng! Later, you can buy new car, like the silver Pajero – there, like your father's friend Mr Liu's wan, the prawn farm tauke. Your new car will have air con until sweat also don't dare come from your armpits.' He repeated for emphasis: '*Sweat* also don't dare come from your armpits.'

'As for myself' – Mr Ng paused for his vision to form – 'maybe I get myself another Rolex. This year collection wan. Then buy new house with air con, better electrical wiring, and longkang that don't block up so easily.'

If Chong Meng had been the kind of person who was prone to reflection, he would have thought of his ah-ma during his journey: her frailty, her chest rising in soft breaths as he stood watching her in a sea of white-sheeted hospital beds.

'Accident,' he would remember whispering as he stood by her bedside. 'She was supposed to be at the hairdresser's.'

'You say what?' Han's father had said.

Nothing, nothing. Chong Meng had said nothing even as Han left for the capital to find Mr Ng – who could believe his cousin would do something so daring as that? Chong Meng knew all along where Mr Ng had gone. ('The green shop opposite the Mustafa Nasi Kandar, first floor, ah-hmm, okay, boy, remember ah? Otherwise, capital so big, where can find anyone again?')

When Chong Meng left Kampung Seng, he told his family, 'Following friend on holiday. Maybe I might be gone long.'

Bintang Jelas arrived at the docks of Bawahsiang just after breakfast.

'Make sure you lock up any valuables,' said a disembodied voice over the PA system.

Chong Meng lacked awareness of how *Bintang Jelas* was moored, but it did, on that cool morning, and a gangway leading to the docks appeared. Swarms of workers waited to board the *Bintang Jelas*, to carry out maintenance work and turn it around.

'This is why you lock everything up. Rats – they steal everything,' the professor muttered, half to himself, and half to anyone in the vicinity who happened to be listening.

'Yah, true also,' Chong Meng said, nodding.

The professor looked irritated. 'Please don't follow me today, I need some space. I'm going on a long walk.'

'Don't worry, Professor, ah-boy won't follow you around,' Mr Ng said, quickly. He turned to Chong Meng and said, 'Now, you hear anot, you better pay attention ah. Don't go play-play and tomorrow never turn up for work. The boat leaves tomorrow morning. If you don't show up, then bye-bye liao, no adventure.' He stopped and looked around. 'Wah, the ship so quiet hor.'

It was true, what Mr Ng said: *Bintang Jelas* had grown silent. Around the quiet ship a nest of activity had formed: workers hammering, scraping, and yelling at each other over the din, in the middle of which *Bintang Jelas* slept, as if waiting for the right moment to wake.

The streets of Bawahsiang wound in tight squiggles along the slope of a gentle hill. People went about their business. Chong Meng had been curious to look around this new town initially, but got bored after the third vegetable cart passed him by. He overheard two aunties complaining that the price of anchovies had risen. 'Now twenty-one per kilo, like that how to afford?' *Aunties, the same everywhere,* he thought. *Now, to find cigarettes.*

At last, at a T-junction where one street met another in an end, a sundry shop appeared to be open for trading. His mummy would have said, Why put your business at the T-junction? Feng shui bad for business.

A man, presumably the owner, was sitting on a stool out the front, reading a newspaper. Around him were large Milo cans piled up to form circular towers, blocking the view into the shop.

Chong Meng stood at the entrance and looked into the darkness. A speck of sunlight rested on the till. Next to it was a glass cabinet where cigarette cartons were displayed. The man said something in gibberish.

'What? What? Speak properly. You can't talk, issit?' Chong Meng said.

'You outsider ah? Can't speak our tongue ah? What brand of cigarettes do you want?' the man said.

'Any brand, I don't care. Cheapest can already.' Chong Meng yawned.

The man stood up and folded the newspaper along its original fold lines. The front page's main headline was SECOND P LANE CRASHES IN THE HEI-SAN ISLANDS.

These were the same islands Mr Ng talked about. Chong Meng picked up the newspaper and stared at the photo beneath the headline. What islands? The photo only showed a green sea, flat like cardboard. He squinted at the picture – maybe wrong photo leh – turning his head this way and that, and then, all at once, he saw islands; they burst onto the photo, as black as stove coal, as black as the night in haunted rubber plantations. How had he missed seeing the islands before? Their angularity protruded out of the two-dimensional sea and ate the flimsy lines of the newspaper.

'You want to pay anot? Your cigarettes,' the man said, now holding a carton of Lucky 7s. He pointed to the newspaper that Chong Meng was holding up to the light, and said, 'You want to read more, you pay.'

After Chong Meng paid for the cigarettes and a fresh copy of the newspaper, the man said, 'Those planes, spooky, huh? Must be the govmen doing wan. Cover up their experiments. Who knows what they are doing on those islands.' The man's voice rose. 'All these planes, this new technology, is unnatural. Unnatural! People are born with two legs; they are made to walk, not fly. If the gods wanted us to fly, then we would be given wings like birds. Instead, we have two legs. Our place is on this humble earth, where we are meant to have a family and live good, faithful lives. These accidents, I tell you now, is because we don't know our place here on earth. Humans have become too arrogant! One day they will be punished; just you wait.'

Siao, Chong Meng thought, shaking his head, walking away. That man spent too much time in the cuckoo factory. There were a few people in Kampung Seng who reminded him of that man. Auntie Fong, his father's cousin's wife, who owned the dobi on the corner, had told the ten-year-old Chong Meng that their family was going to burn in hell because they prayed to the wrong gods, and that her three children were not allowed out after school to play because of the bad influences out there.

Chong Meng's mummy, upon being told this, had said, 'Ai-yah, that Mrs Fong, no wonder her husband left her! So religious, so pious, until she let herself go. Her clothes all ham choi, her hair kerinting, her skin so dark and wrinkled, never put moisturiser. What man would want her?'

Several shoplots down from the sundry shop, a black sign hung overhead that read MASTER WONG.

Underneath, smaller red letters read FORTUNE TELLER FENG SHUI MASTER.

An arrow pointed to a narrow set of stairs squeezed between two shoplots. To the left of the stairs was a forest of empty hawker stalls with no customers. A single teenager was in a shop manning the char siew pau cart. Her eyes narrowed as Chong Meng looked at her. To the right was a shuttered shop front that gave no indication of its trade.

Chong Meng followed the arrow upstairs and found a man sitting in a small office with no windows. The man was about the same age as his mummy. He looked out from the depths of his blue shirt, a wrinkled collar weighing his neck down. A brown stain marked the top of his breast pocket. A brush painting of eight galloping horses hung on the wall behind him. Choy Sun Yeh looked down upon them from a small altar perched above the man.

'I am Master Wong,' the man said. 'I can tell your fortune.' Air conditioning blew at his hair.

'How much?'

154

'For you, quick reading, only twenty. I can tell you three things.'

Chong Meng nodded.

Master Wong started by asking for Chong Meng's birth date. He said, 'You will take a long journey.'

Chong Meng was irritated. That, he knew already.

'You will have no luck with women.' Master Wong's voice was as solemn as his expression.

'Why you say until like that? How can I improve?'

But Master Wong, unhearing, unheeding, continued, 'There is only darkness in your future.'

Chong Meng stood up. 'What kind of stupid fortune is this?' He threw his right hand out angrily. 'You curse me, bring me bad luck only. How can you expect me to pay you?'

'Tell your fortune is not the same thing as giving you luck. You want luck, you go to temple and pray to the gods for blessings, okay? Go, go! I don't want your money; you only give me bad luck money,' said Master Wong.

Chong Meng ran down the stairs, through the streets he ran, so fast that the rows of shoplots down the hill blurred into a single image. How dare that Master Wong say bad things. Fortune teller, my foot! He continued running down the streets of Bawahsiang, and only slowed to a stop at the bottom of the hill, where the steep gradient softened into flat ground, and there the *Bintang Jelas* still lay on the water.

His local fortune teller and feng shui master would never dare to tell Chong Meng a bad fortune. Mummy always told him that he would be a successful businessman, just like his father. He was going to be a superstar. He was going somewhere in life, even if he was dragged down by his relatives. Now – Mummy had added, as if an afterthought – if her darling superstar son would pay attention so that he could take over the business . . .

It aggravated Chong Meng that no one knew who his father was outside Kampung Seng. Why would a fortune teller want to predict bad things for him? he thought. Somemore I was going to pay him. He felt bitterly hurt, angry, and, most of all, cheated of a bright future.

'Bad luck, choi, choi!' He waved his hands around to ward off any bad luck that had stuck to him. The stink of stale engine oil from nearby ships filled the air, reminding him of prayer oil on altars. Perhaps he should find a temple to make a few offerings.

He spent the next hour searching for public temples but could not find any. Finally, he spotted a payphone in a booth beneath a half leaking roof. Mummy could make a temple offering on his behalf, he thought. He fumbled with several coins, before putting them through the slot, which happily turned the coins into a connection.

The phone at his house rang one time before it was answered. 'Hello, Mummy?' he said, surprised at the quick response.

'Chong Meng ah? Chong Meng, is that you?' The voice was unmistakably his mummy's, but sounded frayed at the edges.

'Yes, yes, Mummy, it's me. Eh, I just want to ask you ah, can you—'

He was cut off by his mummy's choking sob – another surprise. 'Ai-yoh, Chong Meng, you know anot that my mother is still in the hospital?'

'Your mother?' Chong Meng said, momentarily confused.

'Ai-yoh, you stupid or what? My mother meaning your ah-ma lah! Why you gone on holiday so long wan? Your ah-ma, all day in hospital bed, in and out of consciousness. So fast she deteriorate after her fall.' There was a pause over the phone line when she stopped talking to blow her nose. 'Chong Meng, you need to come home now, pay respects, because, you know lah, what would happen, soon.'

Then she hung up, not wanting to speak about bad news any longer. As if it wasn't bad enough that Ah-ma was in the hospital, now they had to talk about why she was in the hospital; as if the very act of talking about death would cause death.

An entire phone call, and Chong Meng never got to ask her about making temple offerings on his behalf. He let the phone drop. His shoulders sagged. He wanted to go home. Too many questions outside Kampung Seng. Sick Ah-ma. Mr Ng. Professor. Tower. Missing planes. Hei-san islands. What did it all mean? More questions were thrown up in the air; too many for Chong Meng to juggle, a man of limited introspection. He wanted to speak to someone; he wished Han was there.

There Was Only the Sea

The next morning, *Bintang Jelas* left the Peninsula. The passengers watched as Bawahsiang vanished to a single point. The smell of the stale water in the port disappeared. The air was brought in fresh with the wind, and the same-same blue of the water was everywhere, broken only by the dragging shadow of *Bintang Jelas*.

It would be another two weeks before they arrived beyond where the maps stopped, through to the Hei-san islands on the other side, Mr Ng said. For now, Chong Meng could enjoy the sea, all the sea he would ever want!

Mr Ng paused, with a sideways look at Chong Meng. 'Are you scared? If you fall off the boat here, you won't be able to swim back to land, you know. Too far away.' He added, 'You know, if you scared ah, maybe you aren't the right person for this important expedition, you know.'

'Ai-yah, scared what scared? You think when I go deep-sea fishing can just swim back to shore ah? I been on so many types of boats before, this is just a bigger type of boat wor.' Chong Meng flicked his hair and rolled his eyes, actions that masked the knot of anxiety that grew in his stomach. *There was only the sea.* Nowhere within the vast metallic caverns of *Bintang Jelas* gave Chong Meng respite from the unshakeable terror that they were going to fall off the edge of the world. With each day, they sailed towards a place that did not exist on the maps he knew.

He did not tell Mr Ng this. Mr Ng and every one of them, even the foreign workers, would sneer at him for being so kampung, so jinjang, so uneducated. They would say, 'This is modern technology you know. Ship very advanced wan. Somemore you think the ship is going to fall off map. Wah, you still believe in this kind of old folk tales ah?

'You know lah, kampung people all like that, very super-stitious. No wonder they can't advance in life. Technology like-that-like-that also scared.' There would be some satisfied nodding; a confirmation of the stereotype that everyone knew.

If Chong Meng had been less defensive, more self-aware, he would have noticed that the crew avoided him, too. Who wanted to speak to a cursed man? Bad luck was contagious, especially this type of bad luck. The crew had heard too many stories from the Hei-san islands.

In the game room, there was no one to avoid and no one who avoided Chong Meng, and there Chong Meng was to be found when he was off shift.

One day, Chong Meng walked into the game room to find Frank the oiler kneeling on the worn-out, dark blue carpet.

160

'The Archie game console is missing,' Frank the oiler said. 'Must have forgot to lock it up when we docked at the port. Oh, well. Someone else needed it more.'

'What are you doing here?' Chong Meng said.

'Same reason as everyone else. To make money.'

'I mean, why you here, in the game room?'

'Same reason as you. No one wants to talk to me. They say that I am a White Ghost. So I come in here, I chill a little. No one stares at me here.'

'What you mean people don't want to talk to me? You know I'm with Mr Ng and the professor, right?'

'I have never seen you with them. In the daytime you work on the deck. In the evening, I see the professor and Mr Ng eat with the captain, but you eat in the mess room by yourself.'

'Look, I'm not going to argue with you, okay? Everyone knows White Ghosts lie. They drink so much alcohol that they forget how to tell the truth.'

'Not all White Ghosts are like that.'

'You work on *Bintang Jelas* because you drink all your money away, issit? Or issit women?' Chong Meng said. He was reminded of words from Mr Chiew, his father's friend who owned the Rasa Sayang resort: *White Ghosts leave their family, drink and party only. They don't respect their elders.*

'I need to pay off some debt. Hopefully I will have paid it off by next year,' Frank said. 'Are you're getting off at the Hei-san islands? I hear the rest of them talk about how unlucky you are. Mr Ng must be paying your family a lot of money.'

'What you mean?'

Frank got up. 'I shouldn't talk about other people's business; your business, not mine.'

*

As Chong Meng spoke, Mr Ng twisted his lips so that they occupied the left side of his face.

'Mr Ng, I need to ask a few things ah, not to mean any disrespect. Got this worker said I was unlucky. Said bad things happen on those islands.' Chong Meng's voice dropped to a whisper. 'Like – *death*.'

'Why you listen to these ship workers? These workers know nothing; tin kosongs all of them. Listen, I told you already, top-top secret. Got a golden tower somewhere on those islands. You, I, and the professor will be the first ones to find it. Then your name – in the front page of the newspaper! Big boss Mr Lim Chong Meng!'

Mr Ng placed a comforting arm around Chong Meng's shoulder, and Chong Meng felt relieved by the touch of a friend.

Late into the afternoon, a group of off-duty crew – stewards, engine men, deckhands, and even the chief engineer – milled at the bow, pottering on the patch of limited triangular deck beloved by the professor.

The professor was also at the bow that afternoon, standing off to one side. (By then, everyone knew that the professor paced on the bow for hours each morning. They whispered among themselves stories of the hermitic professor, and his bad-luck assistant, Chong Meng. Mr Ng, on the other hand, was a friendly fella.)

It was an afternoon of nervous waiting, and a low buzz of anticipation permeated the air, swelling as black specks on the horizon were sighted by the crew, subsiding when these black specks were later identified as a bird, or a pod of dolphins, or whales that murmured in the beating sea.

162

These whales sang in their many hearts, and they watched as the strange, land-bound creatures swam past, trapped in their metal cage.

They going where? a whale sang.

Land of the Urang Api-Api, an older one replied.

In the end of, end of.

The sun reddened as it sank. There was an air of increasing resignation in the crowd; perhaps the first encounter of the islands would take place at night after all. The sky began to turn, hinting at the many-starred universe, the depths of which hosted invisible planets, spinning balls of fire lonely in their revolutions, and every one of us, specks of dust, flying in the lightless vacuum.

The decline of the sun was almost complete when the first sight of the Hei-san islands appeared on the horizon. The weariness of the crew evaporated as they watched cliffs and peaks bubble up through the placid sea. This was where the maps ended. There was only the sea.

'What you think of the Hei-san islands? Impressive, huh?' Frank the oiler said to Chong Meng. 'It's my third time seeing these islands, but I still think, *Wah, shiok wei!* as you would say. No wonder the maps stop before these islands. Who can draw this dark nothing of rock and water?'

Chong Meng took a step away from Frank, trying not to look at his face. This worker always tried to talk to him, as if they were equals. What if other people saw them talking together, like buddy-buddy? 'Okay only lor. Just islands only what. I seen lots of islands before.'

They were standing by the railings, some distance away from the rest of the crew, and even further away from the professor, who maintained the boundaries of his singular space.

Frank's voice dropped to a whisper: 'I wanted to speak to you. We will be landing tomorrow. Don't get off. Stay on the boat. The Naga Tua island is cursed. When people return from Naga Tua, they are possessed by ghosts. I read that there was another plane crash in those islands. People like yourself, young men and women, they disappear on the island. They don't return.'

Chong Meng heard the same kind of pity in Frank the oiler's voice that was found in his mother's tone whenever she spoke about foreign workers: Ai-yer, those workers, those immigrants, so poor, so dirty, sleep twenty people in one room. No better than dogs and cats! Chong Meng, watch ah, you don't study hard, then you become like them. What kind of life they have? Next weekend, we go to their dorm and donate our old clothes.

'I don't need your advice,' Chong Meng said.

Back in Kampung Seng, nobody would dare treat him as if he was some kind of common *worker*. If only they knew who his father was. He was the son of Mr Lim, Kampung Seng's most successful businessman, and one day, he will be the owner of Lim Fishing Company! One day he will come back to this ship, this *Bintang Jelas*, and buy the ship and its cargo and all the workers, and then they will see. He will be the captain, and he will spend most of his time in the bridge. All the workers will gossip about the last time they caught a sighting of the reclusive captain. 'I heard that he just bought all the shops in Bawahsiang,' his school head teacher would say. 'I heard that he's so powerful now that even the mata-mata obeys his orders,' his friends would say.

The Naga cluster of the Hei-san islands came into view. First, the island of Naga Tua, surrounded by its cousins Naga Muda and Naga Besar.

164

Naga Tua was marked by steep mountains in the north that gave the island its name – barren, black cliffs that looked like a sleeping dragon, where only the hardiest grass grew. The north part of Naga Tua was similar to that of the Burnt Islands – the cluster of islands that marked the most northerly islands of the Hei-san archipelago – where its soil had been birthed in a nursery of molten lava and deep fires. Towards the south of Naga Tua, the steep mountains gave way to gently sloping hills, before broadening out to a large valley that fanned into the southern plains. Rivers buried themselves into the depths of its greenness. Houses sprouted in clusters among the verdant, misted wildness. The south felt old; its trees grew with sturdy trunks that had not been blown away, and its grass held the land firmly.

The port of Naga Tua was the only port in the southerly islands. A few tired lorries slept next to the loading yard. Dusty food carts waited solemnly by the pier, their owners taking naps on nearby chairs or absent altogether. There was a smell of burning in the wind; it reminded Chong Meng of the glow of burning joss sticks and the fine curling lines of their black smoke that dispersed in the air.

Frank the oiler was standing on the main deck of *Bintang Jelas*, looking at Chong Meng from above. *Bye-bye*, Frank the oiler mouthed. He looked sad. They would never see each other again.

Mr Ng squatted by the edge of the dock, smoking a cigarette.

'Mr Ng, you promise I would see this golden tower. Promise-promise only, where is it? Here this place like end of the world like that,' Chong Meng said.

'Kan cheong for what? Look at you now, you sailed on a modern ship. You think your cousin, that one with the dead mother' – here Mr Ng salivated – 'got such an *opportunity* anot? You should be grateful to me.' Mr Ng, with his keen nose and intuition for weaknesses, had sniffed out Chong Meng's resentment. With a few choice words, a stray comment here, a casual remark there, Mr Ng had placed many barbs with the mastery of an experienced practitioner. Cucuk-cucuk sikit. This world was a zero-sum one, where Chong Meng could only win if Han lost.

Chong Meng was the heir to the Lim Fishing Company, and the only blood grandchild – yet Ah-ma loved Han more. In Mr Ng's barbs, Chong Meng heard the echoes of his mummy's comments: 'There, that cousin of yours, come from bad mother, don't know what background also. Maybe even – but don't say to other people, otherwise our whole family name also kena bad name – maybe even she *prostitute*.'

At the same time, Chong Meng missed Han more than he thought he would. He wanted to tell Han that he had sailed on a ship that was a hundred times larger than any of the Lim Fishing Company's deep-sea boats. (He would skip the part where no one would speak to him and everyone was disrespectful.) He wanted to tell Han that he had met a White Ghost named Frank the oiler. Most of all, he wanted to tell Han about these islands not on the maps, created when cracks had opened up in the sea floor, and out came black liquid; furious, boiling bubbles that burned the air and the creatures of the sea. Mazu saw this and was very angry, for her people were getting burned, so she blew and blew, until the sea was cool, and the bubbles solidified into disfigured shapes, never moving again. At least, that was what Frank the oiler had told him in the engine room.

166

He wanted to tell Han how sorry he was when Ah-ma fell down. He was also sorry that Han had seen him in the same car as Mr Ng and the professor. No one was supposed to have known.

He said to Mr Ng and the professor: 'All I see here is an old port. Where is this golden tower you promised?'

The professor looked at Chong Meng as if seeing him for the first time. 'The golden tower? My boy, you will be the first to enter it.'

Part Five
The Desert of Birds

Capital-to-East-Coast Train

When Madam Chua explained these great trains to Han, he understood them in an abstract way, in the same way that a desert person, starved of moisture and hissed at by hot air, could imagine what the full force of a thunderstorm would be like – that is to say, not at all.

A desert person would not know, for instance, that thunderstorms strike in the sleepiest corner of the afternoon, usually as the maid, lulled by a false sense of security, falls asleep while the day's washing dries on the clothesline. Or that thunderstorms bring so much water that the soil of the football fields took several days to drain; meanwhile, millions of tadpoles hatch in the transient pools, racing to develop into frogs before the water evaporates into hexagonal mud cracks. Or that curtains of rain could fall for hours and sometimes days, but rarely.

No, certainly, Han did not understand what these great trains meant. As Han and Min embarked on the longest train journey in the world, which ran from the capital to the East Coast in a one-week trip, neither of them were moved by the journey's significance. Instead, they found themselves annoyed by the other people who pushed themselves into the train, and their inexperience at protecting their personal space led to them being separated between sweaty bodies and slapping armpits.

The train, like a cockroach who creeps by the reflected light of roof shingles, swerved through the capital's newer high-rises that had sprouted amongst a sea of patched-up shacks. It stopped for schoolchildren, who ran across the tracks through holes strategically cut in the track fences, shaving twenty minutes off their daily walk to school. (Only one out of the eight planned pedestrian bridges had been constructed, to maximise the developer's profits. The civil servants told each other to 'just close one eye', after receiving gifts of Rolexes and large discounts on houses. Who would care? Not the people who jumped across the train tracks every day to get to work, leaving their safety behind in their small, half-lit homes.)

Above the tracks, electric wires criss-crossed in flight lines. These thief wires clamped their jaws onto the train's electric lines, stealing power for their masters' homes.

Some way into the outskirts of the capital, the train stuttered to a stop at a rundown platform, where weeds pushed through the cracked concrete. This was the first of the New Villages – settlements built as isolated clusters during the long war. Here in the New Villages, groups of unsupervised children ran feral in the unpaved streets. The smell of uncollected rubbish and outhouses filled the air.

An official from the train company boarded the train. 'Hot? You say hot? This not hotel okay. You want first class, you go hotel. You go get off train.'

172

The person who spoke originally was a man holding a briefcase leaking perfume samples. He frowned but said nothing else. Around him, aunties looked at their baskets, thinking silent *I-told-you-so*s. No point argue-argue. Why must make trouble? The man with perfumes should have known better. What kind of stupid ask this kind of question?

The train gradually emptied along the stops of the New Villages: hairdressers going back home for their yearly holiday, carrying their scraps of savings in a homemade purse; a grandson visiting his grandmother who was sick; market aunties who made the long trip from the capital to the villages in the Desert of Birds, carrying with them baskets of beauty products ('This moisturiser will make your skin many years younger, confirm!'), clothing ('This bolero is very heng now, all the young girls want to wear, somemore ask me to bring back from the capital') and small household items ('If we don't have brushes to scrub the clothes with, then we have to use stones – so susah').

When empty seats appeared, Han and Min found themselves sitting next to each other, on sticky, cracked, fake-leather cushions whose filling exposed itself to the world. Sitting across from them was Auntie Ong. Auntie Ong was a train passenger with five children living in different cities, so she spent her time travelling around to visit them all. Her youngest son was about Han's age. She looked at Han with an equal mix of loneliness and desire for conversation, so much so that Han felt sorry for her and asked the next, obvious, question: 'Your youngest son, what does he do?'

She brightened and informed him that her youngest son worked as a production assistant at a radio station.

'Aih, he tried to explain to me his job, but so confusing, I hear-hear only also don't understand. Kids these days!'

'Auntie, your son sounds like he is doing well wor. You are so lucky. He is so lucky to have you too – you visit him all the way on the other side of the continent.'

Auntie Ong gave a lopsided half-smile. She sank into herself, the arch of her back growing more curved. 'Yes, yes, very lucky I am.' Her smile drooped at its edges, and her eyes withdrew from the grimy overhead racks, the moving windows of the lowlands, to somewhere else altogether, a parallel life, where history ran differently. Upon sensing Auntie Ong peeking, the parallel world quickly withdrew, leaving the air bonecold. The absence of the mention of a Mr Ong collected in the air like heavy water, suspended in its stillness, threatening to fall apart into millions of drops of rain.

Auntie Ong caught Han looking at her with concern, so she shifted her body away, refixed her smile, and signalled to him that their conversation was over with a well-appointed shrug. Her auntieness lost its bold outlines, her voice lapsed into a washed-out grey colour, and her physical self flattened like leftover cardboard, wet from yesterday's rain. 'Auntie Ong' was no longer; in her place was an old woman with a tight white perm, wearing a blue samfu, her dullness blended in with the boredom of train passengers waiting for the train to take them to wherever they needed to get to.

The next morning, the passengers woke up to find the Capital-to-East-Coast train starting to climb the mountains of the Western Range. Walls of rock rose up at an unforgiving angle; not even moss had time to grow, so fresh and unstable were the rock faces.

Han's ah-ma would have said, 'Ai-yoh, why come here so far from Kampung Seng? Only hantu here. When the triads want to get rid of people, they shoot them and then throw them off the cliff. Don't know how many dead bodies here. Police also scared to come. After the hantu eat your qi and possess you.'

Out of the other side of the train, the mountains of the Western Range sank into lowlands where rainforests grew, carved up by rivers large and small. Tiny tributaries ran amok, before they were captured by the main river – aptly named Sungai Lembik – swollen and lazy like an overfed cat. Its days as a cannibalistic predator were over; jumping over boulders, eating its lesser cousin-streams, before it met its terminus in a muddy estuary, where the salty waters of the sea lapped.

Towards the coast, the rainforests were cut into squares by paddy fields and farms and roads that grew through the land. Han could see the path of the train, its metal tracks strangling the New Villages. He could even see a hazy smear that was the capital, pierced by tall spindly towers.

'Are you okay? You look like you're drowning,' Min asked. The aunties on the train tilted their heads, on the prowl for gossip of any kind ('The girl and the boy, unmarried you know, maybe running off to elope').

Could Kampung Seng even be seen from this distance? How small would it be? Han thought of its main road, Jalan Seng, that gave the village its name. He peered out of the window; he desperately wanted to find Kampung Seng. His eyes followed the coastline up north. Was it that cluster of black dots over there, surrounded by patches of farms? But he could not find the hills that surrounded the village.

The train jolted. Baskets on the train floor rattled. The view of the Peninsula shifted.

Han's eyes searched until he found two black lines running parallel, like an equals sign in mathematics – the two rows of shophouses (handphone shops, snooker cafes, kopitiams) that flanked both sides of Jalan Seng. He looked for the river mouth that led into Kampung Seng, lined with factories and fishing docks, where he once sorted fish into boxes. His eyes fastened onto a village which he was sure was Kampung Seng. He squinted to find a patch of grey dots where his home would be, with Father inside. He continued squinting, not wanting to lose sight of his home for a second time. Still the train rolled on, turning into the Western Range again, in one of its many turns. Kampung Seng dissolved into the brown of the newly cleared farmland, into the green of abandoned tin mines, into the villages along the coast, boats, towns, farms, forests, hills. And then, just like that, Kampung Seng was simply nothing. It disappeared into the green of the lowlands. He had given away his Kampung Seng, without ceremony, only to discover that it never belonged to him in the first place; it belonged to no one.

A voice crackled over the PA system. 'Entering the Spirited Pass in a few minutes. The Desert of Birds next.'

If someone had sat down next to Han, and explained what they would both soon see, then perhaps Han would not have dreamt of the Spirited Pass for many years after. Perhaps he would have seen the Spirited Pass for what it truly was – a crack.

The Western Range were new mountains, hardening to become the spine of the Peninsula, and this Spirited Pass was a long crack in one of its vertebrae. As the spine was being pulled apart by tectonic forces, some cracks, like the Spirited Pass, had grown until there was more crack than rock, and together they had formed a continuous, thin crack splitting the Western Range along its entire width. These cracks were passageways to the highlands on the other side. There were other cracks that lay south of the Spirited Pass, such as the Giok Canyons, Kelabu Gang, and also in the north, the Crossing of the White Bulls, where the Hilang River began. Perhaps there were a few more passes up north, but no one knew for sure, for those were the lands of the White Ghosts.

The Spirited Pass was the only passageway in the Western Range that was wide enough to lay down train tracks through its entire length. For this reason, goods came through the Spirited Pass.

During the last extended drought, the desert people in their thousands had walked through these passageways to cross the Western Range. *Water, any water at all*, they said, their lips cracked from the sun, their determined feet dusty. *My child needs water*, they said. The child was often more alive than the parent, as the parent would have given their child most of their water. Local police were tasked to stop the desert people from moving from the highlands into the lowlands, but the police were often parents too, and they saw the desert people with dusty feet and listless children, and their hearts wanted to give them shelter.

Han knew none of this, or even that the Spirited Pass was a passageway. When he looked out of the train window, he noticed that the train appeared to be heading directly into the rock face of the Western Range. Han looked around the carriage frantically. None of the other train passengers paid any attention. If Min had been there, she could have explained that they were entering the Spirited Pass; but at that moment, she was making her way back from the third carriage where the toilets were.

177

'The train – going the right way ah? Seems like going to crash in the mountains only.' His voice shook.

The view disappeared. There was only dark. Still the old man three rows ahead slept, still the two aunties sitting in the corner continued to talk, still Min was not there in the carriage. He raised his left hand, expecting it to disappear too, like the rest of the world. Was this a hole that the world had fallen into and there was no way to get back out? He felt watched by the darkness outside and remembered a story that his ah-ma had told him.

These must be where the sanctuary caves were. During the long war, people had hidden in the caves in the mountains of the Western Range. When the long war ended, some of the people who hid in these caves had refused to return to the lowlands. They had been living in these caves for so long, they said, they knew no other home. They wanted to die in the caves.

'They had hidden themselves so deep that our world could not touch them anymore,' Ah-ma said. 'They could not find their way back.'

When they finally died, it was said that their spirits refused to enter the underworld. Even in death they could not leave the caves. At night, Ah-ma said, when the wind blows from the mountains to the sea, if you listen carefully, you can hear their howls – whether of contentment or of sadness, no one knew. Were these spirits sad to be stuck in the caves, or were they so content that, even in death, they wanted to remain in the only home they knew?

Min was sitting next to him. Han did not remember her returning to her seat.

'This train smells like spilled perfume,' she told him. He wanted to tell her about the sanctuary caves, but she continued: 'And dried red dates, and pickled mustard plants, and badly permed hair from those aunties over there. Their feet are up on the seats, and they spread their toes to air the smell out. Their slippers are made from silk, maybe fake-silk. What an easy life. On foot, these mountains take days to cross, weeks if bad weather. This train takes just six hours!'

She frowned so hard at the dark windows that Han was afraid to talk to her. Instead, he let time slide under his feet, feeling the train's vibrations.

A flash of light from outside distracted them both. This light appeared in the distance, a lip of black that circled a shining mouth. The dark walls faded away, and now the patch of light was the entire world.

They had come out of the other side. There was brown dust everywhere. The mountains of the Western Range stopped rain from falling in the empty, middle highlands of the Peninsula. Parched trees sprouted like orphaned children. The air was thin. Here the Desert of Birds awaited them.

The Town of Winds

This is the Town of Winds. The children of the town leave for the coast every year, and they do not come back. One day a big storm will blow through the town and nothing will remain.

The locals have a different name for their town, in their own language, a tongue-twisting multisyllabic name that had been inherited from their ancestors. But their name is not the official name; it is not what the maps say. The maps say that this is the Town of Winds, deep within the interior of the Desert of Birds.

The people of the capital say, We cannot use the local name, otherwise its influence will spread to the capital. Before we know it, we must use their names for everything: for trains, for trees, for the sky, for food. They will insist on speaking their language. They will insist on a translator. As if it is their birthright. Insist! Like a woman's period, their dirty influence will spread like a stain on our proud traditions. Their language will be pressed upon us, and soon their way of thinking. Every aspect of daily life in the capital will change. The fruit seller will sell perfect hairy fruit with sweet flesh that will no longer be called rambutans, the char kway teow man will fry cockles and kway teow and prawn and egg and taugeh and his creation will no longer be called char kway teow. Our names will be taken away, italicised, stripped of their original meaning, translated into a different name in a different language, lost to history. We will become their servants, their maids, their drivers; we will sweep the streets for them. Our names will change too. There will be new dreams, new songs, songs of what we have lost and how we are, now, strangers in our city.

We cannot let this happen. We must build walls that keep them out. Physical walls and cultural walls. We must keep them in this desert that shows no sympathy for living things, keep them thirsty. Sell them opium that they will smoke with shame. Hide their name for this town, laugh at them, until they themselves are ashamed of this name, as if the very mention marks them as uneducated, uncultured. Tell them, 'Why you so backward, go back to the desert lah.' And if they let their name for this town slip through their lips and touch our pure air, bury them and their children in the bare sands and rock of this place.

This town has one name only: the Town of Winds.

The train platform, usually empty except for a single yellow line on the ground and a warning of 'Stand Behind Yellow Line for Safety', was now filling with passengers dripping from the train, as if someone had left the tap running. The conductor stood at the steps of the front carriage, the top half of his

182

body twisted inside the train as he spoke to the train driver. Min and Han watched as the top half of his body reappeared and joined the bottom half.

'Problem with the engines. Train delayed until tomorrow. They need to get an engineer and some parts here. So going to take a while lah. I'm going to speak to the town chief, ask him to open the school hall so you can sleep inside. So hot out here, wah lau.' The conductor used his hand to shield his eyes as he peered out across the Town of Winds, and beyond to the Desert of Birds that enclosed all of them. 'Okay? Okay.'

Min and Han stood among the passengers pooling on the platform, who shrugged off the delay with apathy:

'It's one of those things; the train always break down.'

'Ai-yah, what can you do, just accept it lah.'

'What to do, business like normal only. Complain also complain to who?'

'You think you king ah? Train don't run for your pleasure lor.'

Buildings as fat as corrupt officials gathered next to the platform. Beyond, the sparse land spread out into patches of yellow grass, knee-high and singing wispy lilts, before being settled into sleep by the drifting sand carpets. Cliffs sneaked away in the background like truant schoolchildren, flitting at the periphery of sight.

The heat was dry, different from the muggy, salt-tinged sea heat that Han knew; this was more like an old heat, ancient and sulphurous, from things that had existed a long time ago. Once there were families here that grew green beans in their backyard, hidden from the wind so that the roaming elephants did not smell them; and other families that exchanged their half-empty baskets of grain with the traders from the capital every seventh day. But in the end, they too could not stop the march of the desert, the sand that swept into their homes and their gardens, and when they were too tired to fight anymore, the sand buried the lines they had built.

The train passengers were redirected to the sand-stained walls of the school hall, the largest building in town. Both leaves of the front door hung open, patiently welcoming the passengers into its depths. Inside stood a man with a balding head, wearing a white T-shirt decorated with armpit-sweat stains. He looked apologetic.

'Sorry ah, hall very dirty, wedding yesterday. Youngsters these days want to get married before the Lake Ceremony tomorrow. Auspicious, they tell me. Please can you help to clean. Got people sweeping already, but now need to mop the floors.'

Some of the train passengers had set their bags to one side of the hall and were already wielding brooms. Han mopped the floors until the bucket of water turned grey with repeated rinsing. They took down the paper flower decorations that clung to the white backdrop of the stage. Paper initials remained stuck to the backdrop – *P, &* and *R* – the initials of the couple. Those were taken down too.

A few people were carrying a large arch with elaborate twinnings of flowers and leaves, fragile in their radiance, which diminished slightly when one of the stems broke and dropped to the floor, its folded paper origin laid bare. 'Okay, that one take in the storeroom carefully,' White T-Shirt Man said. 'The town only have one flower arch, import all the way from the capital. Please don't knock the flowers off! Otherwise no decorations for next wedding hor!'

184

Floral centrepieces were carried into the storeroom with similar care, then the stacked chairs, then tabletops with their legs folded under them, large enough to seat ten people in a circle, elbow-to-elbow. Some of the passengers continued mopping until the sandy grit beneath their bare feet disappeared, leaving behind the concrete floor that they would sleep on that night. Old, clean bed sheets were given out. Han wrapped the entire length of his sheet around himself, like fish from the market wrapped in newspaper.

Many years had passed since Min had left the Desert of Birds, but it was not until now, eight years later, when her toes felt again the loose grains of desert sand, that a few tears collected in a watery film over her eyes.

No one was in the small building where a sign on the door announced its purpose: Toilet. Min entered to find the toilet surprisingly clean, except for a layer of fine sand that draped the toilet bowl. The air was several degrees cooler, and quiet. More tears escaped, and her nose choked in sympathy with her throat. All these years and she never once cried in front of anyone. She had not cried when she found out that her family and her village would not take her back – would not even look at her. Their words had been thrown like sand in her face: You have been disowned. She did not cry when Researcher Kwan had said that a place had been found for her in the capital, where the chosen people of the Feather Book lived.

Researcher Kwan had added: 'I managed to find you a housekeeper job with one of my colleagues.' (Another new word: 'colleague'. She memorised the sounds for her reference later. This was the first of many new words she would learn during the rest of her life.) 'That is the best I can do for you.

185

You need to be a good girl, okay? Scrub floors, wash clothes. Don't cause trouble. Otherwise you will be sent to the orphanage instead; you don't want that. Children are forgotten there.'

She did not cry when she arrived at Professor Toh's house to start her new job. She carried no expectations, no possessions except for the layer of desert sand that clung to her. She would be a good girl, a quiet, obedient, hardworking housekeeper; she would keep her head down and everyone would leave her alone.

Min took a few deep breaths, and eventually her breathing evened out. She blinked several times and wiped any watery residue from her face. *I will be all right*, she told herself.

As she stepped out of the toilet, she noticed that the cliffs of this town, this Town of Winds, were purple-black, just like the cliffs of her home village. The dry heat of the desert rushed to meet Min like an old friend. So long you have been away. So nice to see you again. It wrapped its scratchy tendrils around her and told her to stay. Even as she shrank away from its embrace, she realised that it was here, in the desert, where she felt most at home. Back in the capital, the air was so humid that her face had a permanent oily sheen. She had to take three showers every day or the professor would complain that she smelled.

'I can't have my housekeeper walking around the house smelling like that. You are not living in the desert anymore. We're not savages, you know,' Professor Toh had said.

Three showers a day! In her previous life, it was wrong to use water to wash more than once a week. She had been allowed to clean herself only by wiping with a square-shaped cloth, dipped and rinsed in a bucket of water, which was the same bucket of water that had been passed around the whole family to clean themselves. When everyone had had a turn, the water, now grey from sweat and dirt, was splashed onto the plot of vegetables at the back of the house.

Always, for the rest of her life, the crunch of vegetables made her think of the bucket of washing water, grey like the dreams of desert people.

The Lake of Unheard Words

'She said can hear ghosts? Like real-real can hear ghosts wan?' Han whispered to Min.

'She said spirits, not ghosts.'

'Same thing wor. Sometimes people translate differently that's why got confusion.'

Min, Han and most of the residents of the Town of Winds were standing on ground that sloped gently into a large, flat, basinal depression. It reminded Han of a sloping beach, leading into the flat plains of a vast lake that was devoid of any water.

'Lake of Unheard Words,' the White T-Shirt Man said, helpfully. Today, the white T-shirt that he wore appeared to be free of armpit stains, although new patches of damp were spreading.

Han whispered to Min, 'Eh, you heard of this lake before ah? You said you grew up in the desert. Thought all lakes got water wan. Who knows in the desert got no rain until lake also can become dry.'

Min said quietly, 'The desert is bigger than you know.'

'The ceremony will start soon, need to be quiet,' the White T-Shirt Man said. 'Otherwise we cannot hear the spirits hor.'

'I have never heard of this Lake of Unheard Words before. And even I haven't seen a lake this dry,' Min whispered.

Indeed, Min had never seen a lake as dry as this, even though she had seen many desert lakes in her past life. She had seen lakes in various stages of drying up, but never completely dry. There were stale lakes, with no activity except the flies that busied themselves over the months-old turbid water. And there were the lakes where fish burrowed into the drying mud until the rain came again, which it did, eventually.

Lakes were where animals returned again and again, checking the state of the waterhole, where waters once ponded. Or perhaps, as her tua ku explained to her many years ago, the animals returned because it was in their blood, in their ancestral memories, passed down from generation to generation. Even if there was no water, and even if it had not rained in months, they returned because some primal instinct beckoned, invited them home. They arrived at these mud-filled waterholes looking for water – once upon a time there was water here, but not now; there had been no water for months.

Because, you see, Min, they are just dumb animals, her tua ku told her. Dumb enough that they will do something over and over again. That is why we hunt in muddy lakes.

The White T-Shirt Man heard Min speaking and turned to look at her. She felt the weight of his look and wondered whether she had inadvertently offended him. Suddenly, the

190

clothes that the White T-Shirt Man wore were insufficient to describe who he was, or who he could be.

'Sorry, sir,' she said, automatically.

'No need for sorry. Sorry is like the dry sand that covers everything and never settles. Why waste your words with saying sorry? This lake will only fill up faster,' he said. 'The desert is a harsh place. People live, people die. Their bodies die in this sand, their bones are buried with time. Their names evaporate with the morning sun.

'Our only worth is the words we create. We give these words to our children, they give them to their children, and with time, these words that we have gifted our descendants will be all that is left of us. A man who jumps off a cliff, and realises, too late, that he cannot fly. What happens to his cries for help? A mother looks for her lost son and cries out his name. But the child cannot hear, for he is far away, and he will die soon. What happens to her cries? When a grandmother prays to her god for rain, but there is no god and her prayers are unheard, what happens to her prayers? No one hears them; they will not be carried along by families and friends. They are like abandoned dogs with no master. Orphans with no family. They come here, to this lake, the Lake of Unheard Words, where they settle among millions of other words that are unheard.

'And now you understand, now you know why we are standing here. You have your Cheng Meng festival, right? That day when you lowlanders pay respects to your ancestors? In the desert, we do not remember our ancestors; they are sand in the wind. We have this lake instead.

'Every year, the lake grows. Once upon a time, the lake was only the size of a small spring. Now, it extends past the

191

Crossing of the White Bulls in the north. The river that used to run through the Crossing has now been consumed by the lake,' he continued.

Several people had moved closer, towards the lake. Their feet touched its edges. Nothing about them had visibly changed, their faces calm, their eyes staring at a distant horizon; and they appeared to be . . . listening.

The White T-Shirt Man went on, 'One day, if we are not careful, the lake will grow until it reaches the White Ghost Line further north, the Western Range in the west, the Valley of the Fish in the south. It will grow until it reaches the Jagged Mountains in the east, where the rock is so black that it eats up all light, and still the lake marches on, until Jagged Mountains cease to exist. Next, the field of sand dunes, next the eastern coastal towns and its people, next, next, next! Until the lake meets its cousin – the sea.

'The lake is careful at first, prodding at the edges of the sea with gentle tendrils. After some time, the lake realises: the sea is no match for words. These unheard words are more powerful than people, or the mountains, or the sea, and there is nowhere else for these words to go. So the lake spreads into the sea's depths and fills the deep sea with fine layers of unheard words.

'The whales are curious about this new invader of the sea. They ask the lake in their slow language, "When will you stop?" The lake tells them, "I must carry all the unheard words of this world. Unless someone listens to these words and takes their weight away, I can never stop." The whales swim away, to the cold seas in the north, only to find the lake there too. Then the lake will eat the icy wastes and the whales, and everything in the sea: the fish, the plants, the primordial

192

dreams, from which simple organisms once dreamt of being something more.

'The lake grows, to the end of the maps, far to the east, where it meets the thousand-Hei-san islands, and it eats them one by one, like children's sweets. However strange the words sound, however foreign these words are, the lake must carry them; still it grows, until there is nothing left but the Lake of Unheard Words.

'So we must not let this happen. We come here once a year – once a year, because that is all we can do. We gather at the Lake of Unheard Words and listen. We listen! These words will be unheard no more. This lake will grow no more. And we will carry these words with us, through the years of our lives, as must our descendants.

'But there are too many unheard words to hear them all, so will you help, will you listen with us?'

How Lucky You Are

The train was repaired the following day. Min and Han continued their journey. The carriages rumbled through the thin air of the highlands, the train's joints creaking, its body warped in the metallic heat. The scenes of the desert continued unchanged; rock islands above the sand. They slept and they sweated in silence. Even the aunties stopped talking. Nothing to see. Their clothes, worn for several days, had the smell of days-old oil used for frying bananas.

Bushes grew slowly greener, and strands of water began to carve their escape to the sea. A haze appeared in the distance. This was the Eastern Port. They had crossed the Desert of Birds.

There were no celebrations, just under-slept passengers dragging their bags from the train. They shrugged off their epic train journey, crossing the entire Peninsula casually like walking to the betting shop to buy 4D lottery numbers for that week. The vast, seemingly infinite landscape of Min's childhood, where people had died of thirst and failed crops, now seemed like an inconvenient footnote. Thousands of kilometres struck from her history. *It was always that easy*, she wanted to shout at someone. *Those trains could have sent us more water and food.*

Han was already lost between the carts of steaming noodles that crowded the platforms. Winds swept in sand from the Desert of Birds through the streets, and a salty breeze rushed in from the sea. The collision of winds resulted in a haze, a permanent veil that occluded the lie of the Eastern Port. Nothing further than a few steps could be seen. Buildings existed like forgotten graves – present but invisible.

'You lost ah? You got mouth right? You ask people where to go. Here people in the east friendly wan lah. Not like the west,' the tau foo fah woman told Min and Han, her advice given as part of their transaction. She took their money and handed them bowls of warm tau foo fah. The silken white tau foo were like whole unbroken continents, floating in the sweetness of palm sugar syrup.

They ate their tau foo fah with small spoons, breaking the continents up into something that looked more like an archipelago of pale, bitty islands in a dark sea. The woman continued to ring her bell, alerting potential customers to her location in the haze.

Scenes of the Eastern Port glimmered briefly around them, before dissolving. Obstacles on the road – potholes, hidden steps, errant children – were spotted too late; the haze possessing a playful side that some would say was malicious.

'This haze is all we have,' the train driver had said when they got off the train. 'Around this city lies only poor farming

196

land, where the soil is so light, so porous, that any rain washes the soil away. Our vegetables are frail; one bad sandstorm and dead plants decorate our houses, their naked roots hanging out for all to see. We have seawater that is too salty for our pigs to drink, let alone for us. There are tiny streams that trickle out of the desert; we drink their dusty water. Fishing, you say! You are thinking of fishing in the west. Here the sea is too hot, the plants do not grow in rich, wavy beds, and so the fish do not swim here either. There is no food for them.

'Do you know why the western lowlands are fertile and populous? You have winds that bring rain. Your winds are born in the west far beyond the Peninsula, in the nest of the Boatbreaker Seas. When they are big enough, they get restless, and they want to leave. They lift seawater into the clouds; around they swirl, until they see the giant Peninsula, a super mass of land where there are new toys with which to play.

'Old motorcycles are flipped over, and coconuts are shaken from trees. Careless schoolboys drown in swollen rivers; vegetable farmers cry for their lost cabbages. These winds, they do not care for the little people. They see the Western Range in the distance, and they think, If we climb those mountains with this load of water, we will die. So we will rain onto these lowlands until we are unburdened from this water. The winds bring the rain in the morning. They rain on old atap-roofed houses, the roof collapses, muddying the children's pristine white school shoes, saved up for for several months and only worn for four weeks.

'But the winds, they do not care. They are now light and free. They fly up the vertical slopes of the Western Range. They carry the fine sands of the Desert of Birds in their breath. You've seen the Sandman cartoons, where the Sandman blows sand and sends everyone to sleep? That's what it's like, you know. Every day, clouds of sand flow over the Eastern Port, mix into our food, in our hair, over our sleeping children. In the dry season they march at us like sand golems as tall as mountains. The haziness that you see around you is sand grains suspended in the air.

'But you have never thought about this, have you? You just grew up where you grew up and you never thought about how lucky you are, to have water instead of sand that spits at your face. How lucky you are, how lucky you westerners are.'

There was no shame or sadness when Han spoke about his life in Kampung Seng. Min heard about the warehouse where Han packed fish, and the yard where boats were hammered into seaworthiness. How his ah-ma wanted to make otak-otak but forgot the pandan leaves, and so Han had to go out to the morning market in a hurry, but there were no pandan leaves there, so in the end, she made the otak-otak in the pot, and there was no smell of pandan.

She heard about his dead mother, about how his mama arrived as an outsider to Kampung Seng. Drowned at sea when he was five. She felt uncomfortable – speaking of the dead was bad luck.

'You know ah, it was not an accident,' Han said. Min did not understand what he was trying to imply. He added, 'Mama went out to the sea deliberately.' No shame in his words either, these words that told of a person choosing death over life.

She had been afraid to say anything – where to start even? What words should she use to convey sorrow, empathy, understanding; which words were the right words, and which were wrong – she did not know.

198

It was only as the ship left the Eastern Port, and their lungs were released from the heaviness of sand, that Min understood what Han had implied.

'When you said you were a baby when your mama arrived at Kampung Seng, did you mean – and what I'm trying to say is – your father, he's not your real father?'

'My father is my father,' he told her, as if she missed the point completely.

'But he is not your real father? You said your mama arrived in Kampung Seng with a baby . . .'

He looked at her; he scratched his head, and he said, 'And then Mama met Father.'

These lowlanders, whether they came from coastal villages, or the capital, or the New Villages, or the farms of the south, they were all the same. They accepted strangers like family. How lucky was his mama. No need to prove she was worthy. No need to prove that she deserved to be loved. She had to just be herself. That was enough – enough! These lowlanders did not understand that the Desert of Birds was a place of emptiness. Or how it felt to go for years without hearing from your family.

'They died in the last drought? The sand buries us all. Who saves us?' the desert people would say, with some sadness, but only for a moment, in the brief pause between breaths, for everyone down to the smallest child understood the truth of this place: people were temporary. Every day the sea of sand raised new waves to drown their village; every day the people fought back, but one day they would drown too. The bodies of the desert people will shrivel in the unrelenting sun. No tombstones to mark their names or their bones. *Who saves us?* There was no place for softness in the desert.

Min would not tell Han about her family, nor the test, nor the Bone Fields.

When she was eight years old, her second brother, Kuang, went missing one afternoon. She liked him very much; unlike the others, he never teased her, and he always showed her where to find lizards (in cool, shady nooks next to abandoned streams). On the day he went missing, no one said anything about Kuang, nor at any other time after that; not Ma, not Pa, not her eldest brother Liew nor her sister Shuen, not even as they slept on their mats that night, and she had rolled onto her side, counting the sleeping bodies in the room.

One: Min

Two: Ma

Three: Pa

Four: Liew

Five: Shuen

Six: (there was no sixth body)

Even his sleeping mat was gone: a sand-free rectangle exposed a fresh face of floor in his absence.

The next day, Kuang remained missing. Min asked her teacher where he was.

'Kuang is not one of your family. He failed the test. What did I teach you?'

'But where did he go?'

'He never went anywhere. He is not a Mesulei. He was never one of us.'

Her ma told her: 'No more speaking of Kuang.' Min never heard Ma saying the word 'Kuang' again. Her pa beat her with leather strips when she spoke of Kuang at dinner. Liew and Shuen looked away, so did Tua Ku, who was sharing dinner with them that night.

And the next day, and every day after that – the blank faces, the unsaid name – until, many sunsets later, Min rolled over onto her side and counted only to five. The rectangle was gone; in its place, a carpet of sand lay undisturbed for what would feel to be many years. Ma was snoring, hyenas howled in the distance, and the night touched Min's skin. When the morning came there was still no Kuang; perhaps there never had been.

Min was twelve years, six months and eighteen days old, when an old man and woman came to her classroom and called out her name. She was surprised by the gentleness of their voices that floated in the air.

The other children looked at her and looked away, glad it was not their turn today.

She was prepared as well as she could be, which was not at all, for she had not wiped herself in days (the village's four water tanks had run dry) and the edges of her clothes rubbed against the salt that had grown on her skin. It had been a hot night yesterday, so she had not slept either.

They told her everything would be all right. Liew had passed the test safely a few years ago, and Shuen passed last year. Kuang's name was not mentioned. Perhaps they did not remember him.

They led her out of the classroom, and they walked towards the Mountain of God. It rose in the distance, with its conical top rising above the red-brown sand dunes.

Today, the Mountain of God was serene, with no tears of liquid fire running down its sides, and even the Noses That Spoke of Hell appeared to be resting: their characteristic snouts of steam were floppy, leaning to one side, like a sleeping lion taking a nap. Min felt pleased, even smug, for today was a good day and she was blessed indeed.

If Min had been a bird, the far curve of the horizon would have shown her that the Mountain of God was not unique. Rather, it was a stray child, some distance separated from a large family of black mountains in the north that disfigured the uniformity of the desert. If Min had been a bird, she would not have known that these two-legged ground creatures had a name for the black mountains: volcanoes. And if she had been a bird, she would only be scared of hyenas, leopards, and other four-legged creatures that ate her eggs, not these immoveable rock giants. Hundreds and hundreds of volcanoes would not chase her babies to their deaths. These volcanoes were no threat to her. She would view the volcanoes with indifference, other than to find sheltered ledges where she could lay her eggs in peace.

Indeed, to say that Min could be a bird would be to limit her perspective. Perhaps she could be a cartographer instead – a human with capacity for imagination and feeling for the sublime. She would be able to measure just how big this family of volcanoes was, and recognise that there was nothing else like it, not anywhere else in the world, except for perhaps the Hei-san archipelago. And perhaps, if she was a cartographer, she would have known that the black mountains marked a significant boundary, the White Ghost Line. To the north of the line lived the White Ghosts, and their villages, and their cities.

But she was neither a bird nor a cartographer, nor any other being that would give her a larger perspective beyond her human vision. What she saw was the ground beneath her feet disappearing in front of her. Beyond that was a precipitous drop. Her feet wobbled with the full and certain knowledge that the ground did not exist several breaths away from where she stood.

Only now she realised that they were standing at the Cliff of the First Wei Leep. It was here that the ground beyond had been erased, whether by the shaking of the earth, or by the running of a river of liquid fire, or by sand, wind, rain, or everything else besides. It did not matter. What did matter was that there was no ground beyond.

'Here we will say a prayer,' the old woman said.

What were they praying for?

For the survival of the Mesulei, they prayed. May our way of life hold through these turbulent times. May the First Wei Leep bless the Test-taker today and welcome her as one of the Mesulei.

Then the old man and woman walked to the very edge of the Cliff of the First Wei Leep and looked over.

What did they see? Min joined them, curious but careful, her feet picking their way to the edge, as near as she could get – only to find herself falling.

Did they push her? No time to think. Instinctively, she extended her arms and legs to catch air to halt her fall. A bird, a flying owl. The ground rushed towards her in a frightening blur; then, something happened, something that she could neither explain nor fully understand; perhaps she dreamt it, or her mind made up the memory in terror, for her fall began to slow, to halt in the air even, and for several seconds it felt like she was floating above the hard desert ground. She did not know why, but she thought of her ma then, her characteristic smell, the way she always held Min's hand.

All of this must have occurred in compressed time, for Min found herself falling again, then a tearing pain, and then nothing.

When she woke up, her first sight was the bones around her, bones of children who were pushed over the Cliff of the First Wei Leep and did not survive.

This was why it was called the Bone Fields, Min realised. She started crying. Not from the sharp pain in her legs – she would cry from that, later – but from the realisation that Kuang's bones were somewhere here, too. He was dead; he was really, truly dead.

Part Six
The Tower,
Many Years Earlier

She Had Not Always Been Alone

The girl – who would one day be known as Swee – was born in the tower. On her ninth birthday, the grandfather decided it was time that he told her about the tower.

He started, 'Once upon a time', and stopped, aware that was how fairy tales started. Nevertheless, he had no other words for the story that he was about to tell the girl.

Once upon a time – now, ah-girl, you must know there is no happy ending to my story, okay? I tell it like how it is. Because you are old enough to understand. Once upon a time, there were more people in the tower. More people, more than you and I and your mama and your papa, and the other boy. More people than you can imagine.

We have not always been alone, the grandfather said. You were not always the girl. There were other girls here too, girls like you. Once upon a time, people lived in all the sectors. Yes, all of them, not just where we live, in sector five. They lived in

207

their tens of thousands in their individual sectors: sector one, sector two, sector three, and all the way up to sector twenty, where the mines were, back then.

The girl's eyes were bright, curious to hear more of this strange world that she did not know. Her questions came furiously, while his answers were slow, plodding.

No, each of the girls had different names.

No, you couldn't just live anywhere you wanted to, not like now. You were born in a sector, and you lived in that sector for your whole life.

What if you were born in one of the older sectors? Well, that was too bad. That was where you were born.

Of course it was not fair. That is life, ah-girl. You don't get to choose where you are born, do you? Some people are born into modern sectors. Some people are born into older sectors where all the aleum has already been dug out of the air.

Some are born in ships, and some in towers. The grandfather thought this but did not say this to the girl.

'If there were so many people in the tower, like you say' – here the girl shot him a look, for she was sceptical of the grandfather's story – 'then the stairs would be crowded with people. How would anyone move around? Were they all very skinny?'

They used the lift trains to travel between the sectors all the time. There used to be much more aleum then. Yes, there was enough aleum to wing people around every day, all the time. Up-down the mines, up-down the sectors. To start their shifts at the mines. To the simulation rooms and canteens.

'How many of people?' the girl asked.

'Thousands and thousands. Maybe more.'

'How long ago?'

208

'Hundred-plus years, maybe nearly two hundred.'

'As old as you are!'

'No lah, do you think I'm that old? I'm only eighty-nine-years old. Way before my time.'

'Were they the ones that left all the rubbish and old things?'

'They could not take many things when they left the tower.'

'You told me that we could not leave the tower. We will lose our souls in the bottom floors if we leave. That's what happened to the Crazy Man, you said.'

'Ah-girl, they left from the top of the tower. Where the effects of aleum were strongest and the air thinnest, and the aleum protected against the losing of their memories. They left in the ships that we had, once upon a time. That had always been the plan.

'When the company first arrived on this planet, their first task was to install a memory wall which let knowledge in but not out; a one-way, invisible barrier. We can leave the tower, but we cannot carry our memories with us. That was why there is only one stairwell in the bottom floors, for no one is supposed to leave the tower that way.

'See, this planet is a flower planet. The original people of this planet are flower people, which means they are primitive. They are not like us. They don't know about aleum, even as it exists in the air around them. They don't know about ships and space travel. They don't even know about the other worlds.'

The grandfather paused, aware that this was a lot of information for the girl to take in. Grow lights dimmed in the space around them.

Then she said, 'Do the flower people think they are alone in this universe? Are they also very lonely?'

209

'They don't know any different. The memory wall protects them – from us.'

The girl was silent for several moments, before asking the grandfather to continue.

After the memory wall was set in place, the grandfather said, the company continued to build the tower from the ground up, in stages. First, the bottom floors were built as filler levels, to get the tower high enough to access a substantial concentration of aleum. Then, they began the real work of building the sectors. There were five sectors in the first phase, a kind of pilot phase—

'Pilot phase?' the girl interrupted.

'Think of it as a test phase for the tower. To see if enough aleum could be produced. In this test phase, a limited number of miners were brought over from their home worlds. Your great-great-great-grandparents, ah-girl. Like so many others, they migrated from their home world because they were promised that this would be their last job – they would make so much money that they would be able to afford not just an ancestral hall, but an entire planet! They would mine for several years and be rich. They would have enough money for their children, and their grandchildren. Mine for your family line, the company said.

'The miners were split into the five sectors of the tower. Each sector had an active mine, and their own living quarters, canteens, farms, schools, clinics, so that if one sector failed, the failure could be contained in that sector. Do you know why you cannot enter sector three? My great-grandmother, my chor-mah, told me that a fire started in the farms and destroyed the crops, before spreading through to the canteens. They turned off the pools in the farm and shut down sector three completely.

210

'Once upon a time, our sector five was the very top of the tower. In the receiving halls of sector five, there were once cargo ships that docked there, in the very same bays that now cradle the lift trains. Now you know why the lift trains of sector five always seem so small, so lost, in the giant bays that were once meant for massive cargo ships that travel in the emptiness of space.'

After several years of mining, the company decided to expand. The change did not happen overnight. The tower needed more miners, more seeds, more tools, more cargo ships, and these had to be shipped from the home worlds, a journey that took tens of years in our time and stretched over distances of hundreds of light years.

In the meantime, the mined cubes of aleum that were loaded onto the cargo ships were about to take the reverse journey; they would leave the tower, sail through space, and bring the first cargo of aleum to the home worlds. This was a huge, resource-intensive process, for though these ships had enough aleum to power their flight, they would be the target of every pirate in the neighbourhood.

Many pirates around here, the grandfather added. They like to hide on the millions of asteroids in the Opulent Belt, ready to hijack unsuspecting cargo ships.

'But that is illegal!'

They are pirates; illegal things are what they do.

Years passed, and the tower was awash with babies that had been born to the first wave of miners. Our family came from the first wave, like the rest of the sector five families. Then they came, the second wave of miners, in their exuberance. They were eager to get off the cargo ships. They felt a sense of being chosen, one of the few people to come into contact with a flower planet, even if indirectly: 'We have landed on a flower planet,' this second wave of miners whispered to themselves, and they spoke in reverential tones, having touched a world that was strictly off-limits, glimpsed only in documentaries. They marvelled at the blueness of the planet as their ships approached, and gazed over the limited networks of civilisation that spread thinly across its surface, like a film of oil blooming over water.

And, it was also whispered, in the unmonitored corners beyond the hearing of the company, that the scanners had detected the motherlode of aleum right above the tower. 'That is where we will be mining,' they told each other. The estimates came back wild, feverishly large, they said, larger than the aleum field at the Parallel Lakes, larger than the Jumping Chimera field, larger than all the fields on the On-Ton planet *combined*. Something about the mineral composition of this planet. The miners' eyes glittered. Surely this meant that they could sneak away a few aleum cubes, even sniff a few pinches, and no one would know; surely the company would turn a blind eye to these hard workers missing their home worlds.

The tower was built higher and higher into the sky, high enough that they struck the promised motherlode, the primary aleum vein, and they thought, *This is it*. There was aleum, and it was everywhere.

They thought the aleum would last for ever. They had sniffing parties at night. But the company knew better. After 250 years of mining (they even had a fancy anniversary dinner for the workers, Chor-Mah had said), the aleum had grown thin like watery porridge. The company declared that the mines would be shut. The people had to leave the tower. So they left.

And thus ends the first part of the story, the grandfather said to the girl.

Too much story for today, Grandfather, she said, yawning. She had just turned nine after all.

'Can you sing me the song?' she asked. The grandfather only knew one song, which he sang to her, as she closed her eyes in the dimming air and he stroked her hair.

Blind sheep they go.

Blind sheep a-oh.

Go in the fields they go, in the valleys they go, in the lakes they go, in the seas they go.

These sheep of dreaming woe.

Power Cubes

The girl ate power cubes every day. It was like eating paper. The last working farm, in sector eighteen, had stopped producing new mangosteens ever since its irrigation system broke down. No more mangosteens for her.

The grandfather explained that the food technicians of the past had removed taste from food so that the workers would not overeat. 'Once upon a time, the farms used to grow many more fruit. Cempedak. Pomelo. Guava. Duku langsat. Rambutan. We were only allowed two fruits each day-cycle, but all the power cubes we wanted,' the grandfather said. 'Would you prefer a power cube, or a mango swollen in sweetness?'

It was not entirely correct, what the grandfather said about power cubes. There were faint flavours in the power cubes, shy, and yet familiar. Even the food technicians of the past, in their fancy labs, could not completely destroy the origins of the power cubes. The power cubes had an earthy tang, one that brushed the roof of her mouth, which, although the girl could not know this, was a flavour derived from roots that grew in soggy mangrove swamps on the planet Tenuang. Then a singular, bitter note that was derived from an edible flower that only grew during the warm seasons in the startlingly purple seas of another Gould Belt planet. Even the brown colour of the power cube derived from two original colours – the brilliant yellow of sulphur vents, and the reflection of the red sky that draped across the planet. A ghostly remnant of a ghostly scene. Long time ago, somewhere else.

The food technicians of the past would have been able to explain to the girl that the power cubes contained all the nutrients that a human body needed, like protein and fat, and would have supplemented the food from the farms.

'Yes, yes, I already know,' the girl would have replied.

'Did you also know that these cubes contain an optimal serving of soul nutrients?' they would have continued, their chests puffed with pride.

A whiff of nostalgia, the taste of a stray raindrop, a spoonful of the quietness of broad, open spaces – the necessary ingredients for a healthy soul. Your ancestors would have tasted these nutrients, and they would have passed these memories to you, in your blood-dreams, in this sparkling wave of humanity that you have been born out of. Perhaps you could even say that these nutrients evoke the ghosts that have lingered in time and space and remind you of worlds far away that you never knew and could never know.

Soul nutrients were only discovered after the first workers of the tower died. You see, ah-girl, we never built a tower quite like this one before. There are other towers in other worlds, but they were built as temporary structures. Never was one built to mine aleum on a flower planet, certainly not one so far away that the journey to the tower took years. Never had a tower been so cut off from the home worlds, where workers and their children could easily live out their entire lifetimes. Only in this two-hundred-year experiment we have discovered the effect of this isolation.

You see, after many years here, depression and anxiety infected the workers. These workers did not want to work. They were restless; they wanted to go back to their home worlds. 'We want to touch the soil that our ancestors tilled,' the workers said. 'We want to breathe fresh air that has not been recycled through climate control systems.'

Pinches of aleum calmed them and numbed them temporarily: a brief intervention before their eyes glazed over, and the workers drifted through their shifts, working ghosts in the mines of the tower.

Then, the food technicians realised that when the farms were producing at their maximum output levels, the workers' anxiety and depression eased; the crunch of a guava, the burst of a pomelo pip, as their ancestors would have eaten in their home worlds. *We are connected; we are stardust*, the workers of the tower thought. Conversely, when the produce from the farms fell, and the workers had to get most of their calories from the power cubes, they grew anxious and depressed again.

These bursts of *connectedness* could be brought about by certain foods. With time, the food technicians would isolate the specific 'soul nutrients' – as they came to be named – that were responsible for these feelings. They would add these soul nutrients to the power cube mix. Enough to avoid depression among the people of the tower, but not too much to generate a deep longing for their home worlds. Just enough to produce industrious and engaged workers for the mines.

The girl did not know these stories of soul nutrients. The last food technician had left the tower with the last ships nearly two hundred years ago. There was no one else in the tower but the girl, the grandfather, and the other boy.

The grandfather, though caring and kind, was a man of limited imagination. He had his routine, there were things to do, and he did them every day. He was bound by an unspoken promise to the girl to keep their lives alive for as long as he lived. In the peripheries of his being he felt the pressures of chaos filling up around him, imprinting uncertainty upon this careful life he maintained for himself. He ignored the chaos as best he could. In his free time, he tinkered with the ageing systems of the tower, now failing with regularity. Still everything mostly ticked along.

There were three recent occasions when the grandfather had ventured into the simulation rooms. Each time, he sat in front of the glowing white screens. Each time he tried to retrieve a video of the Eviction Years, a task that Chor-Mah showed him how to do once, a long time ago. Each time, his hands froze even as they reached out for the screens, not wanting to sign the commands; each time his eyelids clamped shut, looking at nothing. Locked down, shut for business. He could not do it. He did not want to make a mistake, even though there was no one left to scold him for doing it wrong.

In the quiet day-cycles, in the long moments of nothing, when the climate system was creaking along, and no new leaks had sprung from the waste lines, when the grandfather had some space to think, he cried.

How long could he keep it up? He felt his world shrinking with each breath. Was he brave enough to leave the tower? They could not keep living as they did, as the tower gradually died around them. But he was too old, he told himself, so he clung to this unchanging, unforgiving tower that he had tried to preserve so carefully with his hands. He hated himself for being weak, for not being a different person altogether.

His story had been written out for him, and he was destined to stay in the tower until he died.

The girl, however, was a very different person. She was curious, with an edge of fierceness and bravery, that resembled nothing of the grandfather's dullness, nor the dreaminess of the other boy, who spent his time skipping down the long stairwells, and sleeping in abandoned beds. A bit dim, that one, the grandfather often said.

'Those ships must have arrived on the home worlds by now. It has been so long since they left,' the grandfather said. And then he added, as an afterthought: 'We have family on those ships. Third cousins that I do not know.'

Third cousins. They were long gone, the girl thought, a long, long way away, drifting through space in ships, or on planets. Some remnant of her genes out there. She had been separated from these cousins whom she did not know. She felt the ache of these broken connections, frayed, lost in the

219

passage of time. If their fates had just been slightly different, perhaps she would have been on the ship, and they would have been trapped in this tower instead.

That night, she dreamt that she was on a ship, and the floors and walls had evaporated, as had her hands and feet, until she was no more than a hazy blue streak flying through time and dust.

The Eviction

'What is the second part of the story, Grandfather? How does it end?' the girl asked.

The tower was emptied of people in what came to be known as the Eviction Years, 185 years ago. The company had told the workers, 'We will help you resettle in your home worlds.' When the workers, both first and second waves, protested, the company said, 'You knew this posting wasn't permanent. It has been at least a hundred years already. For some of you, it has been much longer. Look around you, we have stripped all the aleum from the air until there are only dregs left. You can't stay here for ever.'

So began the Eviction Years, and each sector as per schedule packed up many lives' worth of possessions, to be parcelled away into one of the cargo ships, to be sent back to their home worlds. The company added, 'This is not the *Eviction*, this is the Return. Why are you sad? You always talked about

221

returning to your home worlds, with the money you earned mining, and now the Return is here, look at all of you! Moping, whining, complaining that you have to leave the tower. You workers never change. You never know what you want.'

True, the workers nodded. They wanted to show their children the night skies of their youth. They wanted to hear their home language again, not in the shrivelled, dying form that limped on in the tower, but as vibrant words that grew with the young ones into adulthood, incorporating not just their understanding of things, but also their perceptions of the world.

There is no future in the tower. Anyway, you have no choice. We cannot leave anyone on a flower planet, the company told them. We are going home.

The Planetarium

The girl was twenty-seven years of age when the other boy reappeared outside the sector five simulation room. He had been missing since the day the cable on sector nine's lift train snapped. He needed some time alone, he had said.

The grandfather and the girl had often speculated on whether they would see him again. Sadness or the bottom floors – which one would it be? 'I vote for the bottom floors,' the grandfather had said. 'He's always wandering off somewhere. Stairwells, lifts, sectors, mines, you name it. Might as well wander out of the tower.' They had laughed, a little sadly.

On his reappearance, the other boy said, 'I found a planetarium in sector eight. Last one undamaged.' His hair had grown long and straggly, intertwining into his beard. 'Too beautiful not to tell anyone. Thought you might appreciate it.'

These words were delivered with his characteristic calmness and marked the beginning of feelings that the girl could not explain.

'Take me there,' she said.

'It'll take two day-cycles to walk there. No lift trains or local lifts working. Sector seven is closed off completely now – do you remember when the waste vacuum exploded?'

She froze. Two day-cycles. She didn't have time, she had things to do. She needed to figure out what was causing the grow lights to flicker . . .

He sensed her hesitation and said, 'Never mind. You and the grandfather are always so busy with maintenance.'

'The tower will fall apart if we don't—'

'The tower has already fallen apart. Nothing you do will change anything. Don't you see? You, me, the grandfather – we will die here.'

Wrong, she wanted to shout at the other boy, he was wrong. He was wrong, and he was lazy. She squeezed her eyes shut but a few tears eked out from the corners. 'Bring me to this planetarium of yours,' she said.

The planetarium of sector eight was the only one left undamaged by the towerwaves.

'Its ceiling is so delicate that it's a wonder that this one even survived until now,' the other boy said. 'You would have thought the architects would have planned for this, perhaps designed a buffer. Maybe they did not know much about this world, or the towerwaves. If you look carefully, over there, you will notice that the panels do not quite align, and the stars of the Gould Belt are ever so slightly offset through its spiral.'

The girl had been to a planetarium only once, when she was a child. It had never occurred to her to seek out other planetariums. What else had she taken for granted, she wondered, as around her the stars tracked across the shining blackness.

Giants and supergiants burned. Their bright lights danced around the galactic centre, turning. Nebulas of collapsing stars of long ago, dying in a flash, and giving birth to new atoms – dust that made up the building blocks of all their beings.

'I can't see our home world,' she said.

'That's our home world's star, on that sparse outer arm. You can just about see it. And here, look over here, look at this star.' The other boy pointed to another dark region.

She could not see. She waved a hand, and the planetarium obliged by panning its omniscient camera close, and several stars appeared. A yellow dwarf lingered in the fringes, accompanied by a respectable number of planets. Rocky ones, gaseous ones even. Surely not a solar system that she was familiar with, not any of the solar systems of the home worlds, or that of the original planet.

Then, she understood. The planetarium was showing them a simulation of *their* solar system. *This* planet. *This* tower. And the star of that solar system – that was the same star that gave energy to this tower.

We are so small, she thought. Instinctively, as a child looks for her mother, she looked for the tower on the face of the planet, even though she knew that there was no chance of spotting such a feature.

What did she know about this planet anyway? Not much. This was a flower planet, one of the first worlds to be colonised at the start of the Space Age, when humanity spread like flowers – very slowly, one world at a time. They journeyed from the original planet, the first home of humanity, to colonise the nearest habitable planets, then the next, and so forth.

Ships were primitive then. Aleum had not been discovered yet. Even communication between the planets could take

225

decades, while interplanetary travel took several lifetimes. Babies were born, grew up, gave birth, grew old, died in ships sailing through space. Every one of those ships was effectively a self-governed colony. Like an island in the middle of a hostile sea, crossable only in a three-hundred-year odyssey.

By the time the ships reached the new planets to colonise, the descendants of the crew had had no contact with the original planet for decades. The rest of humanity could well be aliens. They were like wildflowers growing in an abandoned field, and the name stuck – the 'flower people' landing on their 'flower planets'. With time, the flower people forgot that they had once been a space-faring race connected to a larger civilisation. Memory of their extraterrestrial history had become memory of memory, and eventually forgotten altogether.

The settlements committee passed the non-interference law, which stated that the flower people should be left alone, uncontacted. 'These primitives would be overwhelmed from any form of contact and die of shock. We'll mask our signals, so that even if they do develop technologies to see into space, they will not see us. They will think that they are alone in this universe.'

Thousands of years passed. On the original planet, aleum was discovered in the year 80,000 of the Space Age. Aleum, an invisible, nearly weightless mineral existing in an ordered gaseous state, was found in the atmosphere of most planets. *Like magic*, some said. It transformed space travel and started a new era of exploration and colonisation. Travel between planets would take years, rather than centuries. Humanity would spread out once again on aleum-powered ships to colonise new planets, their future home worlds. This time, however, the home worlds would keep in close communication with each other and with the original planet – not repeating the mistakes of the flower planets. The flower planets remained unaware of aleum or that their fellow humans had colonised multiple worlds in the galaxy.

Until the day that a giant vein of aleum was discovered across the surface of this flower planet. A one-time extraordinary exception was made to the policy of non-interference. 'We give you licence to mine aleum on this flower planet, but all environmental and social impact must be kept to a minimum,' the committee said.

The girl and other boy lay in the planetarium, and time was measured in the movements of stars above them, as if they were the centre of gravity around which everything revolved. She touched the arm of the other boy and was surprised that she had done so.

He, too, was startled. The last time his skin had been touched was when the grandfather hugged him after his parents died.

Then she kissed his lips and it was aleumnic. *Aleum* – the words meant 'air-earth' in a home language of somewhere, once upon a time. Air-earth. She felt the beat of his heart. Together they moved, together for several day-cycles, and when they had finished making love, they lay on their backs and watched as the stars burned, little dots against the darkness. They ate power cubes. They slept, they woke, and they watched each other sleeping, watching the other person's chest rising, falling. We have for ever, they told each other. We have the whole tower. And they loved each other.

They maintained little fictions, their inevitable futures denied, only in this space where stars burned for them, this here and now that they protected jealously, even if they knew that their happiness would soon be taken away by the sadness, or the bottom floors. Who would remember these moments when they were gone, or when they forgot? They pulled themselves closer to each other, hoping that somewhere, sometime, someone would remember this little reality that they had created.

Eventually we will burn like the stars, the other boy whispered.

But not now, the girl whispered back.

Do you know? Do you know how my brother and my two sisters died? I thought they were playing hide and seek. I thought I would find them; I kept looking for years, he said. But I never found them.

The girl would learn that the other boy's father had drowned three of his four children and their mother in the muddy irrigation canals of sector nine's farms, and then hanged himself from a noose like a swinging pendulum. After that, the grandfather had sealed up the systems of sector nine. The other boy escaped his father's death sentence for him only because he could not be found for several weeks prior to his father's breakdown. He had been exploring the maze of north stairwells in the powered-off sector fourteen, living off centuries-old power cubes that he scavenged. He had then stumbled through an open door in the receiving halls but found himself trapped as the door swung shut; it could not be opened no matter how hard he pounded at it. Weeks later, he had escaped by crawling through the unsealed vents near the lifts, only to learn that his entire family was dead.

He asked her, Do you know why time is measured in day-cycles? The original planet takes twenty-five hours to turn on its axis.

The side of the planet that faces the star has sunlight – day – and the other side is in darkness – night. The day-cycle of this flower planet is marginally shorter, only twenty-four hours in length. That is why this tower has no windows, which would confuse our body clocks. Otherwise our bodies would be permanently out of sync, cut short, and our lives would run down faster.

We are dying souls in a dying tower, he said. The lights brighten and dim to keep our bodies running for some race that has no end. Every day I run, every day I think, *This is it, this is the ending,* and on the other side, I can start over. But there is no end. Just the infinite simulations, looping again and again, my legs turning over and over, and I can only watch the shadows moving, the ghosts of other people's lives once fully lived. None of this is real.

She told him, I am real, I am here. She tried to take his hands. When he did not move, she closed her fingers around his fingers and pressed them so hard that his skin turned white with the pressure. His hands remained limp.

No stars for us, he whispered to her, staring into her eyes as if trying to find something. Then he whipped his hands away so fast that she thought he was having a seizure, and threw them up at the ceiling.

Instantly the universe above them vanished. She felt as if a towerwave had hit her. The stars, the Milky Way, and the distant galaxies in the planetarium were gone, leaving behind white panels, blank, featureless. One of the white panels had a large crack where once the stars of the Gould Belt had been ever so slightly offset through its spiral.

Once, their bodies were invisible in the darkness of the grand cosmos; now their fleshy bodies were the only solid things left, floating in an empty white space with no markers to define floor or ceiling.

229

This planetarium is made of ghosts of stars and worlds and people, he said. He added, I cannot give you the real.

I know, she said, her skin tingling. Her papa and her mama had once said something similar. Of course I know this planetarium is just a simulation. Do you think you are the only person trapped here, in this tower? You are always so selfish! She shouted her last words at him, hoping to provoke him into feeling anger, indignation, anything. But it was too late.

He was curled up in a tight ball, rocking himself back and forth. He did not seem to care that she was watching him, for it did not matter; nothing would matter to him from that moment on. There would be no more stories from him. His emotional highs dissipated into a flat wasteland, where no new peaks would form, and the todays and tomorrows existed as the same, never-ending flat lines. Just as it had been for her mama and papa. That was when she knew that the other boy had passed over to the sadness.

Some time later, he stood up, emerging from a nest of their accumulated things, which shook loose to the floor like detritus in the aftermath of a towerwave. He would carry nothing in this next phase. Even his backpack remained where he left it. He was finally free, or lost, depending on one's perspective.

The girl watched him leave. She would see him several months later, for the last time, and by then they would be standing in front of the door to the bottom floors.

For now, she was too sad to move, so she sat on the sleeping mat that they had shared in their short time together and wondered when her turn would be. Would it be the sadness or the bottom floors for her? Above her, the panels remained white.

Stories

When he was a child, the grandfather was often found hiding in the corner of Chor-Mah's room when the world overwhelmed him. I think you are like a sponge that has soaked up too much water and needs to sit in a dry place to heal from your fullness, Chor-Mah often said to him, smiling at the gentle boy. They both needed to pass time, so she would tell him stories of sneaking into mines when it was strictly forbidden, jumping into the pools of the rice farms, queuing for the lift trains in the morning, listening to the storyteller as she sang songs of their home worlds, and even creeping down to the bottom floors, camping in some of the empty floors overnight.

'You know, you don't lose your memories until the very end. So, it's safe to go to the bottom floors, despite what your teachers tell you. As long as you don't open the last door.' Chor-Mah shook her head. 'Not that I would go there very often. It's a dirty place, full of ghosts and spirits and the Crazy Man.'

'Where does the door go?'

'Outside. Outside the tower.'

The grandfather, as a child, could not understand what Chor-Mah meant. There was no concept of *outside* for him.

'They are out there. Three of my brothers and one of my sisters. The rest left with the ships in the Return,' she added, as an afterthought.

That was how the grandfather spent his time as a child, listening to stories of days past and people who were no longer in the tower. He would repeat these stories to the girl, for stories are only kept alive as long as one person remembers them.

Sometime after the girl's eleventh birthday, the grandfather said, 'I will tell you Chor-Mah's stories. But I don't know whether they are pretend stories or real stories.'

'It doesn't matter,' the girl said.

The Little Boy and the Wavy Line

Once upon a time, there lived a little boy. He was a normal boy, except that he loved to climb towers. One day, he slipped and fell.

The little boy caught the tail end of a small aleum vein and, instead of hitting the ground, he floated in the sky. At first he was scared. There was no wall to contain him, no ceiling to limit him, and no net to catch him. But then he felt brave and free. He heard his papa calling him to return, but he pretended not to hear. The little boy floated through a large aleum field where hundreds of towers were built to mine it, before arriving at the fringes where the farms lay, so primitive at the time that the irrigation canals were not gridded;

232

instead they danced in wavy lines, their walls made of moving particles.

Again, Papa called him to the ground, for it was time for the little boy to have his dinner. 'Come back or you will be having power cubes instead,' Papa said.

Still the little boy pretended not to hear. The people and the towers on the ground had grown so small; they were like toys. Even Papa had shrunk to the size of a doll. The little boy continued to float over the farms. He watched as the wavy lines of the irrigation canals danced with each other, until, one by one, the larger lines ate the smaller lines, and then the larger lines ate each other, until there were no more lines except for a singular, large, Wavy Line. Soon the Wavy Line ate everything up – the ground, the towers, the farms and the people. The little boy was cold and lonely and missed his papa.

'Bring Papa back,' he cried to the Wavy Line. The Wavy Line did not answer and only turned its world-large blue head away, as stubborn as the little boy was.

Magician or God?

Once upon a time, a Gamut cargo ship was sailing near the Opulent Belt, when a pirate ship intercepted the cargo ship and stole their last aleum fullblock.

The navigator said, 'We cannot drift and wait for help. There are more pirates waiting in the asteroids of the Opulent Belt, and they will attack us when we power down. There is a flower planet nearby. It was last in contact with the original planet approximately 20,000 years—'

'A flower planet? They won't even know what aleum is,' said the captain.

'We believe that there are aleum fields on this planet. The rumour is that pirates sneak there to harvest blocks. We can land there, cut a block and fly off within the hour, and no one would know.'

'We wouldn't even know. When the police catch us, they will erase our memories,' the captain said. Unapproved aleum harvesting was extremely illegal, while any contact with flower people would trigger the ultimate punishment – the complete erasure of their memories, and their families' memories.

But she knew that the cargo ship would not last even three day-cycles out in the open. Better to be alive and without memories, than dead. She made her decision to land the ship in the middle of a large, sparse desert on the flower planet. There was little chance of encountering any of the natives there – and, more importantly, nearby was an aleum super-giant field that formed the core of a chain of volcanoes.

'We'll send the five youngest members out there as ground crew – they have the fewest memories to lose if we get caught,' the captain said privately to the navigator.

Their ship landed among large veins of aleum ripe in the air, its characteristic scent wafting in the wind. Sparse grass washed across the landscape. The air was arid but breathable.

The ground crew had just cut a fullblock from a lightly depleted aleum vein – likely depleted because of the pirates, they thought – and clipped it to the ship, when three people emerged from wooden huts thought to be abandoned, and walked towards them.

Three people. Three flower people, their bodies battered from the sharp winds, their bones small and fragile. They stood staring at the crew members, separated by no more than a few steps and 20,000 years of no contact.

How forbidden, how dangerous, how exciting to come into contact with people who had been left behind in time, abandoned to their own evolution. What if their places had been swapped? What if it had been *their* ancestor who had arrived on this flower planet? What if they had never known the stars, and space, and the multitudes of home worlds that made up the Galactic Civilisation, like these nearly naked flower people in front of them?

'You were taking the fruit of the sky,' one of the flower people said.

Their language was archaic, and yet comprehensible to the translators. Fruit of the sky? Did they know about the aleum veins?

The crew on the ship watched. 'We have no time,' the captain said. 'The longer we stay here, the harder it will be to erase these records. We have to leave now.' She nodded in the direction of the crew on the ground. 'Without them.'

The crew on the ship felt overwhelming relief. The captain had made the decision for them. Perhaps their crime would not be discovered. Perhaps their families would be saved. Something was lost in that moment, and they would spend the rest of their lives thinking about what they did to their friends.

The remaining crew on the ground were shocked and angry to see the Gamut cargo ship fly away, even though they knew they would have done the same had their roles been reversed.

For now, the ex-crew of the Gamut cargo ship were faced with a more urgent issue – the three flower people in front of them.

The most senior crew member said, 'We have come down from the sky. Who are you?'

We are the Mesulei, the three flower people said. We have lived in this desert since we were exiled from the lands of rain and water. This is the Desert of Birds, they told the crew members. This is the Desert of Birds, so high that only birds and the Mesulei live here.

'We can teach you to fly,' the second crew member told the Mesulei. This new place contained so much unused aleum that he could float through the aleum trail for several days. It would not be a bad life. 'You may refer to me as Wai Lip,' he added, as an afterthought.

'Wei Leep,' one of the Mesulei repeated, and then asked, 'Are you a magician? Or a god?'

The Baby

The grandfather woke up. He felt himself ripped from a gentle, oscillating slumber, torn away from dreams that he could not remember, into this place where there was just him and the cold.

Simulation screens surrounded him, their faces blank. The tips of his fingers were numb. For a moment he imagined himself on a ship, wrapped by thin shell walls that separated his body from space. Not even air, nothing existed beyond this clutch of conscious atoms in the ship. They were broken things floating in nothingness. Then he realised that this could not be possible, for the ships had left a long time ago, before he was born, and what he had dreamt were merely reproduced simulations that he had watched when he was a child.

So then where was he . . .?

The girl sat across from him. She appeared more tired than her twenty-eight years. There were blankets in her hands and they moved.

A baby, he realised. The image registered at once, but not its significance. A baby. A baby. Baby. The baby.

The baby. 'How? But you were . . . you were . . . only just showing when I last saw you,' he said.

'I am okay,' she said, even as her right pupil and left pupil drifted apart from each other, as if they were unrelated cousins. 'I am okay,' she repeated, sighing. Her left pupil wandered back around to join her right pupil, before focusing on the grandfather in front of her.

Suddenly she laughed. 'The birth machines, all of it, they really do work! The extractors, the cleaners, the midwife. They work. After all these years! We did a great job at fixing them.'

The grandfather only stared at her.

'After your heart stopped, I had to put you in a sleep. The systems told me to do so. They kept you alive.'

He could not remember that his heart had stopped. 'How many day-cycles has it been?'

Her left pupil moved. 'I was too scared to try and wake you up, even if the screens said you would probably wake up. What if you woke up dead? Then I would have been alone, truly alone, my footsteps the only living sound in the tower. I needed to wait until this one arrived safely.' She paused. 'A hundred and eleven days.'

Hundred and eleven day-cycles? All the time he had lost.

The baby was placed in his arms, a mewling small thing. It shocked the grandfather, for the baby was a likeness of him, as if he had seen himself in the mirror as a baby. Their likeness was so complete it was as if time had folded and they were the same person. It felt like the beginning of something. The baby's cheeks were pink, warm and bloomed with the delight of being alive, even as he stared at the blurry person who held him.

'The other boy. What about the other boy?'

Her head dropped.

At once, he understood what had happened.

She moved her lips, mouthing two syllables that they both knew too well. Sadness. 'He finally succumbed several weeks before the baby was born. He never saw his own child. Perhaps he did not want to. Perhaps he thought it would be easier if he left the world not knowing what he had given up.'

'He left you. Did you expect any better from him?'

The grandfather remembered the day that the girl announced that she was pregnant. They had been standing in the receiving halls of sector ten. The last local lift of sector ten had stopped moving the day before, terminally this time, but they managed to salvage the aleum that had been stored in its power cell.

He had always tried to avoid stepping into any of the receiving halls as their disordered state distressed him; instead, he preferred to walk or make multiple trips through the local lifts. These trips could take many hours to complete, but it meant that he never entered a receiving hall unless he really had to.

Boxes of broken, abandoned things were stacked up by the walls. Floors were devoid of people and bags. Gone were the haphazard families stumbling over the irritated workers trying to get to work on time. What was left were signs that meant nothing now ('Limited Service Every Ten-Day Cycle' and 'Queue in a Single File. Do Not Cross the Yellow Line'), an empty mezzanine area, and five bays for lift trains that once used to carry a lot more people than just the grandfather and the girl and the other boy.

The girl had tagged a partially used block of aleum to her bag, using the aleum cutter. She was about to slip the cutter away, then paused, and really looked at it, as if seeing it for the first time.

'These engravings – these are the stars in the night sky of our home world?' the girl had asked.

'Yes,' the grandfather had replied, puzzled. The girl knew this fact well; it was one of the few stories she had heard as a child. He himself remembered those days as if they were yesterday. The girl had been so young when her mama and papa were lost to the bottom floors. She had cried in tiny puffs of air. He could not leave her with the child minder – the technician who had created that useless machine of wavy parts must never have taken care of a child before. So he took the girl everywhere with him, even up to sector twenty mines for an aleum restock. A few blocks of aleum took a while to cut. Being a man of limited imagination, he had scrabbled for the closest thing to hand, which was the aleum cutter, and told her stories of it.

His was an old cutter, not one of the newer ones made in mass quantities for the workers of the mines. Chor-Mah had told him the story. How the cutter was older than the tower, how her great-great-grandparents had brought it in their bags from their home world across many light years. *The squiggly lines and the dots are the stars that light up the night sky of our home world. See these loops here, on the shaft? That is our family name.* He could not read it as it was written in their home language, its meaning long lost.

That was then, and now the girl had got up on her feet and waved the cutter in the air. The blade gleamed with its characteristic dull shine, worn down over the years. There was no reason to think that something would happen, and yet the grandfather was overcome by the feeling that something was about to change. The beat of his heart grew louder.

'I'm pregnant,' the girl had said. 'Three months.'

Nothing had prepared the grandfather for that moment. She was only a child herself! He remembered holding the girl in his arms and whispering to this small, sleeping baby, promising that there would be a better future for her. He had watched as she squatted defensively on the dusty floor, pulling her arms around herself, their footprints disturbing the thick layers of this failing, failing tower, falling into the hole that it made for itself.

His first child had left through the bottom floors, his second child died from the sadness. If it had not been for the girl to take care of, the sadness would have taken him too. Sometimes he wished that he was braver, smarter. Sometimes he wished that he could give her a different destiny. In the end, he could not save the people he loved.

He had sat down next to the girl and cried; he held his knees and rocked and wished it away. There is no future, he said. There is no future, he repeated. You should not have to live like this, he said. He took big gulps of air stale and cold, centuries old.

After a few minutes, another thought occurred to him. 'But – how? The power to the reserve banks were turned off before you were born.'

The girl had her answer rehearsed. No justification would be made, no permission asked for. 'The other boy,' she said, with a steadiness that she had practised. Perhaps she said those words a little too steadily, as the grandfather looked at her and said nothing.

There is a third part to the story.

During the Eviction, most of the families of sector five refused to leave the tower, including Chor-Mah and her husband. We

241

will live in the tower; the tower is ours, they said. We will not be evicted. We will not be made to go on these ships.

'If you do not leave now, there will be no ships in the future to rescue you, if you change your mind,' the company man said. 'No way to leave the tower, except through the bottom floors – and you know what happens lah. Be like the Crazy Man.'

We are not planning to leave the tower. We do not know the stars or our home worlds. The tower is our home!

'You choose to be stuck in this tower? Fine. Just sign here and waive your rights. And the memory wall will be kept in place so that you cannot transmit your knowledge to the flower people of this planet.'

The ships left gradually, and when the last of them was gone, hope and busy optimism rose up like steam through the receiving halls of sector five. For the first time, there was no company to tell them what to do. They were in charge of their own destiny, bright like light.

They destroyed all communications with the company, and with the rest of civilisation, for they did not want to be spied on. They set up committees to run the tower: Mining and Aleum Supply, Food and Farms, Climate Control and Lighting, Towerwave Watch, Lifts, Water and Sewage, People, Housing and Health.

For all their pride, they never imagined that their descendants would die out from the sadness and the bottom floors.

Her Name

Not long after he met the baby, the grandfather slipped into another coma, which there was no waking from. The girl wheeled the grandfather to his room, the same one that he had had for his entire life. He would not have liked to die anywhere else. She placed a hand on the grandfather's chest, feeling him breathe in, breathe out, getting slower, while the baby slept and fed. One life beginning, another life ending. Eventually, as a day-cycle turned, his chest stopped. She wept. The baby stared. Nothing seemed different from how she imagined this day would be.

'Just you and me now,' she said to the baby. 'Just us.'

She stroked the baby's head as he slept, wrapped tightly against her, and she was thankful for his warmth and movements. She felt his little hands and how small he was, to be trapped in this ancient prison of nothing, where everything died continuously.

She knew she had to travel to the viewing room at the top of the tower. Her papa and mama had brought her there once, and she had to see it one last time. And it wasn't as if there was anything else to do, she thought, and another sob arose from her throat. She counted the aleum blocks clipped to her waist, out of habit, for she knew exactly how many blocks she had. One, two, three – that was enough for a round trip on a lift train to sector twenty. If it was working, she thought, and she shivered.

There was a lift train in the nearest bay of sector five, an oval tube the height of two people. Her fingers touched its cool surface. What luxury! These trains were made for travelling long distances and consumed so much aleum that, for all but the furthest journeys, they were grossly inefficient. One aleum block could power a local lift for days of travel around sector five and neighbouring sectors, stretching to weeks if she was careful.

It had taken her months to scavenge these three blocks for this journey. Mostly from the farms of sector seven, and the simulation room of sector nine. The planetarium of sector eight had a large supply of aleum remaining, but she had been reluctant to strip the aleum from that place. To do so would be to desecrate something holy, something precious.

Just walk up to sector twenty, the grandfather would have said, if he was still alive. Are your legs not working?

It was not an option for her, not anymore, for the journey there alone would take weeks, and they would be stranded without a way of getting back to sector five in an emergency. As with everything, she needed to think of one thing above all else: the baby.

She unclipped the preciously harvested aleum blocks and placed them in the fuel tanks. When she moved her hands, the doors opened. A breath that she did not know she was holding was released. She entered the grey tube and strapped herself into a seat, the baby still wrapped to her. The door shut, and she felt no movement, only small dings, like polite coughs announcing their presence, and then they found themselves in the receiving hall of sector twenty.

At first, it seemed that nothing had changed. The receiving hall was laid out in the exact same way as the one they had just left. Did the lift train move at all, or were they still standing in the same spot in sector five? Then she noticed, over the entrance, a sign that stated simply, SECTOR TWENTY. Dust flitted in the air and slept in thick blankets on every surface: the air circulation systems had long broken down. The grand-father had warned her about this, but he had not warned her what abandonment felt like, or the despair, or the emptiness that came with it.

One floor up were the docks themselves. This was the larg-est room in the whole tower, once containing giant ships, like the dual-purpose bays of sector five. Here was where most workers entered the tower, and here was where they eventu-ally left, after decades of mining, in the same ships, with chil-dren and grandchildren that had not known the home worlds.

Their full names were inscribed on the walls of the docks, a reminder of the people who had passed through the place. These were home-world names – names that existed only in song, and sung the history of their families and clans. How else would a person know their place in the broad sweep of time? If one did not have a home-world name, no one would know who they were, nor their forefathers, nor ancestral homes. A person was nothing without their home-world name, a speck written out of history.

Where was her name? What was her name? the girl had asked the grandfather, when he told her this story.

The girl had no home-world name, he explained to her. She had not passed through the docks. Besides, their family had abandoned their home-world names when they decided to stay in the tower.

The grandfather had added, 'We took on names that were functional to reflect our future. That is why you are the girl.'

She would always be the girl.

It took her several hours to cross the docks. Since the two-hundred-and-something years that had elapsed since the Eviction, there had been no attempt at maintaining the docks. What for, for what – and the answers came back, for nothing, for no one. There was no aleum here, and they could not repurpose the docks for anything. There had been suggestions of using them as construction bays for lifts, or labs for new food, but these suggestions never took hold.

Things were strewn about, blocking her way. Things everywhere, things that meant something once, forgotten things, dropped things, broken things . . . Things like them. Things with no purpose. Things that had lost their names. Things that did not change, things that did not move, because once upon a time, the families of sector five were too scared of change and did not want to leave the tower.

She was furious. She squeezed her eyes shut and pushed the air from her lungs in a long guttural sound, booming through her vertebral column, from her lower back and up to her neck, radiating outwards through the ribs, shoulders and all the way to the tips of her fingers. The baby shook with her deep physical pain. Why? Why did you stay? she cried at the blank

246

space on the walls. Our names should have been written here! Nothing for us, nothing here, only this tower. We are bits of dust flying nowhere. She knelt on the floor, she shook, and she could not stop. The baby shrieked too, joining her sobs.

When the pain eased, shame overcame her – the shame of disrespecting her ancestors. The grandfather would have been disappointed. *They did, Grandfather. They signed away our return to the home worlds, they left us in this tower for a nowhere-future, small and pitiful.*

The grandfather would say nothing, and instead turn away. She wanted to claw the words back, but a third feeling surfaced – relief.

The shaking of her hands stopped. Something was freed in the gloominess of the docks. She watched as particles of dust turned in the air, waking with her footsteps. She would write herself and the baby new names – somewhere that was not in this rotting tower. For the first time in her life, the girl felt free.

The Viewing Room

Above the docks was the viewing room, the highest level in the tower, with the tower's only window. Like the docks, there were no internal walls or partitions; one large room of nothing but traces of saltish aleum drifting in the air. Here, the walls and the ceiling were the same, arching in a giant dome that stretched from the intersection of wall and floor, into a curve that rejoined the floor as a perfect circle, marking the full perimeter of the tower.

The air was several degrees cooler in the viewing room. The girl had stepped from the docks, still in peak day-cycle, to the dark of the viewing room. No grow lights here. The only light here was primordial light from space, percolating from stars so far away that by the time it arrived, history had already happened. She flicked a finger to zoom in on one of the stars, and then realised that the sky outside was not a simulation.

There was the smell of remnant veins of aleum in the air here, poor quality and watery. Enough aleum to make up several blocks, she estimated. Her hand reached for the cutter, ready to cut out the remaining aleum, and then froze in mid-air, fingers stretched out. She sensed some wordless injunction to stop. *Not hers to take*, a voice resonated from deep within her or from the air, she did not know. Her fingers retreated from the cutter; she would leave the aleum undisturbed.

The baby stirred beside her breast. Perhaps he felt that warning too. His eyes had faded from the luminous blue of a newborn, and was now looking at her, keen, more alive than anything in this tower, grander than the giant docks, brighter than the grow lights, more wondrous than the planetarium of sector eight, more alive than the power cubes.

In the darkness of the star-lit air, a hum rose. Light crept in from a distant horizon at the far end of the viewing room. She was confused by the unevenness of the light, how it cast itself at her feet. Pink and blue light swept through the room, and small shadows gathered: now at her elbows, now her shoulders. She placed a hand over her eyes and turned so that her shadow fell upon the baby, to protect his sight from the slanting light.

These were not grow lights, she realised. This was the star of this planet, rising over the edge of the tower. She understood in abstract that the planet was turning itself to face the star, and yet she marvelled, for it seemed as if the star was rising up into the view of the planet. A word came to her, a word that she had only heard in simulations before and never understood until now: sunrise.

She moved closer to the transparent dome walls that separated her from the sunrise. She could see the planet below, its darkness being pushed away by the light of the sun, revealing their true colours. Green, blue, brown and white repeated themselves in fractal patterns, twisting themselves into shapes that she instinctively *knew*, remembered like a lullaby that had been sung. These were ancient patterns engraved in their beings, all their beings. Her eyes traced the patterns – the sinuous lines, the branches, the geometric forms – and she felt an inexplicable joy, and a sadness, at not being able to join in the planet's revelry. She could see everything, and yet she was separated from it, denied access to it by the walls of the tower.

She decided to give this place a name, her own private name for this grand planet, even if the memory wall would ultimately take it away from her. Her ancestors had come here to mine aleum, so, aleumnia? Aleumium? Alluvium. She liked how the syllables turned.

She had known before, but she was certain of it now, that she was ready for the bottom floors.

Part Seven
Naga Tua

Notes from the Bercahaya Empire

From 'Notes from the Bercahaya Empire', Volume 69
. . . On day seventy-two of the expedition, Rama did not re-appear after lunch. He had been investigating the area around the cliffs. Two junior members were sent out to find him. On the evening of day seventy-three, the junior team members did not return either. Were the villagers right in their super-stitions? The decision was taken to abandon mapping of the northeast quadrant altogether and head back to Suriyang.

From 'Notes from the Bercahaya Empire', Volume 102
. . . It is with some trepidation that I approach this barren ground. Here the rocks are black, in their pure state, un-altered by the frequent rains that characterise the climates of the southern islands. Their unweathered state might be due to . . .

Editor's note: The rest of the document is illegible, possibly affected by water.

From 'Notes from the Bercahaya Empire', Volume 480

... What I am about to say next may sound particularly sentimental, or overwrought with emotion, or fanciful. Hopefully my descriptions will persuade readers that I am neither sentimental, nor overwrought, nor fanciful. For there is no other way to describe these observations: I see a golden tower. There is a tower here, and it is golden. It appears to be contained within a deep, circular depression. The surroundings are empty. The nearest settlement is several days' walk away – the village of Suriyang. I have previously talked to the people of Suriyang, and they are none so advanced as to construct this marvel that I see in front of me. This tower is taller than any structure on Layang-Layang. Many times taller than the Shining Palace.

The question must be asked. Even the asking of this question makes me tremble. What great civilisation built this tower and what more can they do? The depths that separate us! My humble feet touch this exposed ground, the bare rock beneath; I am a caveman, I am an ant, and there are gods.

Editor's note: It is unclear how much of this account is reliable. The author of this account, Junior Explorer Qing, was later found unconscious on the gravel floodplain near Suriyang, having suffered injuries from a wild boar attack. He is afflicted with retrograde amnesia, likely from the shock of the event. He is unable to personally confirm his written account.

From 'Notes from the Bercahaya Empire', Volume 1651

... It is a curious thing, their veneration of forest spirits, and their fear of them: on one hand, the villagers regard the spirits as strange, otherworldly creatures, the rightful inhabitants of the forest; on the other hand, the arrival of spirits is regarded as bringing bad luck, a portent of barren durian trees and dust storms as dark as night.

Most notably, unlike the other mythic creatures in the southern islands, like Datuk Gasing or Urang Api-Api, the existence of these spirits has been verified by previous researchers. Their pale skin has been described in detail, their dull, apathetic nature noted, but their arrival in Suriyang remains a mystery. It is an ongoing debate whether these spirits, with their pale skin, have White Ghost ancestry, or have come from another, unrelated civilisation altogether.

So it is with great excitement that I arrive in Suriyang. My theory is that should these spirits have White Ghost ancestry, their bone structure would be similar to that of the White Ghosts, and not the inhabitants of Naga Tua, or of the Hei-san islands.

Unfortunately, it was too late by the time I arrived in Suriyang. I was notified by the sinseh that the last living spirit had died a week before. It was reported that the spirit had jumped off a cliff into a deep river below, and his body was not recovered. The rainy season meant that the water levels were high and the current too swift, rendering it unsafe to carry out a search. A week later, when the water level subsided, three of Suriyang's best swimmers and divers were sent to find his body, but it could not be found. He must have been swept out to sea.

It seems that the spirit left behind a drawing of a spade. Upon further examination, the drawing looked like something a child would draw, and has no relevance to White Ghost cultural histories.

The death of this spirit is an unfortunate matter. With his death, I will have to wait for the next visit by spirits, and that could be years from now, if ever.

Bercahaya Empire

Several strange things happened as Chong Meng, the professor and Mr Ng camped on the outskirts of Suriyang, the most strange of which was a man appearing outside Chong Meng's tent as the late afternoon thunderstorms petered to an end.

Chong Meng had just come back from peeing on a banana tree, the steam of his warm urine dispersing in the cool mountain air. The man was about his height, and his skin was coffee-coloured, like most of the people who lived throughout the Hei-san archipelago. His age was ambiguous, his hair white as milk, but his face seemingly young, with his skin taut and unblemished by the sun. (Chong Meng's mother would have said that the man ate a lot of tendon clean off the bone, good collagen, no wonder his skin so smooth.) The clothes that hung upon him were a large T-shirt (fake brand, Chong Meng noted), and baggy jeans of a pasar malam kind. One of the villagers he supposed. Chong Meng had been warned about these villagers of Suriyang. They were superstitious folk; they had never seen the bigger world; they held on to their irrational beliefs like a drowning man to his raft. They were villagers, ulu, jinjang, backward, primitive, gullible, suah pah, so Mr Ng said.

Chong Meng said, 'What do you want? I don't have any cigarettes.'

When the man appeared to be confused, Chong Meng added, 'No. Cigarettes. Boh liao. No more.' He waved his hands to show that his hands were empty, truly empty, and that he did not have anything that this man from Suriyang could want.

The coffee-coloured man said he did not want cigarettes but had come to Chong Meng's tent to tell him about the forest. 'The forest. Very dangerous. The spirits will take away your mind. You know the professor? He came here before, he came here many times, with many others like you. They wouldn't listen to me. He brought them into the forest. When they came out, they came out empty.' His words fell quietly, slowly, like remnant raindrops dropping off the edge of a leaf.

Chong Meng stared at the man. He had no shared experiences with this stranger, no common words to share. In the absence of words that they could exchange, Chong Meng shifted his feet in the blades of wet grass.

'Empty,' the man repeated, in warning, as he took a few steps to leave. 'Boh liao. No more.'

'Empty.' His voice tolled in the flatness of early evening light.

That night, lightning flashed in the mountains that surrounded Suriyang, and thunder roamed like wild boars raging across Naga Tua and the rest of the Hei-san archipelago. Chong Meng, in his sleep, did not hear a thing.

The professor, Mr Ng and Chong Meng left the outskirts of Suriyang in the morning, following a river up from the flood-plain, and into the dark mountains of the north.

Mr Ng was jubilant. 'I got all the supplies you wanted, Professor! Hah, see, you leave it to me and I get things done.'

The path grew narrower as trees and their shadows enveloped their limbs. The river grew darker too, its gravel banks shaken loose by the strong current, washing any faltering pebbles away – only the most resolute of pebbles remained – exposing the black rock foundations of the Hei-san islands, in its raw naked state, river-swept, slickly wet.

Mud filled up Chong Meng's shoes and swam up his trousers, leaving leeches sucking at his calves. He tried to walk only on the raised roots of trees, or on exposed rocks, but his feet kept slipping into the slop of the mud. He was glad when they arrived at a small clearing, even if he had to hack away at the lalang before they could set up camp. Mosquitoes swarmed around him as he swung the parang through the lalang. *Stupid leeches, I will chop you like chopping yau char kwai, into big fat slices, and now you cannot slither anymore, and I can burn you in the fire, eat your sizzling meat.*

'Eh you careful, don't just whack-whack the blade only. Later you let go and it hit one of us then how?' Mr Ng shouted from the edge of the clearing, where he was setting up the professor's tent.

That night, as a kettle hissed in the camp stove's flames, the professor spoke with the confidence of a man who assumes that his audience will listen with rapt fascination, and in this particular moment, sitting on a frayed mat as he addressed Chong Meng and Mr Ng, he was correct.

'The villagers are so ungrateful. After all I have done for them. Paid for better roads, electricity and clean water. And how do they treat me in return? Like a pariah!

'They think the forest is dangerous. Why? Old grandmother tales, passed down from one generation to another. People are stupid. They are one sand grain of millions, spat out at the hump where the river meets the sea. Each one thinking that somehow their journey means something, but the truth of it is that they are just a boring old sphere, any distinctive edges rubbed away by the river churn.

'Even my colleagues think I am chasing a dead end in the Hei-san islands. They say, Just another old temple or building from the Bercahaya Empire. What are you going to find, Toh? Another old temple? Another pile of bricks that used to be the royal grain silo? Another ash-blackened stone lion? Maybe you should sign up for the Leong Hobby Archaeology Camps. Only $1,000 for a week of fun in archaeology, meals and transportation included.

'They laugh at me, they mock me behind my back. They say, "Toh, everyone knows about the Great Eruptions. There are thousands of well-preserved records from historians, traders, temple priests." They say, "No need lah, no need for professor to study, even a first-year student can read about it in the history books. Everything is known." They think that the well-preserved records of the Bercahaya Empire are somehow defects, that their accessibility and recognisability mean less prestige. The chicken scratchings of an extinct desert civilisation would be of more interest to them. They would chase ambiguity for its own sake, as if history is merely a puzzle to

262

be solved. They don't realise that there has been nothing like the Bercahaya Empire in all of humankind's short history.

'What? You never heard of the Bercahaya Empire? What do they teach you in schools nowadays?' the professor said gleefully at their puzzled looks, knowing exactly what his next words would be. If he could only tell everyone about the Bercahaya Empire – every child, every roadsweeper, every housekeeper!

'A thousand or more years ago,' he continued, 'the Bercahaya rule extended across the whole of the Hei-san archipelago and its thousands of islands, even on the Pinnacle Islands in the south, even though those islands are nothing but glorified rocks threatened by tides twice a day. Every village, every person on every Hei-san island, could call themselves a Bercahaya citizen. Tax collectors and temple priests were stationed on every island, reminding people of their obligations, both in this life and in the afterlife, to serve the Shining Palace on Layang-Layang island, the heart of the Bercahaya Empire.

'At the Shining Palace, book-keepers, historians, canal engineers, sculptors and high priests worked hard to give birth to plans that would cement the Bercahaya Empire as the greatest civilisation ever. Canals and streets radiated out from the Shining Palace, to connect every part of the Layang-Layang island, and further – in sailing routes that crossed the shallow seas of the archipelago, and the deep oceans of the Peninsula.

'Back in their time, the journey between the archipelago and the Peninsula took months on flimsy wooden ships, not like your comfortable two-week trip on *Bintang Jelas*. Many sailors died in transit. Their paintings show the waves that swallowed the decks of ships and ripped the sails into ribbons. Crossing of the Deep, they said. Any ships that made it to the

Peninsula became fantastically rich, trading clocks and wind fences from the Hei-san islands with the barren East Coast towns, fishing nets and farming tools with the West Coast towns, and spices with the capital of the Peninsula, which was then merely a rural outpost of the Bercahaya Empire. Sometimes these Bercahaya ships even went as far north as past the White Ghost Line.

'Even to this day, there are Bercahaya temples, now in their ruins, scattered along the coast of the Peninsula. They left their mark on us, you see. This language we speak is inherited from their court languages. Their blood is mixed in our blood. Sailors from those ships married Peninsular women in the trading towns, mixing their island bloodlines with Peninsular bloodlines. We are touched by the Bercahaya Empire, every one of us, hundreds of years later.'

Chong Meng was displeased. He had no part in this history. 'I never heard about Bercahaya Empire before wor. Can't be that great. What happened to the people and ships now? Nothing around here also.'

'They died out, boy! The Shining Palace was destroyed, and so were the buildings and the people. The Great Eruptions of three hundred and fifteen years ago did what no White Ghost could have done: destroyed the Bercahaya Empire, burned its people to ashes so that no power will ever rule here again.

'Their scientists warned of the sleeping volcanoes many years before the Great Eruptions began. No longer sleeping, they said. The flat ground swelled into lumpy hills. The volcanic mountains grew in their weight, their sides expanded as if pregnant, waiting to give birth to a new beginning, or as it were, the ending of the Bercahaya Era.

264

'People laughed at the scientists when they moved books and records to our capital of the Peninsula, which then was a town so remote, so far from the Shining Palace, that they only heard of it from the whisperings of sailors. A town on the other side of the Peninsula, where giant waves would not reach, nor would the White Ghosts invade.

'For years nothing happened. Then, one day, bricklayers took an afternoon nap, having laid down the eastern wall of the third courtyard of the Shining Palace. They never woke up. A temple priest in a village to the north of the Layang-Layang island keeled over, and the prayer-goers complained of a smell. Rotten eggs, they said. They fanned themselves and complained about the unseasonably warm weather that monsoon season. They had headaches that evening, and by the next morning, they were dead and their children too.

'The smell of rotten eggs grew stronger on Layang-Layang island. More smells came with it, the smell of burning joss sticks and shrivelling prayer paper, for the gates of hell had opened and the spirits of the underworld had come to invade.

'Exactly as scientists had predicted many years before, the volcanoes woke up, spewing up seas of molten lava. Burning rock rained on Layang-Layang and the surrounding islands, melting skin and hair and bones. Those who could rushed under the clay roofs of the Shining Palace, for anyone who was outside died in the scorching rain.

'For three days, the Shining Palace woke to a grey burning sky. The people wondered what prayers they hadn't said, or what offerings they had forgotten to make, or what else they did that was so offensive that the gods of the underworld had cursed their families. *Forgive us*, they prayed.

'In the end, it was the water that killed them. Layang-Layang had a central lake nestled between the volcanoes, dammed to provide water in the dry season. The entire flank of the volcano broke apart, and giant blocks of rock slid into the lake, filling up the dam until the pressure cracked the dam walls. The Shining Palace, together with the royal family and the refugees, was flattened by the walls of water. They had not prepared for the flood.

'Sailors from the sea approached the last known location of Layang-Layang island, only to find smouldering rock. There was so much mud and ash that the shallow seas were agitated into a turbid black and would remain that way for years. The Hei-san archipelago was now a black smear of burning, floating bodies that popped up in the spaces between their boats, a multi-generational graveyard with no tombstones.

'Clouds of falling rock and ash ballooned and burst across the islands. Monsoon winds would scrub some of the blackness away, until the island caught fire with another eruption. Again and again the eruptions scorched the earth, for there would be no respite in that year of the Great Eruptions as the soil burned, and the plants and the seeds and the people.

'Thus the name Burnt Islands was bestowed upon the northern Hei-san islands, including Layang-Layang island where the Shining Palace and Bercahaya Empire once ruled: now barren, fruitless, empty. There is no reservoir of fresh water on any of the Burnt Islands today; only pallid soil on which the occasional straggle of grass lives and dies.

'We are on the island of Naga Tua, one of the southern islands, sheltered from the worst of the Great Eruptions. And what do they do? Grow vegetables and rice for all of history. Pah! This island was always a backwater. Past, present, nothing has changed.'

266

Even Desert People with Dusty Feet

What a strange, alien beauty! Min thought, on her first approach to the Hei-san archipelago. Over the years, she had come up with an impression of the islands, images painstakingly assembled from scraps of information that the professor threw at her. Two-dimensional, flat pictures. Now she was actually here in person, and she could see the islands bursting out of the sea; she could see their shadows, the hidden depths. It was as if she was seeing a million images all at once, superimposed on top of each other, competing for attention.

Each island rose from the sea like draped jewels. Some looked like they had fallen from the sky and lay in shards. The northern islands were raw, their jagged peaks eating at the sky, while dark sloping grounds paid homage to their majesty. Liquid fire ran down their sides. The other islands had been smoothed by the rain and wind, the black rock weathered as patches of green grew in their cracks. In the south, far in the distance where the horizon met the sky, thick forests grew.

There were not words enough to tell their stories.

They approached the island of Naga Tua, their boat slowing against the waves bouncing off the coastline. What had she been hoping to find on this island? Perhaps she was trying to prove her worth; or she had to see the island where memories were lost – not just some name written in a book, but an actual living island where trees breathed, waves heaved and people lost themselves, even people as tough as Sky Yang. Maybe it was to save Han's cousin from the forests of Naga Tua. Or perhaps she needed to know that adventures existed for housekeepers like her, for ones abandoned by their families, even for desert people with dusty feet.

A lorry took Min and Han from the port of Naga Tua to the village of Suriyang, where they arrived to the crowing of roosters. Smoke drifted in the air, perhaps from the burning of dry leaves. The overnight, sleepless ride on the lorry had rattled their limbs loose, and they stumbled through the village square, looking for someone they could speak to. The streets were quiet, and there was no morning market.

Bong, bong, bong. A gong was struck, and their bones thrummed. Somewhere, prayers were being said for the hour of Breaking the Quiet. And in the square a woman hurried towards them, her hair short and white; she was the sinseh, the same sinseh that bestowed their names on Swee and Han eighteen years before.

'You – not spirits,' she stated simply, disappointed. 'From the Peninsula issit?'

'Looking for the professor,' Min said. 'Have you seen him? I know that he usually comes through this village.'

The sinseh reached out her arms and gripped them both firmly by their elbows. She said, 'Don't go into the forest.'

'We are looking for my cousin,' Han said.

'That young man? He was about your age.' She shook her head. 'They passed through here yesterday. They must be in the forest by now. Mr Ng, I trusted him once.'

Min took a step back, taking her arm away from the sinseh. 'We still can catch up with them. Did they walk in the direction of the smallest river?'

'The forest takes people. There is no telling who will come out and who will not. It's too dangerous, don't go into the forest.'

Min was resolute. Perhaps, if she was younger, if she had never left the Desert of Birds, she would have backed down and taken the words of the sinseh, an older person, as the truth: that nothing can be changed, and that Chong Meng would be lost like the others. But she was no longer that person; she had left the Desert of Birds, and the words of her elders did not pacify her. She would not defer to other people's superstitions and fears. She was no longer that twelve-year-old girl, naive enough to be pushed off a cliff or to let her brother die on the Bone Fields. This time, she would speak.

She said, 'The forest does not take memories at random. I have overheard enough of the professor's monologues to know where the safe areas are, and there are two that the professor might have chosen. Which way did he walk – in the direction of the smallest river, or towards the marbled hills?

The sinseh was taken aback by Min's directness. Young people did not usually speak to her this way. *This girl is too young,* she thought. And the boy, with a face so familiar like she knew it in a previous life. She said, 'He went up the smallest river. Be careful. The professor is a manipulative, desperate man.'

That night, as the sinseh lay in her warm bed, feeling the comforting itch of her blankets resting on her neck, she heard her granddaughter in the next room let out a small cry. She half opened her eyes. The moonlight was sleeping on her chest. A stray memory landed in her shifting consciousness. She jolted upright. The boy! She had met him before. She was sure. It seemed important. But the moment passed, and the sinseh fell back to sleep. It did not matter, for she never saw either Min or Han again.

Sky Yang was the last of the orphans to enter the forests of Naga Tua. There would be no more so-called volunteers from the Mercy Orphanage. Miss Gan had started to receive visits from the police inspector himself. Even a gift from the professor of a new house away from the sewers could not tempt her further.

How does one study memory loss without losing one's own memories? It was a fundamental problem for the professor. 'I would go and investigate for myself, but I might lose my memories, and then who would take my place?' he would tell Mr Ng.

Instead, the professor sent the orphans to sweep a specific area of the forest by walking in parallel lines, from top to bottom. By process of elimination, the professor was able to narrow down the location where retrograde amnesia set in. If the orphan developed retrograde amnesia, the area they walked in would be marked out for further investigation, and subdivided into several smaller areas, and the process repeated with the next orphan. There were many false positives. The terrain was mountainous and the forest dense. Some went missing or were found dead. Was it amnesia or did they just fall off a cliff? Over the years, the professor had narrowed down his search to two areas, and Sky Yang was sent to walk

270

one of them. One way or the other, the professor would finally identify which area the retrograde amnesia affected.

Sky Yang's instructions had been similar to the others before her: start at the bamboo clearing. Walk from west to east, at a comfortably quick pace for a total of seven hours. Stop at the end of the day and set up camp. At the start of the next day, take 830 steps to the north. Then turn and walk to the west. Repeat these instructions, alternating east and west for the turn at the start of each day. At the end of the eighth day, we will meet you (if you reach the safe space, which was not said).

Sky Yang had additional instructions: This is your diary. Along your route, write down if you notice anything out of the ordinary. Different. Not belonging to the forest. And even if you do or do not notice anything, you must write in the diary twice a day, once at noon and once in the evening, after you have set up camp. I have left you instructions at the front of the diary, should you forget what your instructions are (if everything goes to plan, which was not said).

Her diaries would allow the professor to pinpoint the area within a half-day's walk where the retrograde amnesia set in, if he was lucky. His theory was that there was a place in the forest where a person could enter freely but, when they left, their memories were stripped; they were spat out as empty vessels into the forest. He believed that the memory loss was caused by walking through a membrane or a wall – one that let memories and people in, yet kept their memories on the way out.

'It is clear that the memory loss protects something,' the professor had said, in one of his many one-sided conversations, where he spoke half to himself and half to Min.

Maybe, Min had replied.

The professor would never understand. He was of the opinion that the memory loss was protecting a delicate thing, like a new-born child. Min's theory was that the memory loss ensured that any person that learned its secrets would die with them. As long as they stayed in the forest, they were fine. If they left the forest, they lost their memories. One way or another, there was death in the end. Whether death came early through the loss of their selves, or at the end of a trapped life, was their only choices once they entered the forest. They opt in because there is no opting out. Just as there was no opting out of the shadeless Bone Fields, where the bones of children were scattered like lost toys.

'It was their choice. If they did not turn around and try to come back, they would have kept their memories,' the professor said.

Min said, 'You would have to stay there for ever. And if you have children, then they have to stay there for ever too. What kind of life is that?'

'What can you know of life, girl? You are just a house-keeper,' the professor sneered.

When a star is too heavy, the mass of the star pulls the light towards its core. The closer you get, the greater the struggle to escape its immense gravity. Nothing can escape this black hole, not even light. Time passes normally for you, but to the outside world, you are just falling forever into the black hole, lost beyond the event horizon from which there is no return.

'I call the memory loss "the Event" for short,' the professor said, delighted with his brilliance. 'Because that area in the forest is like a black hole, see? See?'

Not a Liar

Han and Min arrived at the bamboo clearing after several hours. They found two soggy tents, a surprised Mr Ng and an annoyed Professor Toh.

'Chong Meng, you ah?' Mr Ng called. 'Why back so fast wan, you lost your way issit?' He stopped when he realised that the footsteps were Min and Han. 'You? What are you doing here? How did you get from the capital?'

'Where's Chong Meng?' Han said.

'None of your business.'

'Min! Who's taking care of the house, then?' the professor said. He looked at Han. 'Is this your . . . *boyfriend*? I knew it. Housekeepers like you cannot be trusted. Boyfriend here, boyfriend there. What are you doing here?'

Mr Ng answered, 'This boy here is Chong Meng's cousin. Sure come find him wan.'

'Oh, you are too late,' the professor said. 'Your cousin went in that direction, into the forest. Why don't you go and look for him?' A coldness echoed amongst the thick, hollow stems of the bamboo.

'I know what you are doing. I know what you did to the orphans,' Min said.

'Stupid girl, of course you know. I told you everything. Did I think you would use it against me? Ungrateful! Anyway, you are too late. That boy has gone into the forest, and when he comes back . . . well, he won't be the same. Don't worry, he will be taken under my care. I will give him a much better life than his life in the kampung. The best private tutors that money can buy. I always pay my dues, you know. That boy would have wanted it. Always talking about leaving the kampung and exploring the world,' the professor said, adding, 'Of course, if you want to, you can try to find him yourself. He has not been gone very long.'

Min stared. 'When did he leave, exactly?'

'Yesterday. It is three days of walking to the waterfall. You could be very lucky and find him before all of you encounter the Event.'

'You are lying. You just want us to do your dirty work for you.'

The professor said, 'I am not a liar, Min. Not like your family in the desert who pushed you off a cliff. I am a professor in search of the truth. I told Chong Meng that he would have a better life if he went into the forest and did exactly what he was instructed to do. I only tell the truth. You know that if you reach him before the waterfall, you will probably be safe. Probably. Just follow Sky Yang's route, Min.' He smiled.

'Why?' Han asked.

274

Everyone – Mr Ng, the professor, Min – turned to Han, surprised. His presence had been forgotten; only the branches of fallen bamboo around him recognised his intrusion, poking at his legs. His once-white shoes were soaked with water. The sole of his right shoe had developed a small hole near where his big toe had repeatedly rubbed. His feet had grown wrinkly and embalmed by the black mud. Around them the ground rumbled, and the air seemed to hiss.

The professor was the first to recover from the unexpected question. 'Why? Why? You are asking why? Why do anything at all? This is a great discovery for humanity, and it will be mine.'

'No, that's not what I meant.'

Min said, 'The professor knows many things. And he does not know many things. He will tell you that this memory loss in the forest existed before the Great Eruptions. How long before, he does not know. He will tell you that three hundred years ago, a Bercahaya Era explorer wrote about the spirits of Suriyang. Their skin, their hair, their lack of memories. They came from another civilisation, in ruins now, conquered by the forest. The professor will tell you that a different Bercahaya Era explorer wrote about a golden tower, deep in the black rock of the Hei-san islands. What the golden tower has to do with the memory loss, the professor does not know. He does not know. No one knows.

'Once, I thought the people of the capital knew the answers to every question: they were the chosen tribe, blessed with the only copy of the Feather Book, and that they were exalted to their position near Tian Gong. Imagine my surprise when I found out that the Feather Book did not exist; it never did. These were just lies that they told to the desert people.'

'You are just hysterical, Min. Listen to yourself,' the professor said.

'Why did you have to take Mama's spade in the first place?' Han asked.

They were all surprised, again.

'I got the spade from this boy. Same family as Chong Meng,' Mr Ng said to the professor.

The professor whispered to himself, The boy's mother? The same woman as the runaway spirit that burnt down a temple?

'Why did you need to steal from our family? We have so little. She only owned one thing in her life. Give back her spade, and we will find Chong Meng, and we won't tell the police about you.'

'You think anyone will believe you? You are so stupid, you don't even know what you have gotten yourself into! Your mother came out of the forests here. She was the last spirit. She ran away from Suriyang with her baby eighteen years ago,' the professor said, frowning. '*Her baby*. Oh, I understand now. Oh, I do. Who are you, boy? Do you know where you came from? You are a spirit, boy, and you came from inside that forest, inside there.' He pointed at the striped shadows of the overlapping trees, into the primeval darkness. 'Do you know who you really are?'

Mama, what would you have thought of all this? Mama, who are you?

A breeze sent shadows skittering, and their faces flickered with ghosts of bamboo leaves. Somewhere in the forest Chong Meng wandered.

Mama, why did you leave? Chong Meng, why did you have to leave too?

276

Han would travel to the abyssal depths of a forgetting forest to save his cousin. 'You don't need to go into the forest, Min,' he said. 'Only I go.'

Min was silent. Then her voice came clear through the air. 'I go for the orphans, for Sky Yang. I cannot let you go into the forest by yourself. You will surely die. Do you know how to survive? For seven days? This forest is dark. Hurry-hurry, we must catch Chong Meng before he encounters the Event.'

Hurry-hurry, the summons came, urgent, ringing, and in the bamboo chamber the echo replied, *Hurry-hurry*, and through the trees and the black mountains and the sky, *Hurry-hurry*, the chant sang. Branches rustled beyond the bamboo clearing, in the forest that seemed both familiar and new at the same time, *Hurry-hurry*, the chant echoed. Only now it sounded more like *hur-hur-hur*, like a person laughing, like ashes burning.

The professor and Mr Ng would never see Min, Han or Chong Meng again. But at that particular moment, the professor was excited and Mr Ng was excited for him.

'All three of them! Three! Chong Meng, carrying the spade and the recording device. Min, with her knowledge of the orphans and the forest. And the biggest surprise of all, that boy, the spirit-baby that came out of the forest with his mother.' The professor smiled. 'I'm sure at least one will survive. What new information will they find?'

Mr Ng said, 'Eh, all this ah, is thanks to me, Professor. Yah? Remember, Professor, how much I help you!' He squinted through the trees. 'I still can see Han and Min. There, there, in the forest. They look okay kua. Haven't lost memories yet.

Not yet gone cuckoo. Means must be safe right? I can go in a bit and see?'

'If you want to. As I have explained, you don't lose your memories on the way in, you lose them on the way out. For all we know, they have already encountered the Event. If they turn around now, they might lose their memories instantly. Sky Yang turned around after three days. Too late for her then. Maybe too late for Min and Han now. Do you want to be another guinea pig?'

The professor could see Min fading into the trees. Stupid girl, always causing trouble that one. Never get another desert girl again, he thought. They were too stubborn, too disobedient, like the desert people were. When he got back to the capital, he would get a housekeeper from the New Villages. The girls there were obedient and respectful, so he had heard.

He shook his head, trying to get rid of Min's last words to him, as she stepped away from the bamboo clearing: 'The gods will punish you.' How dare she? Still, his annoyance did not go away even as evening fell.

I Turn Around Now

The trees were clustered so tightly that sparse light reached the forest floor, and time felt like eternal evening. The green canopy thinned in brief interludes, and in these rare moments, Han and Min saw grey and white clouds chugging their way across the vast plains of the sky, and droplets of rain fell as an afterthought.

Han and Min did not catch Chong Meng on the first day. He was going faster than Min had expected. If she had adjusted their strides to match Chong Meng's, it would throw her calculations off, she explained. Any change to their walking pattern might lead them to accidentally exit the area altogether. We might leave the Event if we are not careful.

They did not find Chong Meng on the second day either. As evening fell and the sky darkened, Min pointed to a small crescent grass plain, bounded by a bank of gravel. 'We should camp here for the night,' she said, and the lines on her face deepened. 'We should find him tomorrow.' They both knew what that meant: it was the third day when the old Sky Yang wrote her final words in her diary; there was really no going back. In the whipping of the rain they set up their tent, and their breath warmed the blankets. The soft, damp mush of the ground gave space to their bodies.

'Are you scared?' Min whispered.

'No-no, where got I scared?' They both knew this was not the truth.

'What will we find tomorrow?'

'Chong Meng, I hope.'

Of course, Min replied.

They tried to sleep, individual in their efforts, collective in their frustration. Min turned and rewrapped the blankets around her. Han lay still, feeling his racing heart and sweaty palms. Eventually, he gave in to his sleeplessness and spoke. 'She was the last of the spirits. What does that make me?'

'Your mother's son.'

'They died young, you said, lost spirits that could not find their way back. And now we are returning into this place.'

'You know, you are very lucky. You don't even know it.'

'Lucky? Where got I lucky? I don't know where I came from, or who my mama is.'

'Your mama loved you. As do your father, and your ah-ma, who took you in and loved you. They loved you as their very own. Why does it matter where you came from? Even if you came from somewhere in this forest, does it change anything? There are people who love you for who you are now and that should be enough. How lucky you are.'

'My mama was a lost spirit, and we were not enough for her. The sea fills up all holes in this world; it is dark, silent and vast, and so was her sadness. Maybe I was the only thread

280

keeping her in this world, and once she found a safe place for me, her duty was fulfilled and she could leave. So she left.'

On the morning of the following day, Han said, 'You think the professor lied about Chong Meng, that he had just left when we arrived, that he was only a day in front of us?'

Min had had her suspicions. She had kept them to herself to keep up their hopes. Now, as Han said these words and made them real, she could feel herself sagging. Maybe Chong Meng had not come this way. Maybe they had entered the forest for nothing. Maybe they would die here, or be found like the orphans before them, like Sky Yang, knowing nothing, without having saved anyone, not even themselves. She started to reply, and then stopped. 'What is that, over there, in the rocks?'

In the littering of boulders they found Chong Meng's bag. Stray drops from a waterfall fell upon them. Cliffs loomed over them like gods on an altar. Have you come to pay your respects? Have you brought us some ang ku kuih or pomelos or sticky rice, or will you burn some joss sticks in our name? Worship us, the rock faces said, and you, most faithful follower, will be rewarded with more wealth than you can imagine. You will be given many children and grandchildren to carry your family name. You will live long and wise years, and your portrait will hang high in your ancestral home. Pray to us, offer us your bowls of sticky rice, your burning joss sticks, your suckling pigs, offer us your devotion, and we will not destroy you. No use praying to your gods here: Tian Gong and Chau Ang Gong and Guan Yin and Mazu; they cannot hear your prayers.

Han said, looking around, 'His bag means that he passed through here. We might still be able to catch him before the Event.'

Min stared at the abandoned bag and the waterfall, and said nothing.

It had not been recorded in Sky Yang's diary what her first impressions of the waterfall were. If one had to guess, perhaps one would imagine her impressions as such:

Out from the top of the cliff, beyond the perspective of human eyes, an errant stream of water peers over the edge. Too late, it topples over and shatters into a million different shards at the bottom, then spins into a giant whirlpool, round and round, where all states of the water are erased, its past and present and future, all of where it came from, and where it had been heading, leaving an angry white churn. The silent trees watch over its destruction.

But nothing ever truly ends, and here in this formless chaos, a new stream begins again. It knows nothing of its great fall nor the destruction that had created it. Its heart is as bright as a newborn, and now it must find the sea.

Sky Yang had not recorded any impression of the waterfall, only that the stream below lay diagonally across her west–east line. The current was too strong and she could not cross it.

'Cannot cross stream. Followed waterfall upstream. Think it's 950 steps northwest, but not sure how much because I climb the waterfall sides. Black rock slippery but made it. Now trying to continue west–east direction. Not 100 per cent sure where I am. Dark already because of storm. Going to find place to camp.'

Her next entry was: 'So dark. I believe I found it. Creepy. Feel like hantu looking over my shoulder. Don't want to write about it. After get cursed. Not going any further. I turn around now.'

That was the last time anyone heard from the old Sky Yang.

Sky Yang of the Before

Sometimes, as evening light shaded the streets of the capital in stripes of dark greys and pale yellows, and the pavements gleamed with residual wetness after a thunderstorm, as the rain gurgled through the storm drains, and the sizzle and smell of fried bananas wafted from the next-door neighbour's kuali, sometimes Min remembered the Sky Yang from before the Event.

She was the only orphan that Min had known in the before and the after. The others Min had only known in the after, when their memories had been cleared and their eyes were empty houses. So it was Sky Yang that Min specifically thought of when she thought of the orphans, and was sad, remembering on behalf of Sky Yang what had been lost, even if the girl did not know herself, much less understood.

The Sky Yang of the before was a survivor of the orphanage. She was found on the streets as a young child. She was

283

thought to be about five; no one knew for sure. When asked who took care of her, she shrugged her shoulders and stabbed the police officer's arm with a blunt pencil. She was placed in Mercy Orphanage, which was not much better than the streets. At least she could get clean water easily, and did not have to sneak into gardens to drink from water pipes, she told Min. That was the only reason why she stayed at Mercy Orphanage.

In the before, she was the small, pale girl who had asked the professor, 'What do I get? I don't do this for free you know? Just walk only in the forest ah? Yah-yah, I know must count the steps, okay how many times you must say? Talk talk talk only. I understand lah! You said you will pay for me to live independently, right? No more staying at Mercy Orphanage, right? I am not going back there you know. Sick of that Miss Gan and all her rules. I do what you say, and then I get my own room outside.'

She shook her index finger at the professor. 'If you bluff, I come and find you, and you die. I know where you live.'

In the after, Sky Yang was just a small, pale girl with nothing to say.

In the after, the professor complained to Min: 'Wasted one of my smartest orphans! And she didn't even find anything. Maybe I can send her again. But she knows nothing now – how will she survive in the forest? Surely she will die this time.'

Chong Meng at the Waterfall

Though Han and Min did not know this, Chong Meng had been instructed to comb a narrower area, switching his east–west direction every one and a half hours, while Min believed they were to switch directions every two hours. By the second day, Chong Meng had already reached the waterfall by the cliffs.

Instead of awe, he felt annoyance. 'Tak kan I must climb this,' he muttered, looking around for an easier route, like a side path that slipped around the cliffs. There was none; the east–west line crossed the cliffs at a near-perpendicular angle, and he had to climb them if he wanted to keep on the line. Professor Toh had told Chong Meng sternly that he was not allowed to stray off the planned route. He felt the sweat beading on his forehead. 'You tell me where, where I must climb? How I climb? So steep leh,' he muttered.

Finally, he saw an apron of fallen boulders, which fanned out on the ground in a gentle gradient. Water trickled over the boulders, their surfaces slippery. Tree saplings grew in the crevices. 'I guess here lor.' He wiped the sweat from his forehead, and sighed. *I eat first then I climb*, he thought.

He sat on one of the drier boulders and ate nuts and one hardboiled egg. He found himself still hungry, so he rummaged in the bag to find the parcel containing bak kua slices. Eventually, his hand ran up against the crisp waxed paper of the stack of bak kua. He pulled the parcel out – it seemed smaller than he remembered – and began unwrapping it with excitement.

It had been surprising to find among the rows of wooden shops in Suriyang, a village so far away from the Peninsula, a place selling dried meat and meat floss, just like the dried meat and meat floss back home. There was bak kua, spicy bak kua, gold-coin bak kua, bak kua made of chicken meat, bak kua made of wild boar meat, and even a selection of dried sotong and fish ('The lorry drivers from the coast always buy the seafood wan,' the bak kua shop owner said). The shop smelled like what heaven would smell like: meat, more meat, sizzling on wire racks, their fat dripping onto hot coals. The right mixture of pork and sugar, and salt. Each slice of bak kua made the old-fashioned way: dried in the sun, then grilled over the coals, thus caramelising the sugar, resulting in burnt edges which were a careful balance of crunchiness, bitterness, sweetness and saltiness.

With trembling fingers Chong Meng carefully peeled the greasy paper away to find only five slices of bak kua left. 'Where did the bak kua go? Two weeks they said the bak kua will last. I only ate one or two hor.' He thought about it harder and said, 'Maybe more than one or two. But I thought surely will last longer.'

286

As the shadows of the cliffs lengthened, Chong Meng felt the minor irritations in his tensed muscles relaxing, like releasing a long, smelly fart. The professor's ignoring of him. Feng shui master giving him a bad fortune. Frank the oiler's warning. Foreign workers thinking they were better than he was. No hot food at meals. Mud. What else? He missed air conditioning when he slept and he missed eating three warm dishes for each meal. Even the ship had served cold food for lunch! His mummy would have been shocked. And he had had no soup since he left Kampung Seng. No watercress pork bone soup. Or potatoes tomatoes chicken soup. Or kangkung and ikan bilis soup. Or chicken ginger soup.

Most of all, he missed Han and he wished that Han was there, so he could tell him, Yah-yah, you were right. There was nothing better outside Kampung Seng, that life in Kampung Seng was good (*damn good lah*), and he sometimes wished he had never followed Mr Ng to the capital. (As for helping Mr Ng to steal Han's spade, Chong Meng did not think that was something to be sorry for; after all, it was an old spade and had no value; did Han really want it anyway? Even the professor said the spade wasn't important, though he did give it to him and said about using it around strong smells – which Chong Meng didn't fully understand.) Why would a golden tower even be in a forest like this anyway? So far, on the island, he had only seen villages smaller and more isolated than Kampung Seng.

Chong Meng was not the type of person to question the claims of someone like Mr Ng, let alone the professor, but he was beginning to suspect that all was not what it seemed – *Why they sent me alone to the tower wan? Why they cannot come also? If so important, then why they deent join? Forest so dangerous wan meh?*

Another voice in his head whispered, Jiang shi hopping around in the forest. Demons hiding in trees. Ghosts that are lost and have not found their way to the afterworld. Urang Api-Api lighting fires in the forest.

Chong Meng observed the black cliffs above him; they seemed to have grown taller, as insurmountable as the sky, and with that, the last traces of optimism fled. Then, as he looked at the meagre five slices of bak kua, something within Chong Meng crumbled – the invisible lines of resolve, stretched to their breaking point, snapped all at once. Tension drained from his body. His arms flapped. Everything was so hard; too hard to go any further. He could not go on anymore. Really too much to climb wan. Food supplies also finish liao.

The professor would call him a kampung boy, which he hated. Mr Ng would call him weak if he came back empty-handed. He could say that his bag was dragged away by the forest monkeys at night, that they stole everything from him: the recording equipment, the spade, everything except the food (the food would be in the other bag, he thought to himself, pleased).

The next few moments would change Chong Meng's life for ever, although he did not know it then. He left the bag with the recording equipment, the spade, and a second packet of bak kua – which he had missed – next to the boulders. The bag would later be found by Han and Min. Had he known that Han was only a day's walk behind him, he would have waited, and perhaps this story would have been different.

He did not know, and so, Chong Meng turned around.

This story can do no more than point out that Chong Meng was very lucky; far luckier than Sky Yang or the other orphans, or the spirits who tried to leave the Event, or the unlucky few

288

who wandered into the forests of Naga Tua, who left behind their memories like misplaced bags with recording equipment and bak kua, unable to be carried beyond the Event.

By any measure of character, Chong Meng did not deserve his luck, for he was far from brave, or determined, or strong, or intelligent, or worthy. So it was not his character or anything besides; no, it had not been anything but pure luck that even after having venturing so deep into the forest, *Chong Meng had not stepped into the Event.*

If either the professor or Min had known this information, they would have been able to narrow down the area. The area between the bamboo clearing and the waterfall would have been designated a safe zone: safe to enter, safe to leave.

Miraculously, with his memories intact, Chong Meng tried to retrace his steps back to the bamboo clearing. He gave up after a day, and instead followed a river that he believed to be one of three rivers leading to the plains of Suriyang, as briefed by the professor.

Most of the rivers on Naga Tua ran to the south, but the river that Chong Meng followed was one of the few exceptions. If he had followed any other river, he would have arrived in Suriyang, and again, this story would have been different. Instead, this river ran down into the valleys of the west, where it soon found the sea.

Ten days later, Chong Meng found a hamlet of nine houses on the coast. The people there spoke in a local dialect that was unlike anything he had ever heard. They pointed him to the port of Naga Tua, which they assumed he was looking for.

Chong Meng was tired of being lost and gave up on meeting Mr Ng and the professor at Suriyang. 'Surely they will scold me kow-kow for losing the spade and recording equipment,'

289

he reasoned. He felt like he had fallen into a pit of failure from which there was no climbing out.

When he arrived at the port a few days later, there was a boat leaving for the Peninsula. Chong Meng boarded it. As the boat edged out from the arms of the island, he looked back onto the mountains of Naga Tua. The 'head' of the dragon seemed to turn to him, its gaze following him out to the open sea. 'Bye-bye, dragon,' Chong Meng said. 'Maybe I will see you or your family some day in the future.' Tendrils of smoke rose from its nostrils. The head appeared to tuck itself into the gentle, green slopes of its body.

What would it have meant to stay on the mission that had been set for him? Would it have made him an important man? What adventure had he missed, what prize did he give up? And then, like others before him, he shrugged, 'Tidak apa lah,' and the question was put out of his mind for ever, with the dream of a larger, grander future washed away in the slipstream. The boat rumbled rhythmically on. A weight lifted off his shoulders. Out of instinct, he fumbled in his pockets for a cigarette, forgetting that he had smoked the last one in the forests of Naga Tua.

The boat took him the long way back to the Peninsula. When he arrived in Kampung Seng, his mother, Mrs Lim, was overjoyed and his father, Mr Lim, muttered a few non-committal words but was secretly happy that his only son had returned. Within a year, fate decreed that Mr Lim would suffer a heart attack and die an early death (eating too much goreng pisang, it was said), and Chong Meng became the tauke of Lim Fishing Company, living happily in the air-conditioned comfort of his home, only leaving Kampung Seng for gambling trips with his friends or negotiations with distributors in the capital. With time, he even found a woman to marry.

Chong Meng would never see the Hei-san islands again.

Part Eight
Beyond

Through the Emptiness, Eighteen Years Earlier

A sign hung at the bottom of the only stairwell in the bottom floors. 'Warning,' it started off politely. 'Warning. All Employees of the Tower Are Forbidden to Leave the Sectors.' Below it, in bright red lettering, it continued, WARNING: YOU WILL LEAVE YOUR MEMORIES BEHIND.

Don't play-play in the bottom floors, otherwise you will be like the Crazy Man.

The bottom floors have a lot of cold wind; bad luck to go there.

Blind sheep they go. Blind sheep a-oh. Go in the fields they go, in the valleys they go, in the lakes they go, in the seas they go. These sheep of dreaming woe.

Once, she had stood at this very same door, with the other boy next to her. She had been eight months pregnant then. The patroller had tracked the other boy to this spot, after weeks of searching. She had to get to him as fast as she could; she had even taken the lift train to get there. It was the first time she had seen him since he left the planetarium of sector eight. It would also be the last. Physically, he looked the same, other than the strands of hair around his chin which had now grown into unkempt patches.

His eyes, though, were a flat, desolate place. Once they had been quiet oases where she sought refuge, but they were now replaced by the emptiness of the tower. He was silent.

She approached him as she did a wild machine that went rogue. 'This is your baby in here,' she told him. She felt the kicks in her belly, and she imagined their baby moving in joyous rolls.

'I know,' he said.

Was there a spark in his eyes; did he escape the sadness after all?

'You should go up to the viewing room,' he told her. A flicker of his old self appeared at the edges of his eyes, in the twitches of his mouth, but even as she leaned in to look at him, the flickers had already disappeared, the lines of his face smoothed out to a blankness.

'Come and live with us in this tower,' she said. 'Remember the planetarium?'

He shook his head, and she knew she had lost him for ever, one of the many lost lives of the tower. She never saw him again. Later reports from the patroller would announce that the other boy died of the sadness in the farms of sector nine, succumbing to his father's curse after all.

Here she stood in front of that same door in the bottom floors once again, but this time she was strong, her mind clear, and she asked: What is out there for me? A question she asked over and over again. The tower is my life and I know nothing else.

In actuality, her decision had already been made for her. There are sequences of the universe that cannot be altered; one cannot swim against the tide that is rushing out to sea. Instead, one has to drift, beyond the waves and froth of the breaker zone, to the deep sea, where the water breathes in with longing and out with emotion. This is where we will bring you, the sea said. This is where you have to go. Do I have a choice? she replied. There can be no change to your story; these are the immutable sequences of fate and destiny that will send you away to a new beginning.

Her baby gurgled, beautiful as babies are. He had no name, because she had not wanted to give him a name that she could not commit to. To name a person is to name a destiny. For her little one, destiny was fluid. They would both forget everything, and a new destiny could be written for them. It was not her baby's fate she was worried about; his fate would be bright and new.

Very well, she thought.

She carried a large bag with her. She had packed it with supplies she had scavenged from the tower. She had climbed through cupboards, closets and storerooms, rummaged through supply cabinets, combed through entire sectors, and taken everything she might need in the outside world. She had power cubes, tools, clothing and, of course, her aleum cutter.

She pushed the door. To her surprise, it swung open easily. Many had made the same choice in the past. On the other side of the door, the floor fell away into darkness, the deepest depression that she had ever seen. Her baby was awake, with his eyes wide open and alert, looking at her and at the darkness.

Little one, do you know what is out there? We are leaving the tower. I don't know what we'll find, but I promise to keep you safe.

He turned his face inwards, towards her, nestling into her familiarity.

We're outside, she said to him as she stepped through the doorway. It was colder here; there was no temperature control in the outside world. A bridge led away from the doorway, just as the books said. She could not see the other end, entirely engulfed in the darkness that was the hole of the tower. When she looked up, there was no ceiling, only stars in a grey sky sparkling in their infiniteness, intimations of the greater universe, holding her distant relatives on their home worlds.

She turned around and looked at the tower from the outside, for the first time. The tower was taller than she had expected it to be: large, gargantuan. She was overwhelmed by its physical magnitude, on how it imposed itself onto the tapestry of reality. Who could have built this? she asked herself, even though she knew the answer. She touched the walls of the tower. They were cold, undefinable in their texture, almost a metal but with a softness that reminded her of her baby's newly washed skin. The little she knew about the construction of the tower came from books.

Her memories of the tower were partitioned into neat categories – sector five, where she lived. Sector eight, where the planetarium was. Sector twenty, where the last operational mine was. This tower was beyond any scale that she had ever known. It was ten times, no, twenty times, thirty times, higher than any of the ceilings that she had known. It was higher than the ceilings in the docks, larger than the giant bays. Her thoughts brought up comparisons to things she had seen or known, until she realised that, by definition, it was the largest structure she would ever know, because it contained all the structures she had ever known.

Her eyes followed the tower upwards until they found slivers of sky, where clouds were being blown across in a high wind, and the tower lengthened in sympathy. Beyond, the star around which this planet revolved hung low. We are continually dying and it is cold, she thought, and she kissed the smooth cheeks of her baby. Her feelings, for so long kept compressed, exploded in a supernova.

I am not just losing my memory, I am losing our collective memories. The home-world names that I did not have, the home language that I hear in dreams, the stories of our home worlds, of who we are and how we came to be. For we are stardust – we are merely a minuscule physical manifestation of larger processes, planets forming from bits of rock and dust, plants generating oxygen, comets and asteroids delivering water, volcanoes spewing aleum, creating homes for humans to find and populate; we are one sentence in a larger story, one whose ending has not been written yet. To lose this history is death.

All those years ago she had been told what would happen when someone left the tower through that last bottom door. You will forget that you had ever lived in the tower. The hole of emptiness that surrounds the tower will keep your memories as you walk across the bridge. You will forget your entire life. You will forget that you forgot. You will choose to lose yourself, and for that, it is suicide.

And finally, they whispered, perhaps you get a second chance at life.

She started her walk across the bridge, with the baby wrapped safely on her chest, through the emptiness and out into the world.

Who am I? As she walked, increasingly, she had no answer to the question.

The Tower

Here they were, Min and Han. In the same-same darkness, and the place was silent. The ground had been untouched for eighteen years. From where they stood they could see the tower rising into the weighty dark clouds.

Here they were. There were no words they could say to each other that could capture what they saw, and how they felt, for the tower was beyond their comprehension. Words were primitive instruments, made of grotesque, disjointed notes with no musicality, shuffled together. They felt like children, unable to express anything of what they saw.

The tower loomed in its fractal symmetry, round and round it went, perfectly circular, unbroken in its smoothness, except for a door that materialised at the bottom. Around and around their eyes followed, but it did not break, it was infinite, forever, magical. Magical, and beautiful beyond their understanding. Also, alien: not from any culture that either of them knew, transplanted from a strange somewhere.

'Don't turn around,' were the only words Min managed to say aloud. The vibrations in the air from her words were dampened by the darkness.

They did not turn around. The black soil held them firmly. They had only one thought, and the thought was the same for them both – that they had not managed to find Chong Meng, not in the three days of walking and scrambling up the black cliffs. Only his abandoned backpack had been found and in it, the spade, but not his intentions, nor the person of Chong Meng himself.

'You have your spade back, at least,' Min had offered.

He had left the spade buried in Chong Meng's bag. He couldn't bear to look at it. Kampung Seng seemed very far away now, across deep seas, across deserts.

'But not Chong Meng,' he had said.

Chong Meng's disappearance would remain a puzzle for them both, even as Chong Meng himself, at that moment, was traipsing along the westerly river with his five uneaten bak kua slices, his memories safely stashed away in his head, unaware of the distress that he had caused.

They consoled themselves that if they were going to lose their memories, they might as well make the best of it.

'What else can we do? Go inside loh. Let's find out what someone or many ones want to keep hidden,' Min said.

They entered together, Han and Min. They approached the door of the tower, the same door from which Han's mother had left eighteen years ago. They were not sure what to expect: certainly not an empty room sheathed in layers of dust. No one had been there for a very long time.

It was clear that Chong Meng had not come this way. In his rising despair, Han very nearly turned back around the door, until Min took his hand and squeezed it firmly.

'You cannot save him now. You can only try to save yourself,' she said.

They scanned the room, its four walls, the floor, the ceiling, and a spiralling staircase that appeared to carry on upwards into the tower.

There was nothing else for them to do but to climb up and up, until they came to an open doorway. Inside, they found themselves in a cavernous room, so large that they almost forgot they were inside the tower, and empty, except for dust. Light glowed from no discernible source – no lamps, no overhead lighting, not from the walls, not even from the floor; instead, whatever light there was appeared to exist in the space around them, bunching in the air like dust particles. In the distance there was a subtle change in colour, the briefest of lines demarcating where the walls rose and outlined this giant room. Other than that, there was nothing in this room, nothing at all.

They continued walking up the stairs. Their footsteps landed softly, absorbed by the flooring. When they arrived at the next room up, they found that this room was empty too, a giant room of nothing, similar to the one before. *We lose our memories for these empty rooms? The orphans, Sky Yang? Chong Meng?*

The next floor up was empty too. So was the next floor, and the next, and so forth, until they reached the fifty-first floor. Here was the start of sector one, and its receiving hall.

Min and Han did not know this, of course. They only saw twisted wrecks strewn across the floor, giant cradles, spider-like objects, the space around them glowing with light. Things everywhere, too much of everything, too little of everything. There were people here once, their feet pressed the floor, and their hands touched these giant cradles; their absence made tangible in these abandoned objects belonging to no one, and owing nothing.

Min, did you feel like this when you arrived in the lowlands for the first time? Desert girl in the wet western lowlands; people, buildings, weather, words, similar and yet wholly foreign? Everything meant something different, where no one spoke how you spoke, and you had to learn everything again.

Maybe. And maybe that was how your mama felt.

They continued their climb up the stairs, passing through scenes of stale pandemonium. The space around them brightened and dimmed in cycles that resembled day and night; they ate nuts and meat floss when the brightness appeared to be at its peak, and when the glow of the stairwell dimmed to the point where they were tired, they ate dried cuttlefish and then wrapped themselves in their blankets to sleep.

Min said, 'They were trapped here. The memory loss was meant to stop them from leaving.'

Han was thoughtful. Nothing that he had seen so far answered his questions about where his mama and he came from, who they were. He was sad for his mama, and for himself, for not only did he not know his mama, he didn't even know the person who had become his mama. And then, what of the people that led to him? His mama's father, his mama's mother, his mama's father's father, his mama's father's mother, his mama's mother's father – the list went on and on, the people he did not know, the stories they had not told him, the names that they had lost.

'No people, only ghosts here,' he whispered.

The tower was coldly mute. No stories for you, it said to him. There will be no stories of digging weeds in vegetable gardens, nor stories of Ah-ma or Mama or Father. Or cousins. You will never know the journeys of your ancestors, the people who have loved each other, who have gazed into the faces of their newborns, the newborns that would become your great-grandparents, and grandparents, and parents, and everyone in your family besides. You are like a tree with no roots. You are the flower people. This world is bigger than you can imagine, and it lies out there, in the riffling of the grass, in the swash of the seas, and the lands, and it goes on, to the sky, to the stars, a large swirling cloud of millions and millions of stars, around which worlds like this revolve. But these stories are not for you. No, there will be no stories for you. There is no one and nothing here for you.

It was then that he realised the significance of what Min had said. 'Then where is everyone? If they could not leave, where did they go? Did they all leave to become spirits, like my mama?'

'Your mama was the last spirit that arrived in Suriyang. And reports say that there were only thirty or forty spirits in total that arrived there over the centuries.'

'Such a large place. You would think there would be a lot of people here.'

The darkness gave Min and Han no answers.

First the nuts ran out, then the cuttlefish, then the meat floss. They had found a packet of bak kua in Chong Meng's bag. They unwrapped the parcel of waxed paper with love. Grease and sugared burnt edges and pork greeted their hopeful faces.

303

'Sure no other food in here?' Min asked.

'I found recording equipment and a blank diary. And the spade.' Han shook Chong Meng's bag. 'Here, see if you can find anything else.'

'Chong Meng likely had another bag for his food,' Min said. She knew that Chong Meng would have been instructed to record everything he saw. His instructions would have been to enter the tower and explore it for a week, before stowing the equipment and the diary in this bag, safely sealed, of course – the professor would have known that Chong Meng's chances of surviving in the forest would be minimal when Chong Meng turned around and lost his memories. The professor took precautions to ensure that any footage and written notes would be saved, even if Chong Meng's body was found floating down the river.

'Is this the spade? This belonged to your mama?' Min said.

When Han had first appeared at the professor's house seeking his mama's spade, Min had assumed that this boy of sun-darkened skin who spoke in a kampung accent, wearing clothes that were even more washed out than that of the orphans, was missing a normal spade – just a spade to dig up soil. Like the cheap, medium-sized spades found in hardware shops. Kampung people were simple people, and from that moment on, she had felt pity for Han. *So poor he cannot even buy a new spade.*

But this – this object was nothing like cheap spades found in hardware shops. Even referring to the object as a spade felt sacrilegious, an earthbound term. How does an ant talk to the gods?

She said, 'You know other spirits carried this object yah? This . . . spade, as you say, was the only thing they carried.

They usually took it with them when they went to their deaths. That is why I have only seen it in drawings until now. Your mama was the only spirit who left her spade in this world.'

Her hands felt the coolness of the object. It pulled the heat from her fingers, and the muscles in her body trembled as her toes grew cold. Like falling into an abyss on a dark night. The grooves on the shaft were old, worn, familiar, once well-trodden paths. She examined the patterns, turning the object around again and again, willing herself to understand their long-abandoned meanings.

Some feeling arose within her, some echo that sounded of her ma's voice, of home and desert and innocence. These were syllables and rhythms that she had not heard since she was a child, and she wanted to return, before she remembered the Bone Fields and her stomach grew hard again. *This is how we worship our god.* She could see the black rocks of the Cliff of the First Wei Leep, and the roughness of Ma's palms as they pressed into hers, hardened from many years of hauling buckets of water from the nearest water tower. *This is how we worship our god*, Ma used to say, as she scraped at the rocks with her puller.

The parcel of bak kua had been as thick as a phonebook at first. Though they were careful to stretch out their supply, the parcel dwindled as they made their way up the tower. They no longer ventured into every open doorway. They had been climbing for some time, according to the light around them dimming and brightening – perhaps a few days.

'What's here? Nothing here, Min! If we leave now, our memories will die like Sky Yang's. Or we stay in this tower for ever and waste our lives away in this nothingness. What kind of choice is it?'

'Let's continue to the top. Then we decide,' Min said.

The parcel was down to the last few slices of bak kua. It would not last much longer. Perhaps their decision had been made for them. It would be easier if it was so.

If a man jumps off a cliff, and realises, too late, that he cannot fly, what happens to his cries for help?

If a mother looks for her lost son and cries out his name, but the child cannot hear, for he is far away, and he will die soon, what happens to her cries?

When a grandmother prays to her god for rain, but there is no god and her prayers are unheard, what happens to her prayers?

Who will hear us? Who will hear us in this silent tower?

They secretly believed that the hush-black stairs would go on for ever, and the walls of the stairwell would hold them in the tight curl of its cylinder for perpetuity. Maybe this was the real curse of the tower, and their feet would climb the same-same oval steps for the rest of their lives, always nearly but never quite reaching the top.

But like everything mortal, the stairs did end. A doorway greeted them in the ceiling. They climbed into the space above and found themselves in an unbroken sea of a room, similar to the early floors, with no internal walls to break the space into a comprehensible size.

'Do you smell something in the air?' Min said, looking around the empty room. 'Like the smell of wind from dried-up lakes?'

There was a faint scent, perhaps salty like the sea, but it vanished so quickly that Han wondered if he had imagined it.

They could have stood in the room for two hundred years and it would have remained the same, if not for the light – the light was different; it came sweeping past their feet, in long angles that rested on their sides, choosing one side of their feet over the other. Their shadows had differentiated from fuzzy orbs into long, linear shapes, announcing the beginning of an end. Here, a decision had to be made, a path must be taken; no longer could they revel in a cloud of possibilities.

'We are at the top of the tower,' Min said. They were and they felt free. Clear glass walls arched their backs into a dome, enclosing them. They stepped close to the dome walls, and the outside was so near that they felt they could touch it.

The world outside sang to them in blue, green and white that ran across the horizon: in the seas that ran up against the grass of the land, in the wind and sand and rain, in the clouds that swept across in layered curtains. Their souls were uplifted as the world bent around them; they were happy, they were sad, they were at the top of the world, they could see everything, they were gods. How could they leave now? How could they choose to forget? These memories would die as soon as they turned around and left. Whatever choice they made would lead to a sure death.

Min was waving her hand through the windows. She said, 'Han, these glass walls of the dome – they are not really glass or walls. Here, stick your hand through one of these panes. You can feel the bitter cold of the air. *You can feel the sky.*'

Han did as she asked, and his hands slipped through the clear walls of the dome, with the wind rushing around the tips of his fingers, turning them blue. 'This was how they left,' he whispered to Min. 'The people that used to fill these dusty rooms – this was how they left, through these walls that are not walls. Do you remember, Min, those halls below us, with ceilings as high as hills, and giant cradles that could fit rows of town houses? Min, I think those cradles once contained ships of people. That might be how the people of the tower left, through ships that flew from the top of the tower.'

Min stared. 'Your mother didn't. She was found as a spirit in the forest. The Event traps everyone here in this tower. You cannot escape it.'

'Maybe on the ground, the Event is a wall that traps memories around the tower. But somewhere here, somewhere up in the sky, somewhere above or below us, perhaps the Event does not exist anymore. The Event can't be infinitely high. Those ships of people must have left with their memories intact.'

'Or not. Han, those people could have lost their memories too. Blank vessels, living graveyards of people floating in the sky, with no idea of who they are and where they are going, and with no one to help them remember.'

They were silent, horrified by what this could mean. Ships of people with no memories, like mindless schools of fish, driven only by food and light. Their dreams empty like the cold, abyssal plains of a lifeless ocean.

'It doesn't matter anyway. Not like we have a ship also.' Han shook his head. 'Maybe my mama didn't have a ship to fly her out of here either.'

He tried to imagine his mama. Since he had only the faintest of memories of her, it was surprising that an image of Mama arrived to him now, full and crisp: his mama, standing here at this very spot, as the sun fell across her shoulders and her hair. He could see her face, where the tips of her lips turned up in a smile, and her deep eyes softened as she watched him, and he watched her, over years and distances, as present and past slipped into each other, and there was love.

Mama, he whispered, *I am sorry. Sorry for returning to this place that you escaped. Now your sacrifice will mean nothing.*

I'm proud of you, my son. Proud of you for trying to save your cousin. She looked at him, and then whispered, *Aleum.*

What was that word? The vision of his mama vanished in an instant, folding back into whatever spaces of the past or the afterworld that it came from.

'Aleum, you said.' Min stared. 'I heard that word before, in another life. In the Desert of Birds, when I was a young girl.'

'My mama said that word to me. In a . . . dream.'

Min said, mostly to herself, 'How was I supposed to know what it meant? Could it be?' She turned to Han. 'That object – that "spade" of yours.'

He gave his mama's spade to Min, who took it, and turned the spade over and over, feeling the inscriptions carved into its handle. 'That smell – I know that smell,' she said.

They both sniffed the air as hard as they could, and as they followed the scent with their noses, it grew heady, spirited, like birds soaring. So much of it, until all they could do was sit down in its turbulent waves and let the scent wash over them. For the first time upon entering the tower, or perhaps even for the first time in his life, Han felt the most alive he had ever felt, and he laughed.

Min laughed with him too, and for a long time after they rolled around, belly-hurting, big-laughing *hur-hur-hur* that would have caused any schoolteacher of Han's to clip his ear and mark his name down for rubbish-picking detention at recess. *Don't laugh anymore. You think this funny ah? You laugh laugh somemore, I send you pick rubbish, see you laugh anot. No respect.* They continued laughing at the stern air, and the clear walls of the dome reverberated with pleasure, for many years had passed since it had heard laughter. *I tell you don't laugh anymore! No respect for elders. You think this place what? I hantam you boy.* And they laughed, and they laughed, and they were birds soaring.

Min picked up his mama's spade and tugged it through the air. Then she extended the spade, its blade pointed at him, its flat side facing up. 'Here,' she said. 'Move your face above the blade. Then inhale deeply.'

Han was floating. His body had lifted off the floor, and his arms dangled. He leaned backwards and found himself drifting. 'What—?'

He tried to look at Min. He flipped over instead, and he found himself facing the floor, and he could now see his shadow, a dead thing trapped on the ground. His arms and legs kicked about wildly. He slipped in the air and continued to roll. He felt like he was drowing. He gasped, and he scrambled, trying to slow down his rolls, his hands cutting through the nothing, trying to breathe. It was all air everywhere, and he could breathe anytime, his mind told him.

Min stared at him from a distance. 'Like . . . swimming.'

Swimming. He knew that word. His arms and legs made large sweeping strokes, and eventually he stopped slipping.

She started crying into her hands. 'Min?' he said.

She shook her head, wiping her eyes with the back of her hands. 'Air has much less resistance than water. A small movement can send your body drifting a long way away.'

He was floating a considerable way away from Min. He made a small wave with his left arm and found himself drifting back towards her.

'How do you know this? What have I inhaled?'

Min was silent for a few seconds before answering, 'This is aleum. It is invisible; you can't see it. You can only smell it, and you can feel the boundaries of it or dig it up with a special tool, like your mama's spade. Every single one of the adults in my village used it. My ma used to sneak me some.' Her voice was soft, and she said, 'She loved me. But she let me lie in the Bone Fields. We used to float for days, my hand in her hand. I convinced myself that they were just dreams of somewhere, sometime long time ago. I was a child. Superstitions, folk tales, fairy tales, as the professor would say. Why didn't my ma tell us then? We were only children. We didn't need to die.'

'No one needs to die!' Han said. 'We can fly, Min! We can leave through these permeable walls and escape the tower with our memories.' He flapped his arms in the air, like a bird, and laughed. *Hur-hur-hur.*

'Aleum doesn't work like that.'

But what if it did? What if this started at the Cliff of the First Wei Leep? *Her fall began to slow, to halt in the air even, and for several seconds it felt like she was floating above the hard desert ground.* The years of dusty pain and abandonment had led her here, to the top of the tower. She did not believe in coincidences, but of all the people Han could have met, she was the only person in the entire capital who knew how to use aleum to break a fall from great height. Because once upon a time in a distant desert she had failed her coming-of-age test, in the eyes of people with hearts as hard as rock. Maybe this had been her destiny all along. Maybe this was the moment she had been born for.

Far away, the echoes of her thoughts were scattered across the salty mirrors of the Lake of Unheard Words, waiting to be heard.

Min cut out the remaining aleum as a block and attached it to her left wrist, as she had seen her ma do in the past. She reached out to Han, floating nearby, and looped their arms together in a tight hook. They both took a large breath in the dregs of the aleum streak, and with that her feet left the ground and they kicked towards the edge of the dome. They felt the clear panes of membrane with their wandering hands, and with one last kick and one last breath, they were in the air, in the space outside the tower, hurtling towards the ground. Fear, ice in their faces, pulse racing in their veins, blurs of blacks and greens and blues, while the tower and its shadow disapproved, for no one had thought to leave the tower this way before. (Certainly, now that this loophole was exposed, future towers on other mines would need to have impenetrable membranes for their dome walls, to prevent workers from leaving their towers whenever they wanted, with their memories intact.)

Han and Min were still falling, their bodies tumbling in an uncontrollable spin. Swim-swim, swim-swim – but it was too hard to swim, as their arms and legs felt as if they had been torn out of their sockets, and they were nauseous, their heads whipping back as they struggled to follow around on the turn, tangled in turbulence.

Min gritted her teeth. She could not nearly die again. The ground loomed like that of the Bone Fields. With the last of her energy she managed a sweeping stroke with her left arm and leg. In her dizziness, it was many moments before she realised that they had both stopped their uncontrollable descent, and they were now just . . . floating. The dark grounds of Naga Tua stopped hurtling towards them and instead stared back with a quality resembling calmness. They were outside the tower, and they were floating in the air.

Naga Tua Erupts

O ver valleys and hills and rivers, over vents of rising steam and trembling black cliffs, they floated. They drifted up and down with the winds and leapt over jumping rivers, as near as they dared. They turned their faces upwards to watch the clouds overtake them. Their shadows chased them through the green paddy fields of the west. The sea waved at them from a distance as they tumbled, feeling the sea winds pushing against the hot air of Naga Tua, as they yelled to each other – Here, these houses are like toy houses, perched on the side of the cliff. Can you see the mountains; they huff and puff as if they are angry! Look, they blow smoke! In the distance, there, do you see the port? And there, the sea! Do you see that glistening speck far away there, leaving white trails in the distance? That is a boat! A boat! Can you see it?

As they flew, they checked on their memories constantly, not believing of their luck. They prodded and pushed, looking for a gap, an absence of memories. Did Han remember the night when he won three hundred in chor dai di? Did Min remember how to suck water from a root as Kuang had showed her? Memories were pulled up into the open air, examined, and found to be undamaged, although if they had been damaged, how would they have known?

It did not matter anymore. Min laughed in her giddiness. *Hur-hur-hur*.

Their floating bodies dipped towards the coast. A lorry driver who had been scanning the mountains saw Min and Han flying, mistaking them for gods. He asked for their blessings and prayed that they would calm the waking Naga Tua, angry and hungry from his long sleep. Later that morning, the lorry driver would tell the rest of his friends that he had seen the gods blessing the people of Naga Tua.

Was he sure? For Naga Tua was furious today, his friends asked.

Of course he was sure, he saw the gods with his own eyes, the lorry driver replied. He was sure it was magic. How else could they fly?

Maybe it was black magic, one of his friends said quietly, not wanting the lorry driver to lose face.

Another friend said, I heard that the Peninsular scientists are talking about evacuating the island completely.

Yet another friend said, I heard the next boat from the Peninsula is only arriving in a week's time. They can't get here any sooner.

Min and Han, unaware of the debate they had caused, carried themselves to Naga Tua port. Their feet touched the wooden planks of the docks. They looked at each other. They had escaped the tower. They had not lost their memories. And they laughed again, first in chuckles and then in full laughs bubbling from their bellies, and they continued laughing. *Hur-hur-hur!* They stamped on the ground, they threw their hands in the air, they sank to kneel, and they tasted the salt of moving water.

We got out, Han said, in gasping laughter.

We got out, Min said.

We are safe, Han said.

We saw the tower, Min said.

'What are you laughing about? You think this is funny ah? Nowadays young people no sense wan. Show a bit of respect.' A woman, likely in her sixties, was standing next to them.

'Sorry, auntie, just happy today,' Min said.

'Happy what happy? You happy to leave ah? You must be foreigners. I live here my whole life. Never left the island before. Want me to go on boat somemore. Coming next week, they said. You think my old legs can take it? Die here also better.'

In the afternoon of the 450th year of the tower's existence, or eighteen years and four months since the girl had left the tower, or twenty-six days since Min and Han first set foot on Naga Tua, the volcano finally entered its active phase. They could see the putrid, ballooning volcano from a distance, a benign infection metamorphosing into a strange gangrenous thing, dark and twisted and rotting. *Hur-hur-hur*, the swollen lips of the Naga Tua volcano leered, its walls starting to split and lava oozing from its deep core. *Hur-hur-hur*, the ground trembled. Naga Tua was awake, and the people despaired.

The magma chamber beneath the volcano of Naga Tua had built up immense pressure. It would be a big one, the vil-

315

lagers of Naga Tua were warned. But they did not know how little time they had. In the next hour, jets of high-pressure water, gas and magma were ejected into the air, coalescing into dense clouds. Bigger and bigger they grew, until the clouds became a single, vengeful ghost visiting from the underworld, eating everything in its path. The entire island of Naga Tua was cast into darkness. The greyness smothered the swaying green fruit trees and choked the wispy stalks of paddy.

'We will die if we don't leave,' Min said.

'No boat coming for another week,' Han said.

'We could float to the neighbouring islands?'

They could see the dust clouds spreading to Naga Muda and Naga Besar, the other islands in the Naga cluster.

'The next cluster of islands are the Pinnacles. Those islands are small, and they do not hold much fresh water. The Professor's books say that the population in the Pinnacles bounce from feast to famine and are particularly hostile to outsiders,' Min said.

What about the other islands? The Jadi-Jadi cluster was directly north of the Naga Tua volcano and south of the Burnt Islands. There was a reason why villages in the Jadi-Jadi islands were built above a certain elevation – tsunamis. The hills in the Dahun cluster were too low. The other islands . . . Her mind raced as she struggled to remember the individual details. Not the Solitary Island. Not the Burnt Islands. She ticked the islands off one by one.

Han said that he had seen islands to the west of Naga Tua as they arrived in the port. 'I saw trees and water. Surely we could survive there for a week until the boat arrives,' he said.

316

'That's the Bulan-Bulan islands. They are flat-lying, with sandy beaches and gentle lagoons that would be washed away by any tsunami.'

'There must be others. There are hundreds of islands. One of them must be safe.'

'Most of the Hei-san islands are small and only just about hold their heads above the tides. Most do not have fresh water. Most would drown in the waves.'

'How about the Peninsula?' Han asked.

How far can we float across the sea?

Crazy cuckoo idea, she said at first. Floating all the way to the Peninsula. What if we run out of aleum and drown in the sea? How about water? How about food?

There were ships coming here from the Peninsula – maybe they could catch one halfway.

They each had a sniff of aleum. At once their heads were giddy, and their bodies were floating through the clouds of ash and molten chunks of rock. They heard the trembling of the volcano as it prepared to explode. Han and Min needed to leave immediately, and kicking and drifting in the air they did, with only a tear for Chong Meng whom they thought was lost somewhere on the island.

Together, they journeyed into the unfamiliar openness of the sea, over the waves that rolled beneath them; together they flew.

The Sea Grows Cold

The evening news was flooded with reports of the latest eruption in the Hei-san archipelago. Father was only half listening, for there were always reports of minor eruptions, especially in the Burnt Islands.

'A volcano on one of the southern islands,' the radio crackled, 'once thought to be dormant, has erupted, triggering massive landslides and tsunamis,' and finally, 'super-volcanic eruption'. That caught his attention. Super-volcanic eruption? The sunset that evening had been a brilliant reddish-orange, an unusual sight, almost enough to make up for the fact that most of the sunlight had been trapped behind grey clouds.

How long will the clouds stay grey? Would the sea grow cold, and would the fish sleep in the ocean? Bad for fishing, he thought.

Father half turned and almost called for his mother – Come, listen to the news of the eruption – before remembering that she was not in the house anymore. She would never be in the house anymore. His chest choked up, and he continued to rock himself on the rocking chair. The room was silent except for the creak-creak of the ceiling fans.

On the altar, embers of joss sticks glowed bright orange, then faded into red, and finally collapsed into dull, dead ashes. The ashes fell densely in the censer, and stray particles settled thinly over the altar, masking the spot where Swee's spade had once stood. Smoke curled in thin strands, floating in the air, bringing Father's prayers to heaven. Good health of the family. Prosperity in afterlife for the family.

Need to speak to my sister tomorrow, Father thought, need to make the arrangements. The burial could not wait for Han to say goodbye to his ah-ma. Who knew how long more until he returned?

The Naga Tua volcano had been sleeping for many years, occasionally blowing out hot air through its nostrils to remind the others that it was still alive, still there, just in a deep sleep while its belly grew. When it finally woke up, it was furious.

There came a moment when Naga Tua could not contain its anger in its expanding belly anymore, so it sent its anger into the world, exploding into white-hot fragments the opposite of rain: solid, sharp, burning rock that fell across the island, searing off the leaves that hung innocently upon tree branches. The air tasted of sulphur, of burning prayer paper at Cheng Meng. Many died on the day that Naga Tua exploded: the ants in their wandering lines died, cows in their ambulating dullness died, the professor and Mr Ng in the bamboo clearing died – with no fanfare and no obituaries in the newspaper – and the people of Suriyang died as they went about their day. It was not the gentle and absolute wall of glowing lava that buried them, it was the invisible poisonous gas that made them faint, keel over on the temple floor in apparent prayer, or fall into a deep sleep beside their napping grandson, or drop down next to their cooking stove, even as the pork bones continued boiling on and on, and the flames leapt to the air, and everything burned; the air burned.

As the eruption went on, the volcano itself failed. Its walls slid down its network of magma conduits, and the largest landslide in the history of this flower planet occurred. Millions of tons of rock failed along a fault plane and slid into the sea, setting off shock waves that grew into tsunamis. One after another, the tsunamis roared in the shallow waters surrounding the Hei-san archipelago. Coastal villages were flattened. The bodies of thousands were torn apart at their joints. Their lungs filled with water and their eyes stopped moving.

Even the Jadi-Jadi cluster, with villages perched high on the hills, were not protected by their elevation. The huge waves of water swept away their cooking utensils and sacks of rice, and thus remained undiscovered the recipes of Mama Shin, whose innovative blend of mountain goat meat, fish and seaweed would have transformed the capital's cuisine, had it been known. Also undiscovered was the little girl, Shan-shan, whose drawings and stick sculptures at the age of three suggested an artistic genius in the making. Their bodies sank into eternal sea tombs, burying them in a fresh layer of death.

Sampans were thrown up by the waves like toy boats, their sides splintering into pieces, joining the army of broken-up dead things that would wash up as strings of rubbish on the beaches of the Hei-san islands, and would continue to do so along the coasts of the Peninsula, for many years after the Naga Tua eruption.

321

The tower was buried with the landslide. From the innards of the earth, the pulsing magma conduits dragged up large quantities of ash and lava and aleum, covering Naga Tua once again with vast aleum deposits that extended high into the sky, just as they had done before in the past, during the Great Eruptions at the end of the Bercahaya Era.

The shock waves of the tsunami raced across the sea and, after several hours, arrived at the giant landmass that was the Peninsula, shattering windows of the Eastern Port buildings and flooding the streets with sand and rubbish-heavy water.

Ash was spread by the winds, advancing like an army of White Ghosts, until its darkness had blanketed the islands in the Hei-san archipelago: the Naga cluster, the Pinnacles, the Jadi-Jadi cluster, the Bulan-Bulan cluster, the Burnt Islands, and the unnamed islands – before being blown further west to the Otherside, running through the streets and their houses, then coming back with the dominant winds to the turbulent Boatbreaker Seas. The wind grew stronger there, and the ash was swept onto the Peninsula, covering the entire western lowlands in blankets of grey. Sunsets remained spectacular for a long time, in shades of red and orange and purple. The seas grew cold from the lack of sunlight and the fish were lethargic.

In the Desert of Birds, the ash blew with the sand, and for many years after that, the desert people spoke of the cloudy night skies. We could not see the stars any longer, they said.

Acknowledgements

Acknowledgements are hard to write for first novels, as there are only so many synonyms for 'opportunity'.

This is a short list of people whom I will be thanking, while recognising that I am leaving out the names of many others who have indirectly contributed in small but important ways, mostly by helping me become a person who has the opportunity to write novels.

First of all, thank you to my parents, to whom this novel is dedicated, for giving me a childhood filled with books, and for supporting me in pursuit of unconventional life choices.

To the person who wrote in the *Star Malaysia* newspaper about financial aid at US universities, which gave a middle-class girl from Malaysia the transformative opportunity to attend Yale. (Yale covers the full cost of an undergraduate education for all accepted students whose families have an annual income of less than $75,000.)

To my fellow workshoppers at Yale, and to John Crowley, for your helpful comments on early drafts. To the Richter Fund, for awarding me the Richter Summer Fellowship to carry out research for this novel.

To Pastor Choong Wah Wai, for graciously hosting me at Pantai Remis, so that I could learn about life in a fishing village.

To Becky, my editor, for taking a chance with this novel, and to the Future Bookshelf team for letting me bring this story into the world.

And finally, to Richard, for keeping the house running, and for your continual love and support through these years.

ORIGINALS
NEW WRITING FROM
BRITAIN'S OLDEST PUBLISHER

2020

Toto Among the Murderers | Sally J Morgan
An atmospheric debut novel set in 1970s Leeds and Sheffield when attacks on women punctuated the news.

'An exhilarating novel' Susan Barker

Self-Portrait in Black and White | Thomas Chatterton Williams
An interrogation of race and identity from one of America's most brilliant cultural critics.

'An extraordinarily thought-provoking memoir' *Sunday Times*

2019

Asghar and Zahra | Sameer Rahim
A tragicomic account of a doomed marriage.

'Funny and wise, and beautifully written' Colm Tóibín, *New Statesman*

Nobber | Oisín Fagan
A wildly inventive and audacious fourteenth-century Irish Plague novel.

'Vigorously, writhingly itself' *Observer*, Books of the Year

2018

A Kind of Freedom | Margaret Wilkerson Sexton
A fascinating exploration of the long-lasting and enduring divisive legacy of slavery.

'A writer of uncommon nerve and talent' *New York Times*

Jott | Sam Thompson
A story about friendship, madness and modernism.

'A complex, nuanced literary novel of extraordinary perception' *Herald*

Game Theory | Thomas Jones
A comedy about friendship, sex and parenting, and about the games people play.

'Well observed and ruthlessly truthful' *Daily Mail*

2017

Elmet | Fiona Mozley
An atmospheric Gothic fable about a family living on land that isn't theirs.

'A quiet explosion of a book, exquisite and unforgettable' *The Economist*

2016

Blind Water Pass | Anna Metcalfe
A debut collection of stories about communication and miscommunication – between characters and across cultures.

'Demonstrates a grasp of storytelling beyond the expectations of any debut author' *Observer*

The Bed Moved | Rebecca Schiff
Frank and irreverent, these stories offer a singular view of growing up (or not) and finding love (or not) in today's uncertain landscape.

'A fresh voice well worth listening to' *Atlantic*

Marlow's Landing | Toby Vieira
A thrilling novel of diamonds, deceit and a trip up-river.

'Economical, accomplished and assured' *The Times*

2015
An Account of the Decline of the Great Auk, According to One Who Saw It | Jessie Greengrass
The twelve stories in this startling collection range over centuries and across the world.

'Spectacularly accomplished' *The Economist*

Generation | Paula McGrath
An ambitious novel spanning generations and continents on an epic scale.

'A hugely impressive and compelling narrative' John Boyne, *Irish Times*